The Magic of the Little Red Cafe

Front cover design: Kathleen Harryman

Kathleenharryman.com

For more information, please contact: magic79.jb@outlook.com

First Published December 2020

The Magic of the Little Red Café

Jenny & Katie

With Love Always

The Magic of the Little Red Café

Prologue

You would have thought that after the birth of our son life would have settled down sufficiently for Lola and myself to begin each day peaceably, harmonising on the challenges ahead. Keeping pace nicely with our souls, blending gently the mix of raising a young family along with the ingredients of what we did know about parenthood and those other as yet unidentified mysteries that were there to amaze and surprise us.

The one known element of the equation that did always affect us and a good many other families in similar situations was the constant tightening of the belt and purse strings, juggling with the temptation of life's little luxuries. Time also challenged, a balance between family, work and leisure.

Most noticeable was the change in Amelia and how she had grown not just is stature, but in confidence passing down some of her new found trust to her baby brother. Now a knowing, all seeing and watchful individual Antonio was sitting by himself on the soft mat surrounded by cushions and toys, his stare following me around the room as though thinking to himself 'I have my beady eye on you mate, I'm watching you.'

As siblings, brother and sister were inseparable and would sit on the mat in an imaginary circle, gently rocking from side to side then back and forth in a playful illusion that they were sailing across the sea on a pea green boat. Watching them play together with Antonio copying his older sister, it was a pleasure to us both to see them happy, they made us both very happy.

Amelia adored her little brother, caring for his every need and she would willingly take over many of the time consuming tasks like feeding Antonio or changing his nappy to help her mother, so that Lola could do the dinner or load the washing machine.

Sharing the same bedroom Amelia would read to Antonio although the little chap never got to hear the end of the story not that it really mattered. Standing on the landing and listening to her read our son and daughter had made our world complete and neither of us wanted them to grow, but stay young and innocent, playing together, standing still time.

Time however would sculpture their future as it did for every living being and in time they would grow and slowly transform Lola and myself. As husband and father it was my duty to ensure that my family was well cared for and looked after. I could not alter the inevitability of change, no more than I could outstare my young son, and the same could be said for the little red café.

Vera had recently declined my offer to become a business partner although as a compromise she suggested that we made Danielle the Assistant Manager of the cafe. Vera, as wise as an old owl said it would demonstrate how grateful I was for all the hard effort that Danielle had contributed in making the café a success and how committed we were in ensuring that she had a good start in life with Martyn. Vera was happy to continue sitting on the side-line and let progress march on ahead without her feeling the pressures of modern day living. With Danielle as Assistant Manager, I could already feel the wind of change blowing in through the café door.

With the extra responsibility Danielle would arrive before me and unlock the café which meant I could stroll to work and walk into a cafe that was already alive with energy, music and the smell of cooking bacon together with a bubbling coffee pot. Unless we had a prior event booked Sundays were always family days, a walk out, swings and park time.

No one day was ever the same and every so often a customer would visit the café, their shoulders burdened heavy with a problem for which they could see nor find a solution. Now whether it was our smiles, the aroma of Vera's cooking or that certain air of magic that had taken up residence, I had still to determine, but they always seemed to leave with a smile.

Customers in the afternoon would say to me that it was a slice of Vera's homemade cake which made you feel good. Vera however insisted that it was the magic and that her recipes were in her head and heart, and none were written down.

Therefore, if you find yourself passing may I suggest you call in and try a slice of Vera's cake for yourself. Maybe you could help identify the secret that makes the little red café so special.

Now as partial as I am to cake, my biggest and most important investment besides my staff was the Fracino Contempo and I could not start any day without a coffee. And just like Amelia and Antonio's boating adventure after a coffee I could ride the wave of change and meet any challenge.

This book is not really a sequel, but more a snapshot collection of how we at the little red café fill our days. How the people, some we know others perhaps not visit the café and like a pilgrim who visits a place of worship they come believing that the café is a haven, a place of safety, a place to come and sit and contemplate.

We laugh, we cry, we try our best to find a solution to a problem and we invest our time in making friends. In the unique cauldron that is our existence family and friends, love and laughter is all that really matters. We hope you enjoy the stories to come.

A Bequest from Darkest Africa

Time marched on and the months had passed by without incident although a relentless nagging thought always seemed to linger at the back of my mind, a constant reminder that we had not heard from our intrepid explorer and friend Alfie Wilson.

Not that we ever expected a postcard or indeed a phone call from Alfie to say that he was safe and well, but I could do nothing to suppress the ball of apprehension growing in my gut. Like a volcano of unsettled activity my fears were justified having received the one and only communication regarding Alfie which had been sent from another old school friend, Albert Anders who so happened to be in Africa at the same time as Alfie and traipsing along the sandy beaches of the Gold Coast.

Albert had written to tell me that he had crossed paths with Alfie at a beach hut bar where they had shared a couple of cool beers together. Albert, not given to over dramatizing any detail or adventure, said that his anxiety had been somewhat heightened when he learnt that Alfie was about to head into uncharted territory where laden with thick dense forest, dark shadows and mystery, the stories that did manage to escape the rarely entered region would make the blood run cold.

Knowing Alfie as well as I did, it wasn't the element of danger which concerned me the most, he was after all an adventurer, a sort of latter day India Jones, but in the communique from Albert he had slipped in that even the local witchdoctor had tried to warn and prevent Alfie from going stating that those who went in, never came out.

Reading down the page Albert went on to say that the bedtime stories, told to local children made reference to eyes being seen in the darkness of night, eyes that would prevent sleep.

Haunting eyes that were said to belong to a lost tribe of head hunters, blood-lust cannibals who would roam stealthily between the tall trees at night like ghosts seeking out their victims using the dense undergrowth and shadows for camouflage. Turning over, I swallowed the lump in my throat as Albert described the tribe. Men and women, even children, their nostrils and ear lobes pierced with shards of bone, animal and possibly human bone and their eyes dark like polished black tourmaline. Rumour had it that what became their prey, they boiled alive in a large pot to eat.

Experienced trackers going out into the dense jungle only ever went in large groups believing that there was safety in numbers. The expeditions were short and overnight camps were restricted to normally just one night. Upon their return they were tell of finding bone fragments embedded into the bark of tall trees. Their grizzly find only helping to fuel the many myths surrounding the dark continent of the Congo.

Now if this wasn't bad enough the word amongst the villagers was that the lost tribe had a particular penchant for white skinned explorers, not only because of the bleached colour of their skin which was apparently very appealing and intriguing, but roasted it tasted like the meat of a wild boar.

Poring over the last page and as serious as Albert's communique was, I ridiculously thought of Alfie as a camel with his outsized itchy feet and a vision materialised itself in my mind of his feet spreading like that of the desert camel as he walked on relentlessly on his quest to find buried treasure. Adventures that so often took him to areas of hostility and trouble. Alfie once told me that without the element of danger being present the journey could so soon become boring and uninviting. As far as I was concerned being captured, placed in a large cooking cauldron and boiled alive for the evening tribal meal was as dangerous as it could get. When I showed Vera the letter later that day, she promptly removed meat pies and pork curry from the menu that week.

Long ago, I had come to accept that Alfie had a natural wanderlust running through his veins and that he seemed incapable of settling anywhere for long and that included London. He had a penchant for treading on the toes of local authority, stating adamantly that rules were made to be broken. Folding the letter and resealing the envelope I did think that on this occasion, somewhere in the darkest Congo, Alfie might have taken a wrong turn in his adventure and upset the wrong people. And just like an unsettled wind he had disappeared. I had every good reason to fear for the safety of my old friend.

Sitting at the breakfast table Amelia frowned as she spooned in another mouthful of her chocolate coated cereal. 'Are you going to Africa daddy to find Uncle Alfie?' Sitting alongside Antonio, her brother fixed his stare upon me awaiting my reply. Telepathically I could see that he was sizing up his options as to which way was best to launch his toasted soldiers at me.

Stirring in the coffee granules with the hot water Lola had her back to us, although somehow she was aware of everything that was happening behind her. I had never worked out whether as a woman or indeed a mother she was possessed by instinctive magic or she was gifted with an extraordinary sixth sense.

The coffee mixed she turned cooing softly Antonio's way, *be a good boy and eat your breakfast nicely*.

Like the obedient cub of a lioness he instantly did what had been asked. Had I cooed like that his eyes would have narrowed and the launch countdown would have been inevitably brought forward. Amelia reached over and helped her brother by pushing his toasted soldiers back into the centre of his plastic plate.

As I watched Lola drink her coffee and Amelia play with Antonio, I wondered how that psychic link worked between the three of them. The ability to see, hear and detect everything going on, albeit from another room had always baffled me even as far back as when I was Antonio's age. First my mother had acquired the ability, then I had seen the same in Lola and now sat confidently next to Antonio, Amelia had almost certainly acquired the gift. It was like a flashback episode of 'Bewitched' all over again, the only difference was my son. Antonio had that look that made me think he also had special powers. At times his big saucer eyes were like that of an all seeing, knowing owl.

'No darling,' replied Lola, 'daddy is not going to Africa to look for Uncle Alfie. Daddy remember has the café to look after with Danielle.'

8

I could almost read the thoughts that were going around inside her head as she worked through the conundrum of my possible departure. Amelia looked at Lola who was watching the bird activity outside in the back garden, before she diverted her focus to Antonio before her stare landed squarely on my brow.

'That's good only you promised to take us all to the park this Sunday.' Goodness, I thought she had grown in confidence. I blamed the influence on her spending too much time with Danielle and Vera. Ever the little lady Amelia had her priorities set.

Lola half-turned and smiled my way. Just like her mother I thought, sharp as a pin and equally as beautiful. Antonio having seen the opportunity launched a sodden soldier at me which promptly landed on the shoulder of my shirt much to his delight. A loud chuckle of success burst forth from his chest encouraged by his sister. I had expected a chastisement from his mother, but Lola continued to smile.

'He takes after his father and never misses a trick!' She wiped clean around Antonio's mouth before cutting his toast into much smaller squares. Staring directly at me my son had me measured and weighed. I wiped the stain clean with the dishwashing cloth.

'Anyway daddy,' Amelia pipped up, 'I thought that Auntie Danielle was now the Assistant Manager, doesn't she run the café now?' Lola lowered her head a little more although I knew she was smirking.

'Yes, most days she does although daddy has to make the really important decisions.' I replied.

Antonio stared again at me as he chewed on a damp piece of toast. Had I not been present when he had been born in the café, I could have sworn that the devil had left him inside when my attention had been elsewhere. With the square of toast half in, half out of his mouth he had clamped his lips shut staring me out until I could no longer look his way.

'Oh,' Amelia responded moments later, 'like what decisions?' Just like her mother Amelia never left a conversation half done. I had to think as I sipped my coffee.

'Well like making sure that the customers are looked after when they come in for their food and their drinks. Making sure that everything runs smoothly with the orders and making the coffee when we have our breaks. Keeping Auntie Vera happy.'

Just like a lawyer deliberating over a big case with a jury watching and waiting for his or her next question Amelia turned to look at Antonio. I could have sworn that I saw him nod.

'Oh okay, only the other day at school the teacher asked the class what their daddy's did at work.'

I felt my heart sink. 'And what did you tell Miss Jenkins?'

'I said you drink coffee and eat Aunt Vera's cake. I told the class that Danielle runs the café now and you just count the money at the end of the day!'

The toasted square gone Antonio was now smiling, as was his mother.

'I don't drink coffee all day,' I replied feeling cornered. 'Daddy makes executive decisions. Decisions that make Aunt Vera, Danielle and Martyn happy.'

Amelia sniffed. 'I told Miss Jenkins that mummy works very hard all the time, except on Saturday when I help her do the dusting and cleaning. I looked at Lola whose smile was huge as she raised her eyebrows and shrugged her shoulders as if to say *that's my girl*. I didn't dare look at Antonio only as far as my son was concerned I disappeared every morning, returned home late afternoon and as long as he got pushed back and forth on the swings over the park upon my return his life was good.

'That reminds me Spencer,' Lola interrupted, 'on the way in this morning to the café can you pop into the estate agents and see if they have anything new on the market.'

I agreed that I would, went up to the bathroom cleaned my teeth, dabbed my shirt where the stain still showed before returning to the kitchen where I kissed and hugged them all goodbye leaving for work.

Standing at the gate I took a moment to look back at the front of the house. I was immensely proud of my family and I was keen to get back home later that afternoon, however in the hours in between I did have a responsibility to run the café, see that the customers and staff were happy despite what Amelia had told her class.

I checked the time with my watch, I had plenty of time before the morning rush would begin. By now Danielle would have the café organised with Vera and Martyn out back in the kitchen if she needed any help.

Standing in front of the estate agents window I scanned the properties on offer. The latest batch had been added to the right of the display. Houses were becoming scarce with home owners wanting to extend and renovate rather than move and when a good house did come on the market it was quickly snapped up. We had both agreed that we didn't need a lot, just a few more rooms and space for the children's toys. It was quite surprising just how much more a baby boy could inject into a house in the way of all manner of oddities, toys, clothes, a buggy and a car seat.

Larry Lawrence, the ever ambitious owner of the estate agents saw me looking through the window. He came from around the back of his desk and was instantly at the door where he shook my hand enthusiastically. 'Come in, come in... I was hoping that you would be passing by this morning Spencer only I've a house about to come on the market, a really good house with potential. I went to collect the details myself only yesterday afternoon.'

Now call me suspicious if you like, but tell me an estate agent that doesn't have just the right house that you are looking for the moment you walk in through the shop door. Letting go of his hand I smiled back waiting for the expected sales patter to begin.

'I was recording the details on the computer when you appeared. Believe me when I say that the house is like a dream come true and the vendor's have instructed me to put it on the market today. It would suit you, Lola and the children perfect. You were the first people that I thought of the moment that I saw the house yesterday. Here take a look Spencer, it would resolve all your space problems in one instant hit.'

Larry pushed across the scribbled details for me to read. The more that I read about the house the more I felt that I had wrongly judged Larry. His

11

detailed description did make the house look very appealing. A bigger kitchen diner than what we had now, an open fire and with an extra bedroom it would give us four in total. The garden was about the same size, but that was not a huge priority as long as it was safe and secure, not that we were overly fussed about the outside space.

'How much?' I asked, a fundamental important question.

The eternal optimist Larry's face lit up. 'The price is within the scope of your mortgage and there's room to manoeuvre I add. The present owners are keen to move as soon as possible so we could negotiate and meet them somewhere halfway.' His tongue was moving so articulately inside his mouth that each word was like a well-rehearsed script.

I eyed Larry cautiously. The estate agent was good at his job, very good. His gleaming white toothpaste smile and his keen eyes sparkled with anticipation awaiting my reaction. I read back down through the description picturing each room in my mind. I had to admit it certainly did look ideal.

'I'll tell you what Larry, finish what you have to do here and get the ad together with pictures, I will call Lola and get her to give you a call. Together you can arrange a viewing.' I pushed the details back across the desk. 'When you say the price is within our price range what precisely are we looking at?'

Larry sucked in thoughtfully through his front teeth resembling a beaver about to gnaw through a small branch, 'no more than fifteen maybe twenty above what you're asking for your sale.'

And there you have the bottom line. Estate agents work in multiples of fives and tens and without so much as a flutter of the eyelids can quickly reach a hundred thousand pounds of your money arguing that in the grand scheme of things, monetary transactions are merely a drop in the ocean. Selling houses day in, day out they deal with big numbers, some say telephone numbers. Sitting opposite Larry my brain was calculating through the mortgage repayments, the interest rate and the risk involved. Breathing in hard I had to somehow make this purchase work.

'Fair enough,' I replied trying to sound confident, hiding my hesitancy. Ever the salesman Larry had a proposition tucked up his sleeve.

'I'll you what I will do Spencer. I'll give Lola a call soon and 'I'll get Katie from our marketing team to pop the details around to the café later this morning. Browse through the finished advert and you can discuss the finer details with Lola. I'll give the vendors a call and arrange a viewing before I put it in the window. I've a good feeling about this house and you will love it. I can't be fairer than that.'

No he couldn't. I agreed. We shook on it and I left with monetary numbers swimming around inside my head like a pond full of frantic goldfish at feeding time. As soon as I was clear of the high street and almost at the café I called Lola. Keeping my voice as calm as I could I phoned Lola and told her what I had agreed with Larry and about the house.

Walking through the park having despatched Amelia to school I heard Lola tell Antonio that he could soon be on the move. His response, as I expected came in the form of a loud raspberry. Come the day that my son started to talk I rather hoped that his auditory level of communication had improved.

'Can we afford it?' Lola asked. I could almost see the pleading look in her eyes as she asked.

'Doing the sums and at a stretch, yes I think it's not beyond us.'

Those last few hundred yards to the café earlier had me thinking it through. Taking on the house would almost certainly mean extending our mortgage although I could use the first quarter accounts of the café to show how well we were doing. Despite an exceptionally cold winter we had done exceedingly well, which I had to admit was down to young Martyn who had taken on the recent responsibility of pastry chef. His jumbo sized spiced meat sausage rolls and tasty treat potato pasties had been serious competition for Vera's cooked breakfast orders.

Lola sighed as she stopped pushing Antonio. 'Larry sounded very enthusiastic and kept saying that this was the house for us Spencer. Do you want me to call in and get the details?'

'There's no need only Katie is bringing them around to the café sometime this morning. As soon as I get them I'll get them to you, even if I have to get somebody else to drop them round.'

'Call me and Antonio and I will come to the café instead. We both want to see the details and pictures.' The call ended with me blowing a kiss down the end of the phone, although Antonio was only interested in the squawking ducks nearby where he had dropped them bread.

The interior of the café was as normal warm and inviting as ever when I arrived. I waved at some of our regulars who were actively talking to one another across the tables. It was always good to see them and just like Larry he had his houses and we had the people who filled them. Between us we had the perfect marketing tool.

'You're late this morning, are you okay?' Danielle asked with a smile as I walked past the counter. I guessed that her asking was more for Lola, Amelia and Antonio than me.

All the same I apologised. 'I stopped off to see Larry Lawrence on my way in. You know how Larry likes to talk.'

'Anything good,' she asked as she raised a hand to acknowledge one of the elderly regulars sitting at the back and in need of a coffee refill.

'Maybe, although you know me Danielle and caution is my middle name.'

Seconds later she was between the tables filling mugs with a free second coffee. I watched as she swayed left and right oscillating between chairs coming back to the counter carrying the coffee pot. 'Sometimes Spence you gotta throw caution to the wind and see what comes back at you.' She certainly had a wise head on her shoulders for a young woman.

I continued to watch as Danielle kept the customers happy, she was no longer the tall thin girl that I had employed some eighteen months previously, instead it was a young and vibrant woman who stared back at me. She had a confidence that seemed to show in her smile and the way she dealt with everything. She also had ambition and was destined to go places. Somewhere hidden deep beneath that exterior was a wild spirit yearning to be set free. Watching her move between the tables she reminded me of Alfie Wilson. Danielle was right, I did need to throw caution aside and take a risk every now and again. Returning to the counter she thumbed at the underside. 'This morning's mail is on the shelf.'

I thanked her. 'I'll have a look once I have said hello to Vera and Martyn.' I poked my head through the kitchen door.

'How are Lola and the little ones?' Vera asked. Since the arrival of Amelia, my marrying Lola and the birth of Antonio, Vera's interest had shifted and instead of asking after me she now asked after Lola and the children. Secretly I didn't mind because we all considered her as an extension of our family.

'They're good thanks and Antonio's aim is improving!' I pointed to the stain on my shirt. Going over to the first aid cabinet Vera took out a plastic bottle of stain remover.

'Here try this, it's good for removing fat and the like.' I rubbed the moisturised ball over the affected patch and read the instructions which said it would dry in about half an hour. I thanked Vera heard about last night's football match from Martyn before going back out front to sort the mail.

There was the normal assorted envelopes containing bills, charitable letters and adverts, the latter of which I added to the recycling bin. The last envelope however definitely caught my eye. The stamp was unusual and franked on the African continent.

I eagerly pulled aside the seal withdrawing from inside a very formal looking letter. I was surprised to read that it was from a solicitor's practice in Kinshasa, a city of the Democratic Republic of the Congo. I made sure that the envelope was addressed to me before I read the content of the communique.

Abdalla Abeeku, Solicitor at Law, Avenue du Chapel, Kinshasa, DR Congo.

Dear Mr Spencer Brand

I have been instructed on behalf of my client, Mr Alfred Harrison Wilson to contact you and to inform you that I act upon his instruction in the matter of his estate owing to the unfortunate circumstances by which he finds himself no longer with us.

You might not be aware, but Mr Wilson and a party of six of our best African porters sourced locally entered the Congo basin just prior to December last. His reason for doing so are best known to himself, although from previous conversations with my client I do believe that his interests were to search for the caves of the legendry King Solomon where legend tells of a hidden cache of gold, diamonds and silver coins.

For myself, I am indeed sceptical that such treasure did ever exist, however Mr Wilson a respected and intrepid explorer was most adamant and insistent that it was there, somewhere deep in the Congo Basin.

As many around here would vouch that part of the Congo is richly overgrown with trees and vegetation and that many who venture inside the darkness never come back out. Villagers living near to the edge of the trees describe unusual events, especially at night and of sightings of a rarely seen tribe known as the Ahumbra who live deep in the very darkest areas of the jungle and who legend has it, still practice ritualistic cannibalism.

Regrettably, no word has been received from Mr Wilson or any of his pack team since their departure and as per the terms and conditions of our contract I am, as instructed writing to you.

A stipulation of his last Will and Testament states that if after three months no word has been received from the hunting party then I am to assume that all members including Mr Wilson are deceased and that I am to sort his affairs and estate.

Attached you will find a document outlining his last affidavit.

I await your further instruction.

16

Yours sincerely, your servant

Abdalla Abeeku

I read the letter over again sitting myself down. I was not only shocked, stunned by what I had read, but completely overwhelmed by what many thought would be Alfie's last adventure. It made me shudder to think that he might have ended up in a cooking pot along with ripe bananas, berries and mangoes. Shaking my head in disbelief, it just didn't seem possible. Alfie was presumed missing, dead. He was always so full of life and energy. He was the same age as me and he still had half the world left to conquer, to explore with treasure to find and books to write. The news was hard to swallow.

Having dispatched a group of postal workers back to the sorting office armed with a bag of sausage rolls and bacon sandwiches, Danielle looked my way rather concerned at the colour in my cheeks. Thinking that I was about to faint she came back over to the counter in double quick time.

'Are you alright Spence only you've gone very white, have you just seen a ghost?'

I handed over the letter, 'here,' I said, 'read this. Not necessarily a ghost although there could be one floating about that we both know.' As Danielle started to read the official letter I read the attached affidavit.

The Last Will & Testament of Alfred Harrison Wilson

Being of sound mind and body on this day of the 27th of December, in the year 2011, I hereby bequeath in the event of my death and my not coming back from my latest adventure, my entire estate to Mr Spencer Marlon Brand c/o The Little Red Café, Oslo Road, London. England.

Signed: Alfie Harrison Wilson

Other details in the document listed Alfie's bank account, where to find the branch, the number of the account and the sort code. Additional instructions stated that the manager had the password locked in a safe deposit box, where I would also find the deeds to his flat. My school friend had thought of everything in the event of his never coming back. Sitting there with the document in my hand I felt quite dumbstruck and mentally I had to ask myself why me of all people. Danielle having read the letter gave it back before she placed two clean mugs under the Francino Contempo.

'Wow Spence, I think we both a coffee with sugar. That's a lot to take in.' She added two fingers of shortbread to the saucers.

'I can't believe it,' I whispered in response. 'I thought that we would see Alfie breeze in through the door of the café sometime around Easter, pitch himself at his normal table and order a fried breakfast as though nothing of interest had taken place during the past six months, except his getting out of bed each day.'

We occupied the two stools behind the counter both staring at the customers who were oblivious to our shock. Had it really been six months it didn't seem possible, although it probably was. Alfie had missed the wedding, last Christmas and Antonio being born. Danielle suddenly reached across and held my hand.

'All said and done Spence, Alfie had a great life.' All that I could do was nod in agreement.

We sat and drank our coffee, devouring our shortbread making small talk, snippets really about Alfie's last visit before I went through to the kitchen to tell Vera and Martyn. When I came back out front again Katie from the estate agents was there to give me the advert for the house. I thanked her and told her that Lola had spoken to Larry.

'You still looking for a new house?' Danielle asked.

'Yes, we are desperate for the extra space and very soon Antonio will be motoring around the place.'

Danielle tapped the envelope. 'I reckon you will be able to afford anything on the market now. Last weekend me and Martyn was over Alfie's neck of the woods where he has his apartment, it's a really nice area Spence and very upmarket. If you considered selling his flat it would fetch a real good price.'

Without her realising it, Danielle was fast developing into an astute businesswoman. She had a methodical brain inside that pretty head of hers, at times she could be a little scatty, but I would not change a thing about her.

'I know, but what about Alfie's effects, his trophies, his books and personal belongings, what would I do with them all?' It was a rhetorical question spoken out aloud rather than at Danielle.

She tapped the envelope again with the end of her finger.

'It clearly say's his *entire estate* meaning the whole kit and caboodle Spence. In my book that means lock, stock and barrel. It's yours to do what you want with it and if you get stuck knowing where to go, give old Gilbert from the antique shop in Tavistock Place a shout. He would be round quicker than a flea on a mangy dog. That old buzzard buys and sells second hand goods all the time.'

Danielle had an answer for every problem. If I did decide to sell the apartment I would make sure that she, Vera and Martyn all got a healthy bonus from the proceeds of any sale.

After lunch when trade had eased Lola popped in with Antonio so that he could see Vera, Danielle and Martyn. My son was fast becoming a recognised celebrity amongst the customers too who I am sure came visiting the café just to see him arrive. Coming after lunch also gave Lola the opportunity to go next door and see how Mary was doing. With Antonio in safe hands I showed Lola the letter and copy of the Will. I watched her expression change as she read through the contents. Slowly her jaw began to drop.

'I take it that the authorities conducted a thorough search for Alfie?' she asked.

'I'd like to think they went into the jungle as far as was safe to do so.'

She shook her head in disbelief. 'What a horrible way to end your life.'

'You mean lost in a jungle or in a cooking pot?'

Her shoulders dropped together. 'Both, poor Alfie.'

'In a way that was the adventure in him and if it did end like that, it's how he would have imagined it. Alfie was a rare breed.'

Lola shook her head. 'No, he gave the impression that he didn't care, but he did.'

We didn't say it out loud, but we both understood how Alfie's bequest would dramatically affect to our future. I gave her the details of the house.

'It looks beautiful Spencer.'

Lola took the estate agent details with her going next door to see Mary. With only an elderly couple present in the café I went through to the kitchen. Danielle had Antonio on her knee and the two of them were happily playing clap along with Vera.

Thanks to my friend Alfie our future suddenly looked very secure and there would be need to show the bank manager our first quarter accounts. We would be able to afford the house that Larry was keen on us viewing, although I would much rather have had Alfie return home safe and sound. Watching Antonio play clap with Danielle made me realise how we have friends throughout our life. Some come and go, whereas others stay the distance and what they feel for you, you never really know, not until it matters.

After tea that evening we took the children to view the house. Amelia immediately fell in love with everything, running from room to room with the little boy whose house it still was until we exchanged contracts. Antonio unsurprisingly slept through the whole viewing although in time he would be as excited as his sister. As for Lola, she was her normal beautiful self, calm and polite she asked the questions that mattered and made everything fall nicely into place.

Much later that evening with Lola asleep on my shoulder, I thought long and hard about Alfie Harrison Wilson, remembering the energy with which he would tell me of his exploits, his adventures making me green with envy. I would listen to the places that he visited, the people he met and what he discovered. At least I had his travel books to look at whenever I thought of Alfie. His memory would live on.

In a way, in his hunt for lost treasure Alfie had followed in the footsteps of Thomas Oliver Barringer, the highwayman. Maybe, perhaps through the mystery surrounding time and kinetic science they had somehow connected and found that treasure. Looking out at the stars beyond the bedroom window I wondered if Alfie was looking back down and smiling at me.

Perhaps Danielle got it right when she had said that Alfie had achieved a lot only never settled in any one place. Watching the stars sparkle every so often I did envy Alfie his energy for life, but travel was never my desire. I liked my feet firmly on the ground. When a star winked at me I silently thanked Alfie for everything and wished him well on his next journey.

It was a couple days later when everybody had left the café and I was about to lock up that I felt a breeze waft through although the door and windows were all shut. I am not sure why, but I sat at the table that he had used on his last visit and asked Alfie to join me.

Anybody walking past would have seen me talking to an empty café and thought me mad, but in my thoughts we had a conversation. In a strange, odd way talking to Alfie and his spirit made me feel much better about the letter, the will and the onerous task of sorting through his belongings. When there were no more thoughts I had an indescribable feeling that Alfie Wilson had planned this all along. Maybe he had just wanted to vanish and made his disappearance in the dark depths of the Congo look like his final days. Alfie was an enigma that could never be fully explained.

Several other times, nearly always around closing time Danielle had also told me that she felt a breeze brush past her as she cleaned and arranged the tables for the next day.

'That's Alfie,' she would say, quite convinced and especially when she cleaned *his* table. We came to accept that Alfie's spirit was happy being at the little red café although when it time to turn out the lights and lock the front door, we would both nod and ask that he look after the place until we returned.

'Do you reckon he came back Spence because the place is haunted or has a magic presence?' she asked.

'A bit of both I reckon. It's what makes it special don't you think.'

Danielle would smile and say goodnight to Alfie, then turn and walk away leaving me to turn the key in the lock. I would also say goodnight and thank Alfie again. He might not have always found treasure, but he made my dreams come true.

I will end this chapter by saying that should you be in the area and have a story to tell, why not pop in and share it with us. I will add your tale to the book and together we will maybe convince a lot of people that magical things do happen. God bless you Alfie wherever you are.

Oh and one last thing before we turn to the next page, I feel that I should mention that I was speaking to somebody the other day who had visited the Congo recently. During our conversation I happened to mention the solicitor Abdalla Abeeku, he responded with a shrug of his shoulders telling me that he had never heard of the man or indeed his practice. What he did tell was that the name *Abdalla* meant a servant of god and *Abeeku* was representative of being born on a Wednesday. It was a Wednesday when our offer on the house was accepted.

Looking up at the clouds as the man continued talking I envisaged Alfie Wilson sitting up there somewhere, enjoying a coffee of his own and grinning. He would have found it amusing to have used the services of a man, a servant of god to have dealt with his last wishes. My only claim to fame was that my name Spencer referred to me as the keeper of the inn or in this case the little red café. From the outside it doesn't look like much, but walk through that red painted door and it can change your life in ways that you would never have imagined possible.

A Thunderbolt from Heaven

First indications that anything was romantically developing between Stephanie Steele and Robert Styles was when we had seen them together at the children's party, which we had held in the little red café. Do you remember the day, only it had a magical feel to it bring us together with Amelia and Angus.

Not uncommon although amusing some of us witnessed Robert hold the door open for Stephanie and her smile of gratitude which said so much more than thank you. That gesture and smile had implications and proved that they had just not met at the corner that Sunday afternoon.

At first there had been the odd furtive glance slowly smouldering into a knowing look and then a stolen kiss no doubt in the vestry after morning service on a Sunday. But, before any of you begin to pass judgement, remember that in the house of the good lord if he so desires to sanction their love, then so should others and since the beginning of time and Adam and Eve, men and women have been coming together for that reason.

How serious they were about one another became quite apparent when Robert came to the café around eleven after his regular Monday morning visit to the old folk's home. Walking in, he activated the small brass bell which hung overhead whereupon Robert clamped his hands together as if in prayer.

'Good morning Spencer. That bell of yours always remind me of the one that we had at home when I was a child. My mother would ring the bell in the hall to announce lunch was ready. My father would emerge from the study and stand to one side as my sister and I descended the stairs from the bedrooms above. Such joyous memories and lunches were always full of chatter, much laughter and later in the afternoon games in the garden outback.' Looking up at the bell as it stopped ringing Robert seemed momentarily lost in his thoughts. 'However, time marches on.' Yes, it did.

He turned his attention back to me and nodded at some of the customers who sat in his congregation on a Sunday. 'My father was a vicar, have I ever told you that?'

It was news to me or least I think it was. 'Perhaps, is he still a vicar?' It would have been a natural rite of passage that Robert did follow in his father's footsteps although not all men do.

'Indeed yes, his church is over in Ellerbury Grange. The rectory, a magnificent house is set to one side with the garden between the church and the house. Spring time is best when the flowers are beginning to bloom once again. His prayers are that one day I would take over his parish.'

'So you would move away from London?' I admit that was surprised as Robert had always said that he felt his place was in the capital helping the underprivileged, the vulnerable and the elderly.

'One I would hope to settle down. Maybe then, I would have to give the thought serious consideration.'

I had known Robert for a good many years, we were good friends and he respected my views regarding religion as much as I had similar respect for what he did and his church. We did however avoid conversations on religion wherever possible unless Lola and Mary were present. I saw his returning to Ellerbury Grange as a shepherd returning home to his flock. Watching as he moved closer to the counter I had never thought of Robert as the settling kind.

'Besides your maker, have you met someone that would help make that decision?' I was fishing as several ears flapped our way.

The expression on his face was full of radiance. 'It is true to say that Stephanie and I have become close of late.' Several customers nearby had to adjust themselves on their seats to stop them from falling over.

'Stephanie Steele from the paper?' I asked feigning innocence.

'*My Angel of Words* as I refer to her, yes that Stephanie.' The silence was immediately shattered as conversations started up again.

'Coffee or tea?' I asked taking two large cups with saucers from the shelf beside the coffee machine.

'Coffee please and a delightful slice of Vera's delightful ginger and orange cake.'

'You know she adds rum to the cake.'

The smile from the other side of the counter was larger than life itself. 'There are times in a day Spencer when a man has to live dangerously.'

Danielle agreed to look after the counter as Robert and I found ourselves a table where we could talk. I launched straight in before he could change the subject.

'So when did the thunderbolt from heaven arrive?'

'Over Christmas really. I have my church, the rented house and my parish work here in London whereas Stephanie has the paper and her rented accommodation. Quite by coincidence her parents live in Lincolnshire and not that far from Ellerbury Grange. Odd that we grew up not far from one another and yet our paths never crossed. God certainly does move in mysterious ways sometimes.'

I grinned. 'So you spent Christmas together then...?'

'Yes and no, although it wasn't easy at times.' Robert ever shrewd, rarely missed anything that went on in his parish including the whispers.

'You're a prominent figure remember, respected and in your collar unmistakeable. I would have been surprised had you not been seen together.' I leant across the table. 'And I think it's about time that you got yourself a girlfriend.' It seemed somewhat odd saying that the vicar had a girlfriend, but this was a modern era.

'I look upon her as my soulmate Spencer. Stephanie and I are soulmates.' His eyes glazing around the inside of the café to be met with several others.

'It's serious then?' I asked.

'Indeed and our union has been sanctioned by the bishop. She was very understanding believing that married vicars have a greater understanding of family issues which helps promote how religion can resolve and calm matrimonial discord. We are to announce our engagement this Sunday and the reason for my visit this morning is to invite you all to the church and a small gathering after the service.'

And there it was as plain as day, entrapment. Robert was as ever the shrewd servant of god and perhaps more devious than I had thought. His invitation was extended to Lola and the children, Mary and Thomas, Vera, Danielle and Martyn. I was delighted to accept.

'We wouldn't miss it for the world.' How exactly I was going to explain that we would have to forego a visit to the park to Amelia and Antonio was another thing. Maybe the offer of juice and cake would help sway the disappointment.

Danielle arrived with Roberts's cake and I could smell the rum from where I was sat. Placing a napkin beside his plate she promptly leant forward and kissed Robert on the cheek.

'I have always wanted to do that to a man of the church.' Robert smiled as eyes turned to our table. Somehow he managed to salvage his dignity and surprise. 'And what prompts such a beautiful moment?' he asked.

'Why you and Stephanie getting engaged of course.' Danielle winked at me then went back to the counter.

Robert leant closer. 'How does she know,' he asked, 'I've only just announced my engagement plans to you?'

I raised my palms. 'You might be all singing, all dancing behind that pulpit, but there are some things that a man accepts in this world and that is that women, females of any age know about things. It's best not to ask how they know because it can open up a can of worms for men. In time you will come to appreciate that not only do the gentler sex have a specific way with words, there are moments when saying or not asking is much safer. They seem to possess a unique gift of knowing exactly what men are thinking.' I paused to check that Lola wasn't walking in the door with Antonio. 'If you want proof, pop round one weekend when you are free, I have two females at home who can read me like a book.'

Robert laughed promising to pay us a visit. 'And Antonio, how is he doing?'

'Just fine. He watches, learns fast and mimics his big sister. I'm beginning to believe that he has more of his mother in him than me, although she would say that it was the other way around.'

He templed his hands together again once more. 'We are all children of the lord.' I noticed that his bible was sat on the table beside his plate. Robert never went anywhere with his good book.

I took the envelope from my pocket and passed it across the table. 'Maybe a few of the flock get lost along the way.' I said. 'Here, read this and tell me what you think.'

I saw his expression change several times as he read the letters from Albert Anders and Abdalla Abeeku. When he was done reading he carefully folded both letters and replaced them back in the envelope then picked up his bible.

'The good lord will watch over Alfie.'

I looked at Robert seeing only the good in his eyes. 'You don't think he's dead, eaten alive!'

'No, I feel his spirit here in the café,' he touched his chest, 'and here too, in my heart. Believe in miracles Spencer and one will appear.' I looked at the bible that he was clutching. We had one at home that Lola had had as a child. Was Roberts's faith so strong that he could feel Alfie's presence. I didn't doubt it. I returned to the original reason for his visit putting the envelope back in my pocket.

'And Stephanie, how does she feel about becoming the wife of a vicar. I mean it's a far cry from that of a successful reporter?'

Robert swallowed a mouthful of coffee which helped wash down a forkful of cake. He used the napkin to wipe the crumbs from his lips. 'She is very happy to keep on reporting after we are married and I support her wholeheartedly. The newspaper editor apparently saw the union as a golden opportunity to run an article on religious marriages using Stephanie as an inside model.'

'Isn't that like Judas Iscariot selling secrets to the Romans?'

Robert laughed. 'No, and the bishop agrees with the editor. She is of the opinion that a page in the local paper could help get people back into our churches. Written by Stephanie from the inside looking out, it might also help quell or diminish myth and legend. Which reminds me, are we still pencilled in for the second week of March to have the children baptised?' I was left wondering what myths, what legends.

'Lola was going to contact you this week and confirm the arrangements.'

Robert checked his pocket diary and pencilled in the Sundays. 'That would sit nicely with my other plans.' He finished his coffee and put down his bible. 'Stephanie and I would like you to be our best man Spencer.'

I felt my jaw drop as my mouth opened. 'I am honoured Robert, but look how we've discussed the church in the past. Am I really the right man for the job?'

Never deterred Robert patted the back of my hand. 'I would not have asked if I didn't think you was the right man. We would like Danielle and Amelia as bridesmaids, along with my sister.'

As if by magic Danielle appeared with the coffee pot to refill our mugs.

'When is our first fitting?' Robert and I both laughed. Danielle had perfect hearing.

'Remember what I told you about that special gift that they possess. Feminine intuition can be a minefield for us men.'

Robert nodded. 'I will remember that when I am married!'

Amelia would be over the moon to be asked and standing alongside Danielle who she looked upon as her big sister, the two of them plus Robert's sister would make a grand trio.

'Thank you Robert, I'll gladly accept.' Robert informed Danielle that Stephanie would be in touch later that day. I watched her dance on the spot wondering if she would get any work done now. Like a flash she disappeared into the kitchen to tell Vera and Martyn.

'We would like Martyn to be our official usher, he's a very sensible and polite young man, and he would organise the guests without any fuss.

'Does Stephanie not have any brothers or sisters?'

'No, she's an only child.' Robert looked towards the kitchen door. 'We wanted to ask Vera to do the cake. Do you think she would?'

'Well let's go and ask her.'

Danielle was still buzzing when we entered the kitchen. I saw Vera wipe her hands on a clean tea towel.

'This is the first time I've had a vicar in my kitchen Robert. Have you come to tell me that I am behind with my church subscriptions?'

Robert laughed as he walked forward.

'Indeed no Vera. As you have no doubt heard already Stephanie and I are to be married. We wanted to ask you, if you would make our cake?'

'Can I add a little alcohol, say rum or brandy?'

'It would make my father's day if you did. And if it was anything like the moist ginger delight that I experienced before I came into the kitchen, mixed with melted syrup and treacle, infused with rum and orange then I would say it will be a cake made in heaven by an angel.'

'Don't go any further,' I advised, 'too much praise and she'll be asking for a rise!'

'Ignore him vicar,' replied, 'I would be extremely happy to make your cake. I'll talk to Stephanie and see what she wants as the bride. The cake will be my wedding present to you both.'

Standing alongside Robert I nudged his arm. 'I told you, they stick together as well.' It was only then that I noticed a small smudge of lipstick where Danielle had kissed his cheek.

Robert took Vera's hand and kissed the back. 'Thank you Vera, your reward will be waiting for you in heaven.' He meant it too.

Vera nodded thoughtfully. 'There is only one thing waiting for me in heaven vicar and one day I'll join him.'

I felt a cold shiver run through me although the kitchen was warm. Alfie or Cyril, they were probably one of many that found the café inviting.

Taking a corner of her pinny she licked it damp and promptly removed the lipstick smudge from Robert's cheek. 'That wouldn't do for Stephanie to walk in now and find you like that.'

Robert rubbed his cheek as it flushed pink. 'My goodness no.'

We went back out and to our table where Danielle had refilled our coffee cups.

'I forgot to ask Martyn.' Robert declared. 'I'll be back in a minute or so.'

I watched him dart between the tables nodding and smiling as he went remembering the first time that I had seen him enter the café, it seemed that a lot had happened in between. When he returned he seemed at peace with the world, a contented man.

'You've made them all very happy, thank you!'

'It makes a change to see happy faces, often the ones that I see other than at a wedding or christening are sad, desperate or standing around the grave. Give me happiness every day in exchange for salvation.'

'You once told me that I had been saved.'

'Indeed yes I did, I remember that occasion. The café, Lola and Amelia were your salvation Spencer and then little Antonio arrived to put a seal on god's belief in you. We are also blessed with friends too, such as Mary and Thomas, Vera, Danielle and Martyn.'

Robert was right although I thought of how my son would greet me with a loud raspberry every time I walked in through the house door. The good lord had a funny way of expressing himself through Antonio. I could however not deny however that the café and my family, and our friends were not a blessing. Like an older brother I had another piece of advice.

'When you go on your honeymoon Robert try to steer clear of churches. Too much prayer and letting him above see all might not be quite up to Stephanie's expectations.'

Robert frowned not quite understanding. 'What do you mean?'

'You will have received god's blessing at the ceremony by marrying Stephanie. You don't need his spiritual presence later... trust me.'

'Oh... I see what you mean.' He put two fingers down inside his dog collar to allow more air down onto his chest before leaning across the table. 'I have already prayed for my sins Spencer.'

I slapped my chest as I laughed.

'Good man, there's nothing worse than you flicking through Gideon's on your wedding night and searching for the right prayer.' I veered myself away from the physical side of his honeymoon. 'Will your father officiate at the wedding?' I asked.

'Yes, we both thought it would be fitting that he did. Stephanie has met my family several times since last Christmas.' I was so looking forward to meeting Roberts's family and especially his father. Two vicars and perhaps the bishop as a wedding guest would be interesting.

When the bell chimed over the café door I wasn't surprised to see Stephanie breeze in and join us at the table. She nudged Roberts and gave him one of her special smiles that she saved just for him.

'Hello Spencer, has Robert told you our news?'

'We are all very pleased for you both. Danielle's not come down from the ceiling yet after being asked to be a bridesmaid and Vera's chuffed to be making your cake, she just needs to discuss the recipe with you. As for me, well I am over the moon to be asked, but I will run my speech by you before the big day.'

'And you'll tell Amelia later?'

'She will want to keep the dress.'

Stephanie smiled. 'Of course, all little girls want to be princesses forever.'

'And you will come to the service to hear the wedding banns read?' I saw the doubt in her eyes as she asked the question.

'I wouldn't miss it for the world.'

Stephanie looked at Robert squeezing his arm. 'Now I do believe in miracles.'

'I was about to get around to saying about the banns when you arrived.'

'Feminine intuition and timing,' I replied giving Stephanie a craft wink.

'What does he mean Robert?'

Wrestling with telling the truth and a little white lie Robert patted her leg beneath the table. 'Spencer was merely explaining before you arrived that there are times when small considerations can say much more than words.' I had to admit Robert was good and so was his quick thinking.

Stephanie winked back which did have me worried. 'Exactly, and I think that that is so important in a relationship.' If the Virgin Mary had walked in at that precise moment it would not have surprised me.

It wasn't the Virgin Mary, but instead Mary from next door with my son in her arms accompanied by Lola. Feminine intuition, it works every time.

'I've caught you speechless for once,' said Lola as she kissed me. I made a funny face at Antonio who instantly blew me a wet raspberry response. I didn't think that there would be a mention of him in the bible, not unless the devil himself had scripted a paragraph. Almost instantly Danielle appeared having heard the bell much to the delight of Antonio. She was closely followed by Vera.

I left it to Stephanie and Robert to give the good news to Lola and Mary as I went behind the counter to serve customers arriving. Every so often I would hear a peel of laughter and look up. The happy couple looked so happy and I was happy for them. They were inseparable and without doubt a match made in heaven.

Looking ahead two years from now Stephanie and Robert Styles would have a family of their own. They would share their love with a son who they would name Angus after a very special teddy bear that brought them both together and then fifteen months later Stephanie would give birth to a beautiful little girl who they would call Carolyn. It would be a loving, thoughtful and fitting gesture to the manager and our good friend from the children's home.

Watching my son being entertained by all in the café, I stood silently behind the counter pondering over how no day was ever the same and that blessings would arrive in all shape, manner and sizes. Magical moments were meant to surprise and did they ever. Whether, as Robert would tell me, it was the lord's work or not, I felt very fortunate to be part of so many happy events and all because of the little red café.

The Last letter Home

The contracts for the house had been exchanged and after what had seemed to take an age the day of the move had finally arrived. Peering over at the clock it was a minute after five. I reached across and depressed the button to deactivate the alarm only my senses were alert enough for me not to want a ringing sound blast through my head so early. Beyond the curtains the birds were already up and happily chirping to one another. The sun was rising and it looked like being a good day.

Sitting on the bed edge I stifled an escaping yawn and stretching hard I felt the fresh oxygen invigorate my muscles. I was ready to take on the challenges of the day. Taking a look at Lola who was still sleeping I slipped silently from the bed covering her with the duvet, she could sleep on for another hour before Antonio was due to wake.

After entering into the world with an almighty scream to let everybody know that he had arrived Antonio would generally sleep through the night and wake around six wanting a bottle, although of late he had taken to staying awake until his sister went to sleep about eight in the evening and surprising us all by waking with the dawn chorus. How the little mite managed to find so much energy to get through a full day of play, eating, drinking and more play baffled me. Lola blamed me saying he had inherited my restless spirit and that Antonio was taking after me. Have you noticed that whatever bad habits children acquire down the years of their growing the father always gets the blame.

Tiptoeing across the carpeted bedroom floor I became aware of a pair of attentive eyes watching me from the cot. Big and round like saucers Antonio watched as I slipped into my dressing gown before he startled to gurgle, the deep throaty chuckling sound coming from inside his tiny chest. I instantly put my finger to my lips, but silence wasn't in the rules of his game. Antonio was about to stick out his tongue and offer his customary greeting when I quickly flicked the tip of his nose hitting his tongue on the way down. I cringed as he laughed.

From the behind Lola groaned as she looked at the clock. 'Did you wake him?' she asked sleepily.

'No, he was already awake before I got up.'

'Where are you going, it's only just gone five Spencer!'

'To make a cup of coffee and do the last of the packing.'

I heard Lola groan as she stuffed her head beneath the pillow shielding out the light and the birds singing. Looking back at Antonio he had climbed to a standing position and was about rattle his toy dog back and forth along the cot sides which normally meant that he was ready to go downstairs. From under the pillows I felt a pair of intense dark Italian eyes aiming daggers at my heart.

'Would you like to take your son with you?' she asked. I didn't smile in response, Antonio did the little bugger. At times he was so like his mother. Kissing the back of her bare shoulder I heard her murmur and curse something in her native Italian. Sweeping Antonio from his cot I told him that we needed the bathroom first and then we would go downstairs where his playpen was yet to be dismantled.

With an assortment of cuddly toys to amuse him Antonio seemed quite happy to ignore me as I boiled warm milk for his bottle. I looked around, stacked in every available space the kitchen looked like a war zone under fire. In under four hours the removal men were due to arrive. Pouring hot water into my coffee mug I feel the panic churning inside my stomach.

Testing the temperature of the milk I picked Antonio up from the playpen where together we watched the birds as he filled his stomach, one eye on the bottle, the other on me, turning his attention to the birds arriving at the bird table outside where they foraged amongst the cake crumbs and segments of fruit that Amelia had laid out for them the night before. Sucking as much as his lungs would allow I wondered how and when my son came up for air.

'Well Antonio,' I said, 'take a last look around only in a few hours from now we will say goodbye to this house and be on the move thanks to your Uncle Alfie.' Antonio stopped sucking and looked up at me as though he had recognised the name. What it possible I wondered. Had Alfie paid the children a visit when Lola and my back had been turned in a different direction.

Sitting on the kitchen chair with Antonio on my lap I let my thoughts wander thinking about my long lost school friend. Out of respect of his memory we had arranged for a local storage warehouse to look after his effects until such time that we felt it right to dispose of them properly and not through Gilbert down at the antique shop. I could not explain the feeling inside of me, but since talking with Robert I had felt different and maybe his faith in god was stronger than my own.

'What do you reckon Antonio,' I asked tickling the underside of his chin, 'do you think that your Uncle Alfie is out there somewhere?'

Astonishingly Antonio gurgled up at me in his own infant language. How I wished then that he could talk as well as his sister. Whatever it was that my son gurgled, it had certainly had meaning that much I could see in his eyes. When the bottle was empty, I winded the excess air from his stomach before putting Antonio in his high chair where the birds could entertain him along with the squirrel that had arrived a few minutes before to steal some fruit.

'You have not been here that long young man, 'I said, as I stirred the spoon around inside my mug, 'and I doubt that you'll ever remember much, but your sister will and no doubt when you can understand one another she will tell you about this house, the garden and our move.' Absently, lost in my thoughts I looked around. 'I will miss the house and its odd quirky creaks and groans, the unexplained noises although I am sure our next home will have a few of its own.' Looking around Antonio was memorising things, the birds, the squirrel and the garden, each vision stored somewhere deep in his young mind.

If Alfie was lying dead somewhere in the deepest darkest African Congo then his audacious spirit was coming through my son. With his tongue pocking out the side of his mouth he was unusually quiet, simply observing. I took Antonio from his high chair sitting him on the worktop so that he could see every inch of the garden. When his head shot round to the door behind he had sensed his mother's presence before I had. She took Antonio from me kissed his cheek giving him an affectionate cuddle.

'Has daddy been looking after you?' she asked. Lola planted a kiss on my cheek as I switched the kettle back on.

'I thought you'd sleep in a little longer?'

'It was way too quiet down here and when you two are together it heightens my suspicions.'

'We were about to finish the packing,' I replied as I measured a spoonful of coffee into a clean mug, 'although Antonio was watching the birds watch the squirrel below the bird table.'

Lola rocked her son in her arms as she nuzzled his belly. 'Yes, we must make sure that the removal men remember the bird house, Amelia would create merry hell if it got left behind.'

The sound of Antonio laughing brought Amelia down from her bed. She yawned coming into the kitchen before kissing Lola and her brother. I pointed to my cheek and received a warm soft kiss.

'It looks like it's an early start for everybody this morning.'

Amelia took her brother from Lola and together they sat on the kitchen rug so that they could play. Despite having had his milk he was chewing on his cloth story book. Lola dropped four slices of bread into the toaster taking the butter and pot of jam from the fridge.

'How long have I got before I pack my rucksack?'

Reassuringly Lola sat between Amelia and Antonio. 'We're good for another couple of hours darling, your only worry is that Angus and Shamus get packed too.'

'They're sitting by the bedroom door and will come in the car between Antonio and me in case they get forgotten.' She watched the toast pop up from the toaster. 'I think they'll miss this house too!' We both hard the tinge of sadness in her voice.

Lola kissed Amelia on the forehead. 'They'll soon be happy in the new house and perhaps when we get there you can draw a picture of how you want the garden to look.'

I grinned at the three of them sitting on the circular mat. The new house was an adventure and all week Amelia had been drawing designs for her bedroom, Antonio's room and the kitchen. Lola had a natural knack when it came to allaying any of Amelia's trepidation.

'That lovely Uncle Alfie left us enough money so that we could buy a much bigger house and so that you and Antonio could have lots of room to play together. Daddy and myself were talking the other evening and we think that all your toys could go in the spare room. Maybe we should ask Uncle Thomas to decorate the room, but you'll have to tell him in what colours.' The smile immediately returned to Amelia's cheeks.

Amelia put a thoughtful finger to her lips already working through the design. 'Antonio likes Goofy and I like Minnie Mouse, but I'll sit down with Uncle Thomas and he can look at my drawings.' I gently nodded in agreement. Amelia was definitely growing and most of her confidence was down to Lola.

Lola hugged her son and daughter. 'We should invite Aunt Mary and Uncle Thomas over for tea one evening and then you can show him your drawings. I am sure that he will do anything you ask.'

On the kitchen table sat one of her drawings. It had been meticulously detailed adding toys and books. There were no empty boxes. Amelia was a funny little girl, extremely happy and calm as long as everything had a place and as long as it fitted. As I watched her sitting with Lola and Antonio there was still some small memories left over from the children's home in our daughter. Of course whether the toy room remained neat and tidy when Antonio took his first steps was yet to be seen.

We at around the table sharing our last breakfast together in the old house. I sat opposite Antonio judging that I was far enough away from his launch abilities. Lola had permission from the school allowing Amelia the day off so that she help move house. When the first of the two removal vans arrived she was sitting on the doorstep armed ready with her rucksack. She had Angus and Shamus safety tucked under each arm.

'I can imagine that despite her growing and eventually becoming a young woman that trio will be inseparable,' whispered Lola as she walked past.

I smiled. Angus was Amelia's hope of making dreams come true at the children's home and Shamus was already a keen favourite of little Antonio. The teddies were cherished possessions in our family.

'Inseparable,' I repeated. I went and sat down next to Amelia. 'The garden at the new house is nice, big enough to include a play house for you and your brother.' It was good to see Amelia's eyes light up.

'Really daddy, would it be big enough to have a porch, so that I can sit on it with Angus and Shamus, and Antonio when he learns to walk?'

'Big enough for you all I guess, plus a few of your big dolls.'

Holding Antonio in her arms, Lola was in earshot of our conversation.

'Will it be there when we arrive?' Amelia continued to ask.

'Not quite yet, although I was thinking that once we're settled in the new house perhaps you, mummy and Antonio can come with me to the garden centre and we can choose a play house together.' I felt the hand of approval rest on my shoulder as Lola stood behind. 'And maybe we can get both nanny's to make you some curtaining and knit a blanket in case the dollies get cold.'

And that was how easy the problem was resolved. We had enough money in the bank to get a good sturdy playhouse, one that would serve both Amelia and Antonio for many hours of play. It would be their garden retreat and a place that they could share without any adults laying down the rules.

When the removal men arrived I made a pot of tea so that Lola could finish dressing Antonio. The only other arrival was David our postman. He handed over a collection of envelopes, nearly all bills to settle accounts before we departed except for one particular envelope. When I saw it I recognised the handwriting. I sat myself down on the stair tread staring at the address on the front of the envelope. Coming down the stairs with Antonio, Lola sat on the step behind.

'What's that?' she asked.

'The postmark, it's African.

'The solicitor. I thought you'd had everything from him regarding Alfie's last wishes.'

'No, not the solicitor. Look at the handwriting, there can be no mistaking it.'

Joining us, Amelia sat at my side. 'Who is the letter from daddy?'

Feeling the butterflies fluttering around inside my chest I peeled back the seal. My heart was pounding like a drum. 'If I am right darling, it's a letter from a friend.'

I was glad that I was sat down with my family. The letter was from Alfie Wilson. I had recognised his familiar style of writing. Unusually it wasn't signed by Alfie, but signed off in the name of *Arris.*

'That was Alfie's nickname at school. He was baptised Alfred Harrison Wilson, but for some unknown reason somebody called him Arris and the nickname stuck. A Greek boy in our class, George Dopolopodus told us that *Arris* meant *great.*'

'Like Alfred the Great,' Lola piped in.

I chuckled. 'Yes. Our intrepid explorer, writer and adventure freak was no ordinary boy and later in life man. I read the contents of the letter out aloud. There was no date or address on the page.

My Dearest Brands

I trust that this letter arrives in time only through various sources I had heard that you are on the move. If you followed the instructions of my solicitor, Abdalla Abeeku you should have uncovered sufficient funds to help pay for the mortgage on your new house and have enough left over for those little extras that always seem to be out of reach.

As you can see from the letter I am alive, contrary to previous correspondence from news from the Congo. However, and for the meantime I must remain a ghost and dead. Do not worry yourselves my dear Brands as you remain the benefactors of my estate.

Things got a bit hairy down in the dark recesses of the deepest Congo and events unfolded much quicker than my legs could carry me and the dense undergrowth is a devil in disguise when you are running for your life. Somehow and I cannot explain exactly how I became detached from my six African guides and regrettably I fear that they are no more. At night and alone I have heard strange noises detecting the smell of cooking much like that of a pork roast dinner on a Sunday.

The Congo was indeed a place like no other that I have ever visited and surrounded in mystery. There was one particular area that I won't be recommending or adding to any travel guide. Devoid of roads the dense forest consists of treacherous vines, tall trees that reach up to the clouds above and mysterious eyes that watch every move you make. Hidden amongst dense undergrowth the shrill noises echo unnervingly and cut through you like a razor. It's fair to say that this place had me and my six companions spooked.

By the grace of god I have managed to escape the suffocating jungle, the enormous snakes, hairy horned spiders, ever-hungry crocodiles and anything else intent on eating you alive although nothing I come across compared to the Ahumbra tribe who would peel the skin from my body piece by piece should they ever catch up with me.

My story began six weeks when I lead my expedition into the region to search for the uncharted caves rumoured to hold the lost treasure of the legendary King Solomon. It was on my hunt for said treasure that I crossed tracks with several members of the Ahumbra tribe. Although petrified, one of the porters acted as our interpreter whereupon we were invited to their village for a feast. What was lost in his translation was that we were the main course.

The women of the tribe gathered fruit and vegetation for the enormous clay cooking pot as the porters were stripped naked and covered in grease. My saving grace was my white skin which fascinated the tribe and I remained clothed. Sitting down with the elders of the tribe I learnt of a hidden temple deep in the heart of the forest which reputation had it was stockpiled with gold, diamonds and jewels of all description. There was however a slight hiccup and that the temple was smack bang in the middle of a sacred burial ground belonging to the Ahumbra and where they buried their dead. Only two ceremonies would allow for the ground to be walked upon, one being a marriage with the tribe believing that the dead relatives of the bride and groom would sell their souls to ensure that the happy couple had a long and prosperous life, the other was to hold a wake.

Wanting to avoid the latter and the cooking pot, and realising that the colour of my skin would not safe me for long I quickly made eyes at the chieftain's daughter. Ignoring the bones protruding either side of her nose she wasn't that bad looking and perhaps at the stretch of the imagination my tribal bride could resemble Sandra Ellingham from school although she was nowhere near as shapely as the delectable Sandra.

Now I had no desires to settle down with some dusky maiden from the Ahumbra, but I did need to get near the temple and marriage was my only option. With my romantic intentions known our courtship was exceptionally short consisting of two days and a boar hunt which was to be slaughtered for the wedding breakfast. Stripped naked and covered in boar blood my bride I was told was waiting at the temple. My rucksack with my money, passport and visa had been taken when I had been captured. I was informed that it was safe and protected from any thieves surrounded by venomous snakes down in a deep pit on the edge of the village.

After much feasting, chanting, drinking and dancing with the other tribal men until sundown I was escorted through the jungle to meet with my bride. The temple was a good mile from the village and without my escort I would never have found my way on my own. Years of growth had virtually covered the temple from sight and unless you knew it was there you could easily have walked by without ever discovering its presence.

The wedding ceremony was even shorter than the courtship, a binding of our hands at the wrist, the cutting of two razor sharp cuts on our right buttocks and we were legally declared man and wife by the tribal shaman. Robert Styles would die laughing if he knew how simple the marriage ceremony was.

There is no point going into detail about the wedding night other than to say that the feast went on for hours, until I took my bride to our wedding hut. Around three in the morning as the tribe slept I slipped from under the rush blanket and into my trousers, shirt and boots. Taking one last look at my bride before sneaking off into the darkness I made my way as best I could back to the temple.

When the first rays of the day arrived I was astonishingly only a stone's throw from the temple. I must have searched every inch of that place, but there were no treasures, no gold nor diamonds, just the remains of some old skeletons and a recent dead monkey.

After finding the monkey I heard a terrific commotion, screams and shouts, some blood curdling way back behind me. I could almost see and feel the anger and lust for revenge in the chieftain's eyes as he saw the tears falling from his daughters cheeks. I ran through the undergrowth that day like I had never run before. Stumbling across a muddy pool I landed in face first, but remembering a film that I had once seen I covered myself from head to foot in mud. It would stop the midges eating me alive and make tracking my scent that much harder. At least that was my theory.

I ran on through the dense undergrowth blind, but boy did I run fast, much faster I reckon than old Thomas Barringer's horse. I hid whenever I heard a noise surviving on a meagre diet of fruit and water for days, who knows maybe weeks. Several times in the night I would hear voices close by as men from the tribe continued the hunt, but lady luck was on my side. There are no bathrooms in the jungle and palm leaves can be very rough on the skin, although I can recommend the mud for good skin conditioning.

Eventually I stumbled across a clearing and civilisation, real buildings not mud huts. A local family very kindly took me in and for a week I lived with them. This is when I penned this letter using candlelight for illumination. When they took me to the market for fresh produce I found a post office where I could mail my correspondence.

I hear you say, why not just go to the police or tell the authorities of my ordeal and escape, but under African law I had been made responsible for the lives of the six porters. If found negligent I could be tried for manslaughter. Therefore in short I cannot leave Africa at the moment because I have no passport or visa to prove my identity.

I have decided to stay in the country and continue my journey exploring this wilderness gradually making my way up through the different territories and African states where with luck I will arrive in Morocco where I can either work my passage on a container ship or stow aboard a tanker and come back to England.

My original bequest to you is legal and binding and I assure you that this ordeal and adventure has made taught me some very worthwhile lessons and the only treasure that I have so far found in Africa are pearls of wisdom.

As and when I do eventually arrive back to England I will take a short rest then begin all over again. You need not worry about Arris because I have a secret overseas bank account that only I know about. There are more than sufficient funds to begin again and using my alias. I might even write about my African escapades as I believe that it could become a bestseller, if I live long enough to see it published.

For obvious reasons I cannot say where I am exactly because the Ahumbra tribe are renowned for their hunting prowess and their relentless pursuit of their quarry. And not that I know of course, but can you imagine the furore if in several months' time my bride tells her father that she is pregnant.

Under the circumstances this is likely to be my last letter for a while as I must keep constantly on the move only if the tribal warriors learn about a white man with scars on his right buttock they will know where I am and groom or not, my life will become worthless.

Enjoy your new house and one day I will come visit, I promise. Arris.

It was the last letter that we would receive at the old house and not that David our postman realised, but he had delivered to us a ghost that many of us thought to be dead. Lola stared at me as she held onto Antonio and cuddled Amelia.

'That is some adventure and powerful reading although very good news.'

Spontaneously I burst into laughter. 'That is so like Alfie and living life on the edge. You wait till I tell Vera, she will split her sides laughing.'

'That's just it Spencer, you cannot tell anyone not even Vera. Alfie's anonymity has to be a secret to keep him safe and hopefully alive. We should go on as normal and wait until we hear that Alfie is back in London before we tell anyone. More than ever now we need to keep his flat clean and tidy, and have the storage company put back his furniture this coming Monday.'

As usual Lola was right. We did our best to keep out of the removal men's way as they loaded our home into the back of the two vans remembering the bird table. Putting the letter safely in her handbag Lola looked at me and nodded. 'Maybe, we can tell just one person, Robert. He can pray for Alfie's safe return.'

Of course it meant getting Robert to keep the story a secret as well because if Stephanie ever heard about Alfie's unusual African adventure and the deadly tribe of head hunters it would undoubtedly be a major scoop for her and the newspaper. If Alfie did return safe and sound and wanted to sell his story then I am sure that Stephanie would get first refusal. Knowing Alfie and his astute business mind, it would run in conjunction with the launch of his latest travel guide.

The move into our new house went very smoothly and despite all the packing and the many boxes we felt completely at ease and very happy in our new home. Amelia was thrilled to have a bigger bedroom and the toy room was set between her and Antonio's room. For the moment he would continue to sleep in his cot in our bedroom, but soon he would move in with his sister until the nursery had been decorated.

45

Much later that day I watched Lola put Alfie's letter in the secret drawer of her jewellery box. It seemed apt because for the moment our intrepid explorer had to remain a secret to protect himself. That evening when both children were asleep and the excitement of the day was done Lola and I toasted our future with a glass of wine each.

'To Alfie, keep him safe and let him come back to us soon.' I chinked the side of Lola's glass as we sat on the settee.

'Do you think that he knew that when he went into the Congo that it would be that dangerous?' Lola asked.

'Knowing Alfie Wilson almost definitely. He has always had a devil-may-care attitude and he lives his life with reckless ease. I had never seen a boy sent to the headmaster for the cane so much as Alfie. When he left to take up full-time employment Alfie and Mr Upton were on first name terms.'

Lola laughed. 'So tell me Spencer, in your opinion is he legally married?'

I gave a shake of my head. 'I doubt that very much and the only reminder that Alfie will carry around with him forever and that he was ever married will be the two scars on his right buttock.'

The next day I was due at work as usual. Standing behind the coffee counter I looked across to the table that Alfie always occupied and where we had seen him last before he left for Africa. I closed my eyes and smiled as the café read my thoughts.

Sceptics might not believe that such things happen, but whatever the reason for his being alive something or somebody, alive or dead had protected Alfie. Taking his travel guide down from the shelf beside the coffee machine I studied the picture of my school friend on the back cover. He was smiling and his eyes were bright and full of life.

One Last Mission

There was no mistaking Mason Harris as he walked in through the door of the café. Built like a running quarterback he was tall, chiselled with broad shoulders and athletically perfect. The lilt in his dialect was enough to make Danielle go weak at the knees as our visitor approached the counter.

'Hi, good day to you,' he smiled. 'I'm Mason Harris, would I be in the right café for Spencer Marlon Brand?'

Supporting Danielle's right arm I instantly held out my hand to greet Mason as an elbow gently nudged me in the ribs. 'And I'm Danielle, the Assistant Manager here!' Mason shook my hand, it was a firm grip giving Danielle one of his best smiles.

'I thought you might be.' She was putty in his hands.

'You're a long way from home friend, what brings you to our shores?' I asked.

His reply surprised us both. 'The café, my grandparents used to come here often.'

'Would you like a coffee?' Danielle asked.

'Sure thing ma'am, black with sugar and do you have one of your famous English bacon sandwiches, I've not had breakfast yet?'

Danielle instantly took his order through to the kitchen needing to tell Vera about the tall handsome American out front.

'Grab yourself a table Mason and I'll bring your coffee over.'

I watched as he weaved between the tables selecting one next to the mural created by Thomas. Sitting himself down two nurses sat nearby smiled to which he responded with one of his own. Like Danielle they went to jelly. Mason was the archetypal Cary Grant of a modern age and no doubt the envy of many.

I took over his coffee intrigued by his visit. 'Do you have the time to join me,' he asked 'it's you that I have specifically come to see this morning?'

'Sure, let me grab a coffee.'

Mason inhaled through his nose taking in the atmosphere of the café. 'Grand, thanks. This is just how this café was described to me. Small although stylishly quaint with...' he took a few moments to find the right words, 'an overwhelming sense of magic about the place. It's no wonder my grandparents liked it so much in forty five.'

'They came here during the last war.'

'They sure did. Pops was a pilot, the captain of a B-17 Flying Fortress. His base was somewhere at Oulton in Norfolk. That's my next port of call after the café. Oulton is where here met grandma.'

He definitely had my interest as I looked over at the kitchen door to see if I could see Danielle with his bacon sandwich. 'We're a long way from Norfolk. How come they picked the little red café to have coffee?'

'They would come down to London when he had a weekend pass. They'd take in a show then grab something to eat after. According to pops they found this little red café quite by chance. It's where pops proposed to grandma.'

We had experienced a lot of emotional moments in the café since I had been the owner, but I had never witnessed anybody going down on one knee. Mason continued.

'Pops was scheduled to go on a dangerous mission the day after they came down to London and he wanted grandma's answer before he went.'

'My guess was she agreed.'

Danielle arrived with his bacon sandwich. It looked extra stuffed with bacon and even had a union jack attached flying on a cocktail stick. She fussed over Mason then begrudgingly went back to the counter.

'I am in awe of the men who went on those missions, so many never came back.'

'Fortunately for pops and his crew they did. Their aircraft apparently got shot up somewhere over France, but none of them suffered anything more than a few grazes and bruises. They were the lucky ones. Pops rarely speaks about the war.

'He's an old man now and spends most of his days in his hobby shop tinkering with a furniture repair or in his study listening to his favourite music. He never listens to the news saying that nothing ever good comes of politics or disasters.

'I was talking to him recently when he mentioned the café. I had to see it for myself.'

'You say your grandma was from Norfolk, how did they meet?'

Mason licked the edge of his mouth where the tomato sauce had escaped the bread.

'Grandma was a dancer in a show at the time and pops was in the audience with some of his crew. The airbase wasn't that far from Norwich and together they would go to the theatre to get away from the war. After a show he waited for her backstage. The rest as they say is history.'

I had met customers before like Wilhelm Wendell and the ghost of Albert Stanley who each had come with their own experiences of the war, but the reason for Mason's visit was different. I had the feeling that it wasn't just to quell his curiosity.

He finished his sandwich and washed the last of it down with coffee.

'Would you like another, it's on the house.' Danielle was instantly at our table with the coffee pot. It was worth coming across from the counter just to get one of his smiles.

'This is my first time in England. I had intended coming over before, but life can get in the way and there's always something more urgent. Grandma got taken ill and she had to go into hospital. That was when pops told me about the café. My wife and kids thought the time had come for me to make the trip.'

'Did you come alone?'

Mason shook his head. 'Yes. Pops wanted to come too, but he couldn't leave grandma. My wife Alyson and our two daughters are looking after him and he'll be spoilt rotten.' He took a photograph from his wallet to show me.' There were two pairs of older men and women in the image.

'That's my mom and dad, and then grandma and pops.'

'You look like your dad and grandfather.'

Mason turned around. 'I like the mural on the wall, who did that?' he asked.

'A friend of ours, Thomas Jones. He was street artist, but nowadays he's a sought after talent. Thomas has paintings exhibited in London and welsh galleries.'

'He's very good. My eldest daughter Bethany, she is studying the classics at Oklahoma University although I believe that her real interest lies in the art of the Red Indian Nation.'

This close to the mural I saw every detail that Thomas has painted, the lines of his brush and how he had cleverly added the smallest detail. There were things in the mural that I had not seen before.

'Bethany inherits her interest from her mom and they spend hours together in the studio painting, drawing or making things out of clay. My other daughter Susan,' he pointed at a younger girl, 'she likes art, but her talent lies in fashion and what she can wear. The brighter the colour the more she likes it.' Danielle would have got on famously with Susan.

'How exactly did you know where to find us,' I asked, 'only London has changed since nineteen forty five.'

From the inside of his rucksack he retrieved a travel book, written and illustrated would you believe by none other than Alfie Wilson. On the front cover overlooking a mountain in the distance was Alfie in shorts, tee-shirt, short socks and walking boots with a khaki rucksack slung over his shoulder. Like a lost penny he kept turning up as a reminder to me that his spirit was never going to be forgotten. Mason opened the page in the book where it had a marker sticking out. 'You're there Spencer...' he pointed to a picture of the café which I had never seen. Alongside was a short complimentary review.

'The wonders of Convent Garden cannot be overstated with an inviting variety of fine cuisine restaurants, talented street performers and scholarly musicians giving free of their time.

'And later, should you by chance have missed lunch I would recommend a visit to The Little Red Café in Oslo Road where the menu and cakes are not only mouth wateringly delightful, but accompanied by a speciality coffee produced by none other than the Fracino Contempo the experience will leave you wanting to revisit before you leave good old London town.

'Spencer Marlon Brand, the owner and his loyal team are always on hand with a cheerful smile and much, much more, only don't just take my word for it, go and see for yourself. You will be amazed at how a visit can turn around your life as if by magic.'

Alfie had done us proud and I was excited to see my name in print in a book.

Mason added a level spoonful of sugar to his second coffee. 'The travel guide was right and there is something about this café. It does have an atmosphere that you cannot quite describe, but it makes you feel calm just coming in.' He let me look at the guide book. 'Grandma had once told me about this magic place in London that she went with pops only I was very young and didn't really take it all in. Dad told me that they both believed the little red café to be their lucky charm.' I gave him back the book which he slipped down the side of the rucksack where it was safe.

'Pops told me before I left the States that I would find something here also that would help.'

I must have looked surprised.

'Grandma,' he replied. 'Pops reckoned that coming here today, I could take back some of that magic and make her better again.'

From my wallet I showed Mason a picture of Lola and the children then another of my mum. He held them respectfully with his fingertips.

'We're together because of the magic in this place,' I said.

'You have a nice family Spencer.' He looked at the photograph of my mum. 'You know she has that same look in her eye that my mum has, a sort of wisdom.' He handed back the photographs.

'My dad died when I was quite young Mason and although I never really knew him I have moments in my life when I miss him and yet I feel him around.'

'That's how pops described this place. He said that he and grandma left some of their soul here when they married and he took her home to the States for the first time.'

Mason was thoughtful as he sipped his coffee.

'Alyson was also keen on me coming, she also believes in magic. I can feel it Spencer. I feel their spirits are still here from over half a century ago. I can see their faces, smiling at one another as they sat at the table drinking coffee, maybe eating a slice of cake and making plans for the future. Marriage was a big gamble back then, life was a gamble. But together they beat the odds and came through it all. If they hadn't I wouldn't be sitting here now.'

I told Mason about Lola working in the florist, how we had found little Amelia through Angus the teddy and about the day that Antonio had been born. I told him of my previous days in prison and how owning the café had transformed my life. Every moment that was ingrained into my soul. I told him about my trepidation the day of my marriage and how my dad had come through to me in my hour of need.

'Sitting here Spencer perhaps where they sat all those years ago I can feel grandma saying yes to pops proposal. I feel the strength of her commitment. Now I know what pops meant.'

'Then take it back with you Mason, go visit your grandma and make her well again.'

He reached down into the rucksack again and took out a framed photograph. It was of an airman and a young woman, a black and white photograph. The people in it looked to be in their early twenties. In the background was a stage door.

'That's your grandparents and when they were in London.'

'Yes. Would you mind if I left this photo with you. This this café is where their love blossomed. I feel that they are part of the café's history.'

'We would be honoured to have it on our wall. Would you mind if I added a few words to say who the people are in the photograph and why only the other customers will be interested to know.'

'That'd be swell, thanks Spencer.' His smile was very approving.

'We would give it pride of place,' Danielle broke in as she appeared at the side of the table to remove the empty crockery. Boy that girl had sharp ears.

Mason laughed, 'you're as pretty and just like my two girls, you don't miss a trick.'

And that was how we come to have a wall in the café just for photographs. A special space not just with any old photograph, but images with a real sense of purpose. Before the end of the week was out Stephanie Steele had found a copy of the travel guide that Mason had brought with him and Alfie's image was also added to the wall. Pretty soon the wall was looking good and a favourite talking point with the customers.

When there was a lull in the morning trade Mason invited Danielle to join us whereby she asked all sorts of questions about America, his daughters and where would be the best places to visit. Sitting back and listening to them talk I sensed the same spirit of adventure in our young assistant manager that I had seen a long time back in Alfie Wilson.

Having left the café with a purpose in his stride I felt also that Mason Harris had found what he had come looking for and that he would return to America a different man.

As for Ada Harris, Mason's grandma she had long known that the café was special and that it would be for her grandson. You see one summer afternoon in July of nineteen forty five she had been told that her fiancée's plane had been shot down over the coast of France. As far as the airbase commander knew the crew were unharmed. By chance a French fishing boat had picked up Noah and his crew and bravely sailed through dangerous waters back to the Kent coast. From that day forward Ada Harris believed in miracles.

I imagined Ada sitting in the café praying for Noah's safe return and soon after her prayers were answered. I never did much praying although I did ask Robert to say one for my family and keep them safe. There was a magic about the café and despite the time spent inside I could never quite say exactly what. I just had to believe like Ada Harris that it made things happen, good things.

Four months after he returned home to America Mason Harris wrote to inform us that his grandma had passed away peacefully in her sleep clutching the original photograph of her and Noah backstage of the theatre. She was joined shortly after in her long sleep by Noah. I was in no doubt that Mason and his family would miss them both terribly, but that they would be happy to know that both Ada and Noah were flying one last mission together.

Jake's Alcohol Problem

Now I will be the first person to admit that I have never liked birds fluttering too close to me and the bigger the bird the less I am inclined to be intrigued or a fan of aviaries and friends with birds as pets. So the day that a large colourful African parrot flew in through the open door of the café I knew then that our problems had only just begun.

Jake as I would later learn was his name was a permanent resident at one of the houses to the rear of Oslo Road. This particular morning however, he thought that he spread his wings and broaden his horizons flying the short distance and into the café.

Danielle had only just propped open the front door to let in extra fresh air when Jake appeared seemingly from nowhere. Initially he perched himself on top of the open door before deciding that the wooden beam that went left to right of the café was a safer option. Alarmed by our uninvited feathered Danielle called me from the kitchen stating that we had a rather unusual visitor. When I looked up and saw Jake I was equally as distressed. We allowed guide dogs in the café, but pets wild or tame were not permitted for hygienic and social reasons.

Jake however seemed quite content to sit on his perch, occasionally walk back and forth surveying the scene below his big saucer eyes taking in everything especially the cake cabinet. Poor Edith Earnshaw who had been quietly enjoying a Danish pastry had to move because like me she didn't like big birds. Moving to a table near to the counter Jake felt the need to comment. *'Hello missus, show us your knickers.'* It brought about a hoot of laughter from a table of workmen sitting nearby.

'Saucy bugger ain't he Spencer, you'll need a ladder to get him down!'

I looked across at Ernie Bambridge. 'If I had one Ernie, I'd still not go up. Have you seen the sharp end of his beak and the length of his talons?' My reply earned another round of laughter.

'You'd best call the RSPCA and get them to send an Inspector. Somebody with gloves.'

Edith however was aghast with horror that the bird had referred to her underwear. 'You naughty impertinent bird, you should be shot and stuffed for saying such an outrageous thing!' Danielle topped up her coffee mug to help calm things.

Jake looked down at the old woman and sniffed bringing his right claw up to his nostril, how he remained balanced perched on the other leg baffled me. Moments later he responded with an ear-piercing shrill wolf whistle. *'Give us a kiss then!'* he squawked, much to merriment of the men.

One of the group climbed up on the table top with a piece of toast to see if he could entice Jake along the beam, but having flown the coop Jake wasn't going to be so easily fooled by a piece of soggy toast.

'Bugger off, get stuffed!' the parrot cried kicking the toast aside. Jake opened and flapped his large wings so emphatically that it almost sent George tumbling from the table top.

'Bloody bird,' George replied as he steadied himself. He raised a clenched fist at Jake. 'Edith's right. Come down here and I'll be the first in line to stuff you!'

The parrot's left eye glared back at George in a battle of will. Rocking contentedly on its perch his vocabulary was extensive. *'Bugger off you fat bugger!'*

Even I could not help joining in the laughter nor Danielle. 'He's got the measure of you George,' said one of the men, 'I reckon it'll take an expert to get him down.' The situation didn't improve when Robert Styles suddenly walked in through the door.

'Cor look,' cried Jake *'it's that bloody penguin from the church.'*

Robert looked up at the offending bird, but calm as ever he smiled up at the parrot. 'Now we have talked about this Jake and you agreed to curtail your profanities.'

'Bugger off,' replied Jake as he raised and dropped his head repeatedly at Robert.

'You know Jake?' I asked.

Robert chuckled. 'Why of course, Jake belongs to Ben Brady from number seventeen Johnson Terrace. Ordinarily we're good friends, but like everybody Jake can have an off day. I have to say that it's rather unusual that he has escaped as Ben is very particular about keeping Jake under control.'

Just to prove that Jake was on fine form and not having a bad day the bird looked over at Edith again. *'Show the vicar your knickers!'* Robert raised a finger at Jake admonishing his suggestion. He turned to face me.

'I'll have to have another word with Ben as he teaches Jake what to say.' He moved to the table where Edith had unsuccessfully concealed her blushed embarrassment.

'Before we try to locate Ben, is there anything that Jake likes as a titbit that will tempt him down?'

Robert looked along the selection of cakes. 'I'd keep your voice low if I was you Spencer only Jake has excellent hearing and they sense danger or trickery. Jake is very intelligent as you've no doubt guessed although he has a penchant for vulgarity despite my talking to him about it on more than one occasion.'

There was a muttering from the beam above. *'Silly old sod.'*

'Jake is partial to carrot cake.'

I sensed a presence behind the counter and saw Vera standing there looking up at the parrot. On cue Jake started to dance from side to side, I knew what was coming. *'Who let her out of the cage.'* It squawked. I saw Danielle stifle a laugh, but her wobbling belly gave it away. The table with the workmen joined in.

Vera who wiped her hands on her pinny sneered back at the parrot. 'Come down here you feathered fiend and I'll superglue your beak together before I put you in the oven.' She then turned to the workmen, 'and you'd be wise to alter your thoughts only remember who cooks your breakfasts.'

Before Jake had flown in the café had been a haven of peace and harmonious conversations. It was surprising how everything could change so quickly. I saw Mary, Lola who had Antonio in the buggy pass the café window heading in the direction of the door. The moment that the women appeared Jake let out another wolf whistle, much to the amusement of my son.

'Does the café have a parrot now?' asked Lola.

'It arrived uninvited,' Danielle replied as she reached down to take Antonio from the buggy. Lola

'That's Jake,' said Mary, 'Ben from seventeen Johnson Terrace calls in once a week to collect the seed heads that I've captured throughout the week. Jake also likes carrots so I buy him some from the market.' There wasn't a bad bone in Mary and she was an angel sent down from heaven. Robert nodded approvingly.

'According to Robert, Jake has a liking for carrot cake.'

Vera who was tickling Antonio's chin looked up at the parrot. 'Well you're out of luck today mate because I've only made fruit cake, a lemon drizzle and a ginger and orange cake.'

Running his pink tongue between his beak the parrot looked down intently starring back at Vera. *'Add rum,'* it squawked.

Open mouthed Vera was astonished. 'How does it know that I mix rum in the ginger before adding the orange?'

'God's creatures know many things Vera,' replied Robert. He templed his palms together. 'The bible includes many apt quotes: *who teaches us more than the beasts of the earth and makes us wiser than the birds of heaven.* As I said Jake is very intelligent, maybe like Mary he descended direct from heaven.' Mary gave Robert's arm a friendly squeeze.

Jake who had now been perched on the beam for the past twenty minutes, had for the past two been exceptionally quiet. He seemed quite content to close his eyes for a nap despite Antonio's gurgles. Cutting a slice from the edge of the ginger and orange cake I put the slice on a saucer then climbed up on a chair. Jake opened one eye and watched me suspiciously. Gingerly I put the saucer and cake on the flat surface of the beam. He waited for me to get down off the chair before edging forward to sniff the cake.

Jake used his sharp beak to break a piece from the slice, gulping it down in one fluid movement. Tasting the rum in the fruit he licked his lips then swaying back and forth began singing a sea shanty. *'Rum, rum show us your treasure and bits, cutlass and gold, my missus you've lovely...'* Danielle quickly covered Antonio's ears.

'Colourful as well,' I said to Robert.

Shaking his head Robert agreed. 'My words often fall on selective ears, even during my sermons I fear.'

I walked and stood directly beneath the beam where Jake was stood. 'If you can't keep a civil tongue in your head you won't get any more cake.' I warned.

Like a scolded child the parrot closed its beak and watched me return to behind the counter. Lola grinned. 'That told him, he's sulking.' She walked over and stood under the beam holding out her arm she asked gently. 'If you're a good boy you can have another piece of cake.'

Just like Antonio when he was having a disobedient moment the parrot shook its head to indicate that no amount of persuasion was going to cut any ice. I hadn't noticed that Mary was missing. Defeated Lola lowered her arm.

'It was a good try,' Robert said as Lola came back to the counter. 'When Ben's late wife was alive Jake was as good as gold, but after her passing he started to swear like a drunken sailor. I think it was his way of venting his frustration and anguish.'

'Perhaps Ben's as well as he teaches Jake.'

'Grief takes on some strange behaviour after losing someone so loved and close, you could be right Spencer. I need to make time to visit Ben and Jake again after today.'

Several minutes later Mary retuned with Ben Brady which was well timed as our busy lunchtime trade was about to begin soon. Ben apologised profusely for Jake's presence.

'I am terribly sorry Mr Brand for this... Jake can be a handful at times. I was cleaning out his cage earlier this morning when he suddenly bit me on the ear then promptly flew out through the fanlight using his beak to open the catch. He really is quite an intelligent bird.'

'So we have heard,' I replied.

'Oh... has he been very vocal?'

'You might need to apologise to Edith Earnshaw if you see her in the street, but otherwise he's kept the rest of us entertained.'

Robert who was standing behind Ben nodded gratefully my way.

'It's my fault, but since we lost Annie, the clouds have seemed that lot darker and the days never as bright. Jake and I talk to keep each other company and I guess I've taught him some naughty words and phrases. It's our way of expressing our sorrow and sadness.'

'He likes sea shanties.' I responded.

'Those I didn't teach him. We rescued Jake from a bird sanctuary the other side of London and he came with a stock of lyrical songs. The file that the sanctuary had on Jake had recorded that he had once taken part as the parrot in an amateur dramatic group play who performed the Pirates of Penzance. Any naughty shanties were probably taught to him by the players. Annie used to laugh when Jake recited a shanty although she knew he was being naughty. I supposed because he did make her laugh I've not discouraged him.' Ben breathed in deep. 'Has he done the rendition regarding cutlasses and gold?'

We all nodded including Jake.

Ben moved to the underside of the beam. 'Hear that you've been a bit of a naughty boy and you've upset Mr Brand's morning trade, now come on jump down and we'll go home for some lunch.' Ben held up his arm for Jake to hop down on.

'Bugger off,' the parrot told him. Ben tried unsuccessfully with several more attempts to coax Jake down only to receive the same reaction. It was then that he noticed the saucer at the end of the beam.

'Has he had cake?' he asked. His expression was one of concern.

We all nodded as did Jake.

'What cake?'

'A slice of Vera's home-made ginger and orange,' added Danielle.

'Did it have any alcohol in it by chance?' asked Ben.

'Rum,' came a squawk from above, *'rum me hearties.'*

'Oh dear,' exclaimed Ben crossing his chest with his arms, 'drink makes him very naughty. In the show that he did he was given a tot of rum every day and refused to perform until he could see that his beaker was full.' I looked up and could have sworn that I saw that bloody bird smile.

'So how do you suggest that we tempt him down?' I asked, noting the time on the clock on the back wall.

'He likes nursery rhymes and they help calm his mood. Jake likes to dance in rhythm with the rhyme.'

'You've got to be kidding me?' I responded, although the look in Ben's eyes suggested that he wasn't.

Robert stepped in to help. 'Any particular rhyme Ben?'

'Humpty Dumpty because Jake likes to fall down at the end.'

I thought that having been in prison I had heard it all, but this was new to me. A bloody parrot that liked to mime then crash down onto the deck at the end of a nursery rhyme. I sensed Lola grinning at me from behind. And so with everybody present we began to sing:

Humpty Dumpty sat on the wall
Humpty Dumpty had a great fall
All the king's horses
And all the king's men
Couldn't put Humpty together again

Like idiots we watched Jake fall sideways onto the beam then get back up. *'Again'* the parrot squawked and so did as we were ordered. We sang the verse six times until Jake decided that he'd had enough. With a flutter of his wings and a single hop he swooped landing on the arm of the buggy. My son who had been busy drinking milk from his bottle sat there bemused his smile allowing the milk in his mouth to drip down his chin.

'Hello,' said Jake rubbing his beak against Antonio's cheek to which he cooed back. I was about to come to the rescue when Lola caught my arm. She shook her head at me. 'It's okay, he won't hurt Antonio.' We watched as Jake danced sideways to amuse our young son. Ben took the opportunity to slip a strong loop around the parrot's claw. At last he we had him under control.

'We were on our way home,' said Lola to Ben, 'if it helps Jake can sit on the arm of the buggy alongside Antonio until we reach your house?'

Ben agreed and tied the loose end over the buggy arm.

Jake arrived home safe and sound just as the first customers began arriving for the lunchtime trade and thankfully the rest of the day passed peacefully without further incident. Looking up the saucer was still sat on the wooden beam a reminder of our drunken visitor. Danielle suggested that we leave it there and every so often add a scented candle to absorb the cooking smells, secretly I think she liked to be reminded of Jake.

It was a week later that Ben Brady returned to the café only alone. He sat at the table under the saucer and order a pot of tea and a slice of Vera's homemade ginger and orange cake. As a special treat we cut an extra slice and gave it to Ben so that Jake could have it for his tea.

'Vera doesn't add so much rum now,' I added as I delivered his cake, 'one inebriated parrot is enough, but Jake might have had an understudy.'

Ben invited me to sit at the table with him.

'The day that Jake escaped made me realise just how much he means to me Mr Brand. We both miss Annie so much, but without Jake around I felt so lost and vulnerable. He can be naughty and especially when he sings, but in the lonely evenings together he makes me laugh. It was strange, but when I looked up and saw him dancing on your wood beam I thought I saw Annie looking back down at me and smiling. This café has a certain atmosphere that makes everything right.

'Robert Styles called around the other day and we had a very long chat. We talked a lot about Annie and he made me realise that her soul is still around to look after Jake and myself. Your dear wife told me that you had moved recently into a new house and that you have a daughter too. Perhaps after school one day your wife could bring the children around to see Jake. I promise that he would be on his best behaviour.'

'They'd like it more if he wasn't,' I replied, 'and thank you Ben, they would love to visit.'

When I had got home later that afternoon after Jake had taken up residence on the café beam I found Antonio sitting on the floor playing with a toy parrot and Amelia reading a nature book on tropical animals.

In the mornings before we get up Lola and myself would hear Antonio in his sister's bedroom gurgling to himself. Creeping along the landing we would watch as he played with the parrot which he held with two hand. What exactly he was saying neither of us had any idea, although I had a sneaking feeling it was reciting a sea shanty that he had heard recently.

Holding the chair steady for Danielle to change the tea light there was one thing from Jakes visit that day which we never dare mention and that was his reference to Vera when she had emerged from the kitchen. There are some things that are best left for solitary moments, when I am with my thoughts or accompanied by Annie and whoever else decides to comes visit the café.

An Ethical Dilemma

Now there are some problems that can easily be resolved by the individual adopting a logical, calm approach, however if the light at the end of the tunnel seems to be fading faster than they can walk towards it the intervention of others becomes necessary to help put things right. I am no different and there was time when I needed a strong hand of support on my shoulder to get me through a crisis. So very often though we cannot always see the answer that stares us in the face.

Perhaps this story is one such case where the dilemma between two ordinary, caring people had become so clouded that neither was actually thinking straight. When this happens lives can be altered and perhaps even damaged, and that the way back seems impossible. The two persons involved were Doctor Adrian Hardwick and Sister Charlotte Moule of the children's ward at our local hospital.

With a busy café buzzing all around me my attention was nevertheless drawn across the tables to a young woman sitting by herself in the corner. For the past ten minutes or so she had been staring constantly at the street outside as though expecting to see somebody walk by or enter the café. As luck would have it Danielle was busy out back in the kitchen so I went across to take her order. Standing beside the table her face seemed familiar although I couldn't remember from where.

'We have a variety of special fruit teas that come recommended to help soothe the nerves and calm stormy waters,' I suggested with a friendly smile.

Charlotte Moule looked up at me, she appeared startled that I had interrupted her thoughts. 'Oh, I am sorry, I was miles away.'

'A good place to be sometimes and I find it helps.' I repeated the offer of a fruity tea whereupon she responded with a wry smile. Her eyes were engaging, bright and full of life.

'I would much prefer coffee please however it comes, I'm really not fussed.'

Two minutes later I took over her coffee and in the frothy top I had patterned a heart. It made her smile.

'If only life what that simple, but eventually the froth will disappear!' That's when I guessed the gazing beyond the window was a search for answers.

'Forgive me and tell me to mind my own business, but sitting here all alone you look as though you're running away from somebody or an unresolved situation.'

She spooned in a sugar and breathed in hard. 'It's the uncertainty that we run from.'

Without being invited I pulled the chair opposite back and at myself down seeing Danielle reappear from the kitchen.

'Ah... that old nutmeg. Life is a confusing puzzle and somebody at the beginning forgot to add the clues. It would be so much less complicated if we could gaze into a crystal ball.'

The underside of her eyes were slightly puffy from where she had spent a restless night crying. 'There's always a solution to every problem.' I added reassuringly.

Her smile was lacking conviction. 'This problem has two halves.' It didn't take a genius to know that the other half was a man.

'On such occasions I go and see Doc Doland and he comes up with one of his special remedies, only I find its best to never ask what is in the bottle.' The smile this time was more joyful.

'Doctor Doland is a good man. Thoughtful and considerate although he is a rare breed.' Therein was my second clue. It helped to do the Sunday Times crossword, our mystery man was a doctor.

'A married man?' I tentatively enquired.

She looked at the ring on my finger and smiled. 'He would be if he could only make up his mind.'

Charlotte Moule was naturally attractive. She didn't need makeup to shine. Through the honey green of her eyes I saw a person willing to give a lot including herself. It was then that I remembered where I had seen Charlotte before.

'Do you work at the hospital?' I asked.

'Yes, how did you know that?'

'We had to take our young daughter along once for a check-up, nothing serious, but Doc Doland wanted to be on the safe side.'

She unbuttoned her coat feeling easier as the coffee took effect. 'I hope that she was okay?'

'Amelia had a chest x-ray which proved that it was only an infection. A course of the doc's special remedy and she was fine again.'

'Good.'

'That and we get a couple of regular nurses in here for breakfast. You all have that look of exhaustion and yet an abundance of hope. That's how I recognised you.'

'This is the first time that I have been in the café, it's nice. It's warm and it has a calming atmosphere.'

'A lot of our customers would agree with you. What would help resolve your problem?'

For the first time she laughed. 'Maybe kidnap him.'

That was one option although I was thinking of a more subtle approach. 'Maybe a touch too drastic and the consequences are not favourable if you get caught. What's holding him back if you don't mind me asking?'

'Australia,' she replied giving her head a confused shake.

'The land of long sandy beaches, surfing and professional opportunity. And he has a job opportunity there I'm guessing?'

'Yes, he's a Registrar in Paediatrics at the hospital. Australia would provide an ideal opportunity for him to achieve his dreams.'

I dreamt every night, some made sense although a lot didn't. I often wondered if we dreamt because they were a sign of things to come, people to meet and places to visit, or alternatively were they cautionary visions. I saw the tear appear before she had time to disguise that it was there. I held out my hand and gave her my name. She told me hers.

'So, don't you fancy Australia?'

The shrug of her shoulders and heavy weight on her chest told me that she was undecided.

'It's not that I have anything against Australia, except of course the spiders, the snakes and the sharks, it would mean leaving here and the children. That's the wrench that is causing the problem.'

I remember looking at all the expectant faces of the children at the children's home from where we had collected Amelia. It was a moment that I will never forget as it tore my heart in half. I understood how she felt. If Lola and I could have, we would have taken them all home.

I held the back of her hand. 'Wouldn't there be others to take your place, there always is...' in essence my argument sounded extremely weak, perhaps even harsh given the circumstances.

Charlotte sighed. 'I know and don't think that that argument hasn't been raging back and forth in my mind, but I broke the golden rule of nursing and I have become emotionally involved with the children whom I care for and their families, it would be like deserting them. Every time I go on duty I face different challenges, but together, the children, doctors and nurses, specialists, we all work hard to overcome the problems that are thrown at us. I would leave a big part of me behind Spencer.' She looked down at her coffee stirring the spoon around absently and through the froth deep. 'If needs be I am prepared to lose Adrian and stay behind, but it's how to tell him.'

Like the challenges that she faced I could see the bricks being added to the wall making it higher. I made an excuse that my coffee was going cold and that we could both do with a fresh cup asking Danielle to do the honours while I made a phone call. A minute or so later Mary arrived from the florist.

'Lola's watching the shop and Antonio is having a great time sniffing the flowers.'

I could think of nobody better to help Charlotte. Having walked into our café the year before lost and confused Mary had changed her stars almost overnight. Her dilemma then had been leaving behind the security of the convent and turning her back on her love for god. It was a heart rendering decision, but she did it and now she enriches the life of as many people through her flowers and the lord is still by her side, as is Thomas. I introduced Mary to Charlotte offering coffee with clean cups.

The two were still talking when a good forty minutes later I saw a tall, smartly dressed man walking down the pavement on the other side of the road, from the way he was glancing behind and sideways it was obvious that he was looking for somebody. He also appeared rather agitated. Instinct and nothing else told me that he was Adrian Hardwick.

Like a Greek waiter touting for trade I held open the door and gestured that he was invited into the café. 'I think you'll find what you're looking for in here.'

When he saw Charlotte sitting in the corner with Mary he thanked me and made his way between the tables. Many of the early trade had left and the café was now almost empty. Seeing Adrian approach Mary made her excuses as Charlotte stood and fell into Adrian's inviting arms.

'I don't think anything else that I say now will make any difference.'

I smiled as I slipped my arm about Mary and gave her a grateful hug. 'What did you say?' I whispered.

'Not that much really as Charlotte did most of the talking. Her dedication to her profession and the children is like my love for the convent and my faith.' She looked up at the clock. 'Goodness, I had best get back to relieve Lola as Antonio will be wanting his lunch soon.' Mary hadn't noticed that Danielle was missing.

'I wouldn't worry too much my son is being entertained next door.'

Charlotte waved to Mary as she went back to the florist and moments later Charlotte introduced me to Adrian.

'We've already met I said,' winking at them both.

'Thank you. You looked after Charlotte in my hour of need. I've been up and down the high street wondering where she had disappeared too.'

Holding onto his arm, she was much happier, content. 'Did you check the embankment as well?'

Adrian chuckled. 'You're far too dedicated to throw yourself in the river.'

'I hear that you might be heading to a much warmer climate.' Sometimes the direct approach works wonders.

Adrian shook his head quite convincingly. 'Not now Spencer. The grass looks greener elsewhere, but the roses here are hard to beat and this one is particular.'

'So you're not going?' asked Charlotte.

'I'm hopeful that in a couple of years they'll be a vacancy for a consultant paediatrician. My ambitions can wait another twenty four months and it's a small price to pay for love.'

The smile and relief in Charlotte's face was something that I will never forget. This time she didn't hide the tears. 'How did you know where to find me?' she asked.

'Going to the various wards I recalled a recent conversation with two nurses who come here quite frequently for breakfast.'

'Claire and Julia.'

Adrian nodded. 'They recommend the café highly, especially Vera's afternoon cake. The little red café seemed the likely place to hide away.' He smiled at Charlotte as she hugged his waist.

'Then when you two have sorted everything, I suggest you come back and try a piece of lemon drizzle or the ginger and orange.'

'We'll be back. I promise,' said Charlotte.

Shaking my hand Adrian pulled Charlotte towards the door. 'Come on,' he urged, 'we have somewhere special to go.' As I watched them leave I had a good idea where.

A week later two familiar faces arrived one afternoon, ordered lemon drizzle cake and coffee. Charlotte proudly showed Danielle and myself her engagement ring before going next door to show Mary.

'There are some things worth sacrificing,' Adrian said as we took the cake and coffee over to the table in the corner. I agreed and told him that he had made the right choice.

Over dinner at the weekend inviting Mary and Thomas our conversation included Charlotte and Adrian. I asked again what Mary had said to help Charlotte.

Bouncing Antonio on her knee she told us.

'We talked about leaving the convent and about others in the order who would pick up where I had left off. Charlotte needed to hear both sides of my argument, the doubt, the anguish, but also how I needed to make the right choice. I told Charlotte about Thomas and that sometimes however hard love will shine through if it was meant to be. I said that there would be children who went home healed and of others who would occupy the beds. Life was a conveyor belt of good and not such good times, but what was right would eventually shine through the gloom. That was when Adrian arrived.'

'Did the café bring him,' asked Amelia, 'like it did Auntie Mary and Uncle Thomas?'

'I reckon so,' I replied. I looked around at the faces looking my way. 'Do you think she would have gone to Australia?'

'We'll never know. She was about to answer when Adrian appeared at the table. Sometimes that magic can be quite secretive.'

Six months down the line Sister Charlotte Moule changed her name to Hardwick and before the year was up Adrian took up a vacant post as a consultant paediatrician. They took their honeymoon in Australia, but neither had any regrets about coming back home.

At times the answer to a problem is right there before your very eyes, it just needs a nudge by somebody else to push it on its way. Mary regularly sees Charlotte on her days off and the two have become firm friends.

Did the café intervene, who knows. I watched Amelia and Antonio play as we took coffee after dessert. Whether or not Charlotte had intended going with Adrian it would remain a mystery, just as fate had intended.

The Dyslexic Violinist

How often throughout life do we take our natural abilities for granted not giving them a second thought. Born into the world we develop quickly mentally and physically absorbing everything about us and accepting what we see, hear and feel as common place. More intricate and advanced than some technology, the body, mind and the senses is without doubt the most marvellous piece of human ingenuity ever created. Emerging from a single biological cell we grow into a living, breathing soul where biodiversity is there for us to be recognised.

As a professional musician you would think that every sound produced was a wonderful opportunity to give back and be part of something very beautiful whatever the listener's preference or taste, unless you suffered from the condition of dyslexia.

Eamonn Kelly was one such young man and I could begin this story by telling you how his dyslexia restricted his love of music, but Eamonn was an extremely talented musician, gifted with nimble fingers in fact the most adept musician that I had ever seen as they caressed the strings of his violin where like a butterfly in flight they would glide up and down the fingerboard as his bow danced left and right.

We met one rainy day when he happened to walk into the café wearing an expression that was as dark as the clouds outside. He elected to sit at the table next to the window putting his violin case on the vacant chair next to his. Danielle went over to take his order.

'I've seen him somewhere before?' she said as I made the coffee.

'You probably have only his name is Eamonn and he's a professional musician. He is normally much smarter than how you see him today.

Eamonn takes a pride in his appearance.' I had to admit that he did look unusually dishevelled as though he had been busking down the corridors of an underground station rather than sitting amongst the orchestra at the Royal Albert Hall. A good friend of Mary and Thomas, Lola and I had enjoyed sitting with them in a box where we had seen and heard Eamonn perform.

Danielle put the order through to the kitchen for two slices of toast. 'He's a violinist,' she continued. 'His case is on the chair beside him.'

'A very talented musician too,' I replied adding a froth to his coffee.

Danielle was watching. 'He reads the newspaper using his fingertip.'

'Eamonn has dyslexia, but he won't let it beat him.'

'Oh...' she replied. I noticed her expression change as she went to the kitchen to fetch the toast. I had known Danielle a long time and seen her mature into a kind, thoughtful young woman. She could turn a bad situation around with just a smile. I watched Eamonn finger the article in admiration of his determination.

Even more surprising was when Danielle took over his toast and sat at the table opposite Eamonn. They engaged one another in conversation for several minutes before she returned to the counter.

'What were you two talking about?' I asked.

'His music mainly. Did you know that he has played in a lot of the big venues up and down the country?'

I did know, but from his appearance today it didn't look like he had worked recently. 'Eamonn was in demand at one time for his violin,' I replied. 'Did he mention where he had played of late?'

Danielle gave a shake of her head. 'He told me that he's unemployed at present.'

'Put his tab in the miscellaneous box, we can afford a free couple of coffees and two rounds of toast.'

'Thanks Spence. Maybe he'd appreciate you speaking with him.'

I made myself a coffee and was about to take it over when Mary came in for a slice of cake to have with her mid-morning break. She saw Eamonn sitting at the table and waved.

'Danielle tells me that Eamonn is out of work. He does look downbeat.'

Mary sighed. 'That's right. He's been out of work for about a month now. Eamonn's dyslexia suddenly made reading sheet music difficult. It's so sad.'

'Has he been to see a doctor?'

'He did see a clinician at the surgery, but Eamonn is a shy man and he felt that he was just getting in the way of others who were less fortunate than himself. He didn't go back and missed his next appointment. Thomas went to see Eamonn last week and they had an informal jamming session without music. He told me that it went well and it made Eamonn smile, but it didn't help cure his recent problem.'

I remembered a boy from school having private tuition to help overcome his difficulties, but without work Eamonn wouldn't have the resources to pay for a private teacher. I scratched my head thinking, there had to be something that we could do to help. I was wrapping Mary's cake in a napkin when Eamonn approached the counter. Mary gave him a friendly hug.

'How are you doing?' she asked.

'Fine, they'll be a job soon.'

Despite his circumstances his optimism was still there to fool others. I saw in his eyes the desperation that I had witnessed many times in prison.

'If you've nothing doing did you want to come to dinner tomorrow night?'

'Can I bring my violin?' Eamonn asked.

'Thomas would be very disappointed if you didn't.' The invitation at least was rewarded with a smile.

'Thanks.' He turned to me. 'I like it in here, it's quiet, friendly and gives a person time to think.'

I passed across the counter his coffee. 'Today is on the house.'

'Are you sure?'

'We always reward customers for their comments and especially when they're complimentary.'

'Thank you, you're very generous.'

'I was heading over to sit with you and take a look at your violin. I've seen you play and would love just to see it. Would you mind?'

'I'd like that.'

Mary went through to the kitchen to see Vera and Martyn telling Eamonn that it would be home-made steak pie and chips for dinner. I knew who would be making the pie.

Protected in a moulding of red velvet was a beautifully crafted violin and bow. There were several sheets of rolled music which looked to have been well-thumbed. Eamonn removed the violin as though it had been crafted by the Italian Giuseppe Narconcini. To my surprise he passed it across for me to hold. It was lighter than I imagined.

'Please, put it under your chin. Until you do that, you can never really appreciate its true beauty.' I noticed that the chin rest was worn where Eamonn had rested his own chin upon the shaped rosewood. He was right and it was a beautiful instrument. I gave it back wary that I could drop it or damage the delicate fretwork.

'I'd like to hear you play it!'

Several other customers who had been sitting dotted about the café encouragingly asked the same.

'Are you sure?' Eamonn asked, the apprehension creasing the lines on his brow.

'It would add a notable moment to the café history and we could tell everyone that we had Eamonn Kelly play in our café.' Mary who had come back out from the kitchen with Vera gave her nod of approval. Thomas often described Mary as an angel who walked softly through a crowd making them smile. I had to agree with him and her smile was full of reassurance and confidence. Eamonn nodded back picking up his bow.

The sound that Eamonn was produced can only be described as an instrumental combination of emotion and harmony. Listening to Eamonn play you could have heard a pin drop. Even the rain outside had stopped to listen.

When he was done Eamonn deftly pulled away the bow from the strings as the last chords echoed about our ears. The café burst into applause as Eamonn bent his head forward in gratitude. Still sat at his table I watched as he carefully put both violin and bow back into the case.

'You don't need to read music Eamonn, the notes are written into your soul.' Unbeknown to me I had not felt a presence standing behind where I was sat.

'And I would be the first to agree with Spencer.'

I turned to see Robert Styles behind.

'How long have you been there?'

'Long enough to hear Eamonn play.'

'You know one another?'

Robert nodded. 'Our paths have crossed.' He didn't elaborate and I didn't feel inclined to push for more. Stood next to Mary and Vera, Danielle whispered to them both. 'Robert always appears at the right moment, or when somebody is down on their luck, have you noticed that!'

'Maybe next time you come to the church, you'll play that same piece. I know of many who would be thrilled to hear you play.'

'I'd like that and the acoustics would be amazing.'

Robert palmed his hands together as though a prayer had been answered. 'Good.'

'There is one slight problem vicar, my dyslexia is causing me some problems and with my reading sheet music.'

Robert placed a hand on Eamonn's shoulder.

'I've suffered from dyslexia for years and when I encounter moments such as you are going through, I put myself in a place where I can let my thoughts wander and rest my mind.'

'You mean with god?'

'No, not necessarily... just somewhere, where I can be at peace with myself. I find that time helps.'

'I've tried meditation, it didn't do a lot for my confidence.'

Unperturbed Robert smiled. 'Can you pop along to the church around five this afternoon, we have choir practice and our organist has been taken unwell with a chest infection, your violin would be our salvation?'

There were two things that I had immediately picked up on. One I didn't know that Robert was dyslexic and the other was that Albert Banks, the church organist had popped in prior to Eamonn's arrival to collect a takeaway a bacon sandwich. He looked to me to be in the perfect picture of health. Hesitantly Eamonn agreed.

'I'd be happy to help.' The arrangement made Mary smile. Robert left saying that he looked forward to seeing Eamonn at five. It was the shortest visit to the café that I had ever known him make. Robert had also gone without his customary coffee and slice of cake. I went back to the counter sensing that our vicar had an ace card up his sleeve.

'Did you see Robert come in?' I asked Danielle.

'Not until he was stood behind you. He's like a ghost sometimes.' I grinned, thinking he was more like a Christian spirit. 'It's the café Spence,' she whispered, I'd swear blind it sends out a signal when somebody needs help.'

Coming to the counter to thank us and say goodbye to Mary, Eamonn looked happier than when he had arrived.

77

'That's the first time that I've played the violin in a couple of weeks. It made me feel good.'

'It made us all appreciate you,' I replied. 'If I had a bigger place like the coffee shops at Covent Garden I would hire you on a regular basis.'

Eamonn smiled giving a shake of his head. 'I played there three weeks back, just to earn some small change. Maybe that is where my future lies.'

I tapped the top of the violin case gently. 'Have faith Eamonn and for every problem there is an answer. I've an idea you'll come across one soon. Come back and see us again soon.'

Eamonn Kelly promised to return. We watched him go, turn and wave then disappear at the corner. 'If I didn't know better I would say that you and Robert had been sent here this morning by a higher order.'

Mary's eyes shone bright in response. 'God works in mysterious ways sometimes Spencer.'

It was my turn to shake my head. 'You've been around Robert too long, he always says that.'

It had to be two weeks before we ran into Robert Styles again, but this time he hid have time on his hands for coffee and cake. I was eager to know about Eamonn.

'He played that afternoon beautifully and from memory without any sheet music. We have choir practice twice a week and for the past two weeks Eamonn has come along to each session. He plays alongside Albert and together they have struck up quite a friendship. It so happens that Albert had difficulty with dyslexia when he was young, but he managed to overcome his problems. He's helping Eamonn grow in confidence again.'

'And what about your dyslexia?' I asked.

Robert grinned. 'God will forgive me that little white lie Spencer. I needed an excuse to get Eamonn to come along to the church to play that afternoon. After leaving the café I went straight round to see Albert to explain why I didn't need him to attend that afternoon. My plan worked a treat, now I think you owe me a coffee and a slice of cake for what I missed on my short visit.'

We found ourselves a free table and I just had coffee as I was watching my waistline.

'What is Albert doing that makes the difference?' I asked.

'We use magnified sheet music which makes it easier for Eamonn to follow. Come each choir practice we've reduced the image. As expected the smaller the magnification the more Eamonn's confidence began to grow. Following the notes across the page he now makes no mistakes. His timing is almost perfect. Another couple of weeks and he should be able to rejoin the orchestra.'

I was impressed. 'God works in mysterious ways.' It made Robert smile.

'Perhaps, although a logical approach was all that it needed.' He washed his cake down with a mouthful of coffee. 'As a young lad I did suffer with my words and it was a music teacher that helped me overcome my difficulties that is when I thought of Albert. You see music has a that special blend of magic and soul, Eamonn just needed to find his way back again.'

How many people pass somebody in a street and on top surface they return a convincing smile, although the other person never truly knows or understands why or what emotional struggles are going on beneath that smile. Eamonn with help from Robert and Albert had found a way to smile again, passing people in the street with a genuine smile. And as Robert explained, Eamonn's musical talent was never lost, it just became a little confused, muddled, but it found a way to be unmuddled. It was a nice way to describe it.

Wiping the corners of his mouth with his napkin I could tell from the look in his eyes that there was something else to this extraordinary tale.

'What else?' I asked, keen to know.

'Love.'

The surprise must been written across my face.

'Eamonn has become a sure favourite with the choir and one member in particular. Vicky was our latest recruit to join the choir coming along to the church because she suffers from anxiety attacks. Singing she find helps and meeting Eamonn together they help one another. Together they have drawn up an unwritten pact. Vicky helps with Eamonn's dyslexia and he is teaching her to play the violin.'

'And is Eamonn getting to grips with the sheet music?'

'Vicky had an idea. She placed a transparency over the normal stark black on white sheet music. Eamonn finds now that the notes and various swirls are much easier to read. It was so simple, but effective.'

Two months later Eamonn was invited back to the orchestra and is enjoying a season of Tchaikovsky at the Royal Albert Hall and true to his word he did come visit us again, only introducing Vicky as well.

The mind is a wonder of biological science, but when things get thrown out of sync through no fault of our own maybe even jumbled, it can take something very simple to help unravel the problem. Eamonn found his salvation through the church choir and love. On this particular occasion however I could not credit the café with having found the solution, suffice to say that something that day did mysteriously bring together Eamonn and Robert, and the choir. If you have any ideas as to what that something was, I would like to know and you happen to be passing by I can promise you a free coffee.

Message in a Bottle

Charlie Dawson walked in the café one Monday afternoon holding a rather small ordinary looking glass bottle. I did think it was one that he had found outside and that he was going to ask me to dispose of it in our recycling bin out back, but Charlie's expression announced that he was otherwise deep in thought.

A black cab taxi driver Charlie knew London like the back of his hand and was a regular caller at all the main line rail stations, theatres and restaurants, but for coffee he liked to relax at the café and take five minutes out of his busy day to read the newspaper. I noticed however that today he didn't have his customary paper tucked under his arm.

'Has trade been that bad today that you needed to hit the bottle Charlie,' I asked as I finished making his favourite Americano with a shortbread biscuit on the side.

He placed the bottle on the counter preventing it from rolling away.

'It's been a hectic one Spencer that's for sure, but if I had to have a reason to be hitting the bottle, it'd be because of my Isabella at home. She drives to distraction at times and being alone in the cab becomes my salvation, that and the afternoon Americano.' He turned the bottle around so that I could see it. 'I found lying on the back seat after my last fare. By the time I had turned around my passenger had vanished amongst the crowd of commuters at Waterloo. It's corked and look, it has a message inside.'

We pulled the cork and banged the bottom of the bottle until the roll of parchment dropped out.

81

'What it a man or woman, your last fare?' I sounded like Sherlock Holmes.

'A woman. Pretty one too. She had a foreign accent, but very light skin. I'd guess she was educated, maybe a doctor. She told me she was heading for Southampton. I checked with the station porters, but I'd missed the one fifty eight by a couple of minutes.'

Charlie pushed his coffee and biscuit to one side as we carefully pulled open the parchment. Inside a flattened rose rolled down the page which had been delicately written. 'You sure we should be reading this, it could be private or cursed?'

I shook my head. 'You read far too many novels and they give you ideas.'

'That's what I told Alfie and look at him, he didn't come back. When I found out that he was visiting the Dark Continent I said to him 'Alfie boy are you sure, that place is full of curse and mystery', and I was right.'

I ignored Charlie and his voodoo ideas and began reading.

My darling Michel

I know that if this bottle ever ends up where it should you will have already left Paris and ventured elsewhere on your quest to find artistic adventure and fulfil your dreams. Without a forwarding address I could think of no other alternative to send you my love than enclose this letter in a bottle in the hope that one you will be walking a beach and come across my message.

Our parting was not as it was meant to be and we both said things that we will regret with the passing of time. I do love you and so will our baby. Yes Michel, as you suspected I am pregnant and I am carrying your child, our love child.

I am going to live with my aunt in Southampton as I need time to think of the future and where best to raise our son or daughter.

If you do find this bottle, perhaps you will have had time to reflect and I will hope that you come back as we had always planned. And there will be two people here waiting for you instead of one.

All my love

Andrea XXX

There was no date or address, but I assumed that Michel knew where to contact Andrea should he want to get in touch.

'What do you think I should do Spencer, put it in *lost and found* at Waterloo or give it to the police?'

'Putting it in *lost and found* will never have it reclaimed.' I rolled the parchment careful not to lose the flattened rose. 'Although I admit, there's not a lot to be going on with is there, we know Michel is an artist and he had wild ambitions elsewhere. My guess is that Montmartre in Paris would be a good starting point.'

Charlie's eyebrows went up and eyes opened wider. 'I'm not going to Paris, blimey, my Isabella would give me hell and more if I told her I was popping across the Channel to France to look for a French woman or artist.'

A big proportioned woman Isabella was not to be laughed at. I could see how my suggestion had made Charlie anxious. Paris however gave me an idea. 'You might not be able to go, but I possibly know somebody who might.' I called out for Danielle to come through from the kitchen. 'Have you and Martyn got a passport?' I asked.

'Yes, why?' Maturing fast into a beautiful young woman Danielle like most females that I knew had acquired somewhere down the line that suspicious streak. She looked from me to Charlie. 'You lost a fare over in Calais Charlie?'

'You saucy young mare,' he replied 'you're as bad as my daughter Jenny back home. You're two of a kind and she has as much cheek.'

Danielle laughed and she had been called worse. 'She would need to have her wits about her with a father like you Charlie Dawson.' She returned her interest back my way, 'so what's with the passport Spence?'

'Are you still communicating with Emily Follingdale in Paris?'

She nodded in response. 'Yes, she regularly sends me used fashion magazines.'

'How would you and Martyn like a couple, perhaps three or four days in Paris with all expenses paid and you'd be doing me and Charlie a favour as well.'

Her face positively lit up. 'You bet your last bottom dollar I would.'

That old café magic had worked its charm again and we had found a possible way to make some enquiries abroad. I winked at Charlie. 'As I said Montmartre would be a good place to start.' I could almost hear Danielle curiosity working overtime.

'There has to be a catch?'

I smiled, beautiful and shrewd, just like Lola.

'It's Lola's birthday soon and there's a perfume that you can only buy in Paris, I know because I looked it up on the internet. You could do some sightseeing and get me a bottle, plus do a little delving for Charlie and me only there's somebody that we need to find for a broken hearted lady.'

Danielle looked at us both not knowing which to believe. 'Delving into what, I know you Spencer Brand and you've got a dodgy past, I ain't getting involved in any shady deal that you two have thought up.'

Charlie looked at me. 'She sounds just like my Isabella.'

At one time Charlie had done wrong like me and received an eighteen month stay at her majesty's prison Wandsworth for dealing in contraband goods. Like me Charlie had changed his stars and successfully attained his licence becoming a London cabbie. Married for almost twenty one years to Isabella, they had one daughter Jenny who not only looked lie her mum, but thought like her too. We showed Danielle the bottle, rose and letter of remorse and hope.

Having read and digested the short letter Danielle exhaled between her lips. 'Well, there ain't much to go on is there other than he might live in Paris and there has to be hundreds of blokes called Michel. Four days might be long enough to find them all.' She was cunning too.

'Maybe if you met up with Emily and had lunch in the artist quarter at Montmartre you could ask around if there was an artist named Michel who had been to England recently. It would eliminate a lot on your list and maybe one who knows of a girl called Andrea.' Now I did feel like Sherlock Holmes. I could appreciate how a detective felt looking for a missing person.

Charlie was in awe of my plan. 'In another life Spencer, you'd have made an excellent bogey.'

Danielle was quick to condemn his use of the term. 'Police officer please. Bogey is disgusting term and this is a refined café.'

Inside I was laughing although I didn't let it show and since making Danielle the Assistant Manager she had made several workmen toe the line, putting a stop to their use of bad language and the occasional moments of bad behaviour. She was definitely a force to be reckoned with. And courtesy of Mason Harris she wanted the café to be recognised as a place fit for all to visit, young or old, retired or working. Charlie on the other hand was born a cockney and he was a Londoner through and through.

'And when you go to one of those posh finishing schools young lady?'

'Living with dignity and expressing yourself eloquently wouldn't do you any harm Charlie Dawson. I think I need to have a word with your Isabell and Jenny.'

This time I did burst with laughter and Charlie had to admit defeat. Danielle turned on her heels to go tell Martyn in the kitchen that they were going to Paris and it wasn't going to cost them a penny. Charlie let a sigh of relief out when she was no longer visible.

'If anybody could find our mystery artist, it'd be her. She's a sharp as a pin although this little trip will cost you Spencer.'

What Charlie didn't know was that I could easily cover the cost and the trip would kill two birds with one stone and the perfume would impress Lola. I would give her some extra to buy something nice for Amelia, Antonio and Vera. Longer than his customary short visit Charlie left half an hour later.

'Time is money Spencer and the punters are due on the three o'clock at Euston, I'll leave the bottle in your safe hands. If I hear anything from the last paying customer I will point her your way.' Somehow I didn't think he would.

Danielle's younger sister agreed to cover Martyn's absence in the kitchen and with Antonio being looked after by his grandmothers on alternate days it gave Lola the chance of a break and for us to work together. Lola said she was to be paid the going rate and of course Vera backed her claim. That message in a bottle was going to cost me dear.

'I wonder when the baby is due.' Danielle asked picking her moment when the cafe was quiet moment.

'Your guess would be as good as mine although we could add a certain amount of deduction to the problem Watson. Say Michel left Andrea recently and the bottle was found today, we can assume that there is a grace period of a few days in which to get over the shock of his going and then to sit down and write the letter. She is at least a month, maybe two months pregnant so adding in the extra seven, sometime around Christmas, early New Year possibly.'

'Who is Watson?'

'Oh, just a figure of speech,' I replied.

'And from your deduction you think that his having an inkling of a baby on the horizon made him do a runner!'

'Quite possibly.'

'If I find him Spencer I'll drag him back by his balls!' I was glad that Charlie wasn't still around to remind her about etiquette and the reputation of the café.

Realising the lady at the table nearest the counter had heard the remark Danielle was quick to make amends. 'The chocolate variety Edna, Vera uses them for toppings on her cakes.' Edna nodded and smiled.

'It's okay Edna's a bit deaf in one ear, so she would only have understood half of what I said.' Danielle put up two thumbs, reciprocated by Edna. 'If Martyn ever did that to me, I'd probably cut his off.' I felt my legs automatically come together.

I doubt Martyn would ever run, he was besotted with Danielle and one day they would make excellent parents. As an auntie and to Amelia and Antonio they were both perfect role models.

Danielle later that evening made contact with Emily Follingdale and they arranged to meet at Charles de Gaulle airport. Lola went on line and booked their flight and hotel. We gave them five hundred pounds to spend and I slipped extra to Danielle for Lola's perfume and the presents. To play his part Charlie took them to Heathrow. I did ask, but as expected he had not heard from any customer named Andrea and about a missing bottle.

We received a text message to confirm that they had arrived, met with Emily and that the hotel was great and that Paris was absolutely magical. I could see Danielle beaming as she tried to take it all in. they were about to take lunch with Emily and then go sightseeing.

That evening I received another text message stating that the three of them had been to Montmartre and they had enquired amongst the numerous street artists there about Michel. Only one man thought he had heard of him, not as a friend, but through a friend. No promise was made that Michel would be found, but the man said time would tell. In France the French never pin themselves down to time, a day or indeed a date, and yet they prosper emotionally and financially. Love as he told Danielle was in the stars and if he was to be found, one would fall from the sky and bang him on the head, making him see sense. Danielle texted that she liked that last bit, I knew she would.

After four fun-filled exciting days the two of them returned home with Lola's perfume, a Parisian teddy bear wearing a red beret for Amelia and a musical book for Antonio, although Danielle had forgot to check that the words were in English, not it mattered as Antonio liked the sounds of the both songs and words were in French, not that it really mattered as Antonio liked the sound of the accordion. Lola said it would help influence the children's love of languages. They brought Vera a beautiful set of lace pillows for her bed. What they failed to bring home was any news of Michel.

For two months the message in the bottle sat on the shelf beside Alfie Wilson's travel guide and we had almost given up hope when soon after lunch on a Wednesday a young suntanned man walked into the café with a rucksack on his back.

'Bonjour Monsieur,' he said as he introduced himself, 'I do believe that you have a young lady working here who has been looking for me?'

Danielle replied before I had the chance. 'Are you Michel?'

'Qui, Michel Bisset mademoiselle.'

Danielle immediately soaked up his accent and his good looks. Taken with Paris, she had quickly fallen in love with the people and the easy lifestyle. During their four day stay Emily had taken them to the top of the Eiffel Tower which had made Martyn go a little dizzy, although not Danielle, and later he declined the climb to the top of the Arch de Triomphe, but agreed to sailing down the seine one evening for dinner.

I let her take Michel over to a vacant table where she let him see the message in the bottle. Slipping two mugs under the Fracino Contempo I assumed they would need one each. When he looked back up having read the letter and looked directly into Danielle's eyes, I think he could her mind. I took the two coffee's over.

'I would have come sooner, but word did not get through to me until I arrived in Tangiers. Antoine, a friend from my school days contacted my brother and good fortune had it that it was his house where I was staying. Leon was the man you talked to at Montmartre. I have been travelling overnight to get here. I tried to call Andrea several times, but she is not there.'

'That's because she's staying with an aunt in Southampton.' Danielle informed him.

'Qui, I know of her. Annie, Andrea's favourite tata,' he apologised 'auntie.'

He glanced down and the letter and the rose.

'Un enfant. C'est une surprise, a grande responsibilite!' he muttered.

Neither of us needed a translation. His eyes alone told us what Michel was thinking and about the baby.

'So what do you propose doing now?' Danielle asked. She had that thoughtful look in her eyes, determined and unwavering. I had seen it many times and no more intent than when she searched deep into my mind the day that Martyn had returned to the café having run from the robbery in the high street. In his favour she had both hands on top of the table.

'I will travel to Southampton and speak with Andrea. We had planned to travel to Paris together, but we had a stupid, a ridiculous argument about life and the future. Had I know about the baby I would not have taken the commission in Tangiers. Do you think that she would still want me now?'

'I think she will,' replied Danielle 'if this message is anything to go by.'

Michel nodded hopefully, then laughed. 'How did she possibly think that a bottle with a message inside would get to Paris in time before I left for Tangiers, incredible!'

He had a good point and indeed it was incredible. Taking into account the tides and the undercurrents the bottle was more likely to have ended up on the African coast rather than the French coast or floating up the Seine. With careful twists he put back the letter in the glass bottle then replaced the cork.

'Would you please do me a favour, would you look after this for me until I return. I cannot explain why, but for some reason it feels at home here and you all went to a lot of trouble to find me. Once I have found Andrea we will both come back and thank you together.'

Danielle took the bottle over to the counter and put it back alongside Alfie's book. Then like the mistral Michel Bisset vanished. Over time that shelf collected a few unusual items, but each had a story to tell. Michel was as good as his word and he arrived in Southampton to find Andrea at the station. She didn't know why she had gone there that afternoon, but something told her that it was important that she met the six ten from Waterloo.

A week later we received a letter from Paris, written in a familiar handwriting.

Dear Little Red Café

Thank you so much. Michel and I, we cannot begin to describe how your kindness made everything right, but it did. We owe you a debt and one day will we come visit and repay your trust in love.

As you can see we now live in Paris and we cannot wait for the baby to arrive.

Our very best wishes

Andrea and Michel Bisset xx

Danielle put the letter behind the bottle.

'I guess they'll come back and collect the bottle when the baby is born.'

I nodded assuming she was right. When Charlie came visiting for his coffee and biscuit we told him about Michel coming to the café and showed him the letter from Andrea.

'I doubt that I will ever find anything as interesting as a message in a bottle on my back seat ever again and all that I have found since has been empty water bottles.'

'Did you tell Isabella about the bottle, message and rose?'

'Yes, she said it was romantic.'

'So how you have a bruise around your left eye?'

'She asked, that if I had known about Jenny what steps I would have taken to have been with her?' I replied, 'bleedin' great long ones in the opposite direction and joined the foreign legion.'

Danielle looked both shocked and disgusted. 'Did you not know that your wife was pregnant?'

'Of course, but I had been arrested just after I found out.'

With that she gave a shake of her head and turned towards the kitchen. 'Other than Frenchmen, you men are all the same.'

The Book Shop

We very rarely saw or heard from Bartram next door in the bookshop and come to think of it neither did anybody else in the area as the emporium of books, mainly old less new, the shop was hardly ever open for business. And a closely guarded secret nobody except Bartram himself knew of his age. It was Vera who had known him the longest and she took a wild stab that Bartram was at least in his late sixties maybe early seventies.

Ted Jarvis, our local postman told me that Bartram conducted most of his book sales through a mail order process and if anybody would know anything it would be Ted only didn't postman know all your personal business. I could not imagine Bartram being conversant with a computer, but always so polite when you did catch sight of him he was indeed a mystery, an enigma. What did come as a surprise was when the *For Sale* sign went up above his shop door.

'The estate agent must have put it there late afternoon,' said Danielle 'and Mary didn't mention it when she locked the florist shop.' We went outside to look, not that similar *for sale* boards were not a common sight especially in the high street where commercial premises changed hands often offering alternative services.

'I wonder who'll buy it,' she mused.

'I was wondering that myself.' I went up close to the window to peer inside. Despite being a bright sunny day the interior looked gloomy.

'Some of the shelves are empty and there are boxes everywhere.'

'My guess is old Bartram knew this day was coming,' said Danielle, 'I reckon he's been running down his stock, knowing the end was in sight. I wonder how long he's had the shop.'

'Well he was here before the florist and café.' I could see that she was thinking. You could always tell with Danielle because she would cock her head thoughtfully to one side.

'A penny for them?' I asked.

'You've the funds now Spence, you could expand the café and knock through the side wall. Think of the custom we could generate with those extra tables and chairs.'

I grinned, ever the businesswoman Danielle had an eye for making the café better.

'It's a good idea. I'll talk to Lola and see what she thinks.'

'It won't cost much,' piped in Danielle, her head still cocked to the side, 'an RSJ to support the upper floor and a bit of modernisation and a couple of tins of paint. We could Thomas to do that.'

'Don't you think that we would lose some of our charm, our atmosphere if we grew too big?'

Her head sat square on her shoulders. 'I hadn't thought of that. I kinda like that warm, friendly feeling when I open up as though the spirits have been drinking coffee and playing cards all night long.' I had never thought of them doing that, but I guess that when we weren't around they had to amuse themselves somehow.

With a click of her fingers she had another idea. 'Why don't you buy it Spence and rent it to Thomas. He told Mary that he's on the lookout to find somewhere where he can open up an art gallery. The front window's all Victorian has that kerb appeal for paintings and Thomas would make the place look great with a few extra lights.'

I nudged her arm. 'Where did you get all interior decorative and have so many ideas?'

'The fashion magazines that Emily sends me from Paris, they're full of ideas.' For a moment she went dreamy thinking of Paris. I knew that however much she liked London, the café, Paris had some of her heart. It would not surprise me to see her living there one day with Martyn, a family and with Emily nearby.

'It's a good idea,' I admitted, 'I'll go see Mary and she can call Thomas while I call the estate agent and find out the asking price.' The other call that I had to make was to Lola to tell her about the proposal.

'It's a great idea Spencer and think of it, we would all be together in one small block. Perhaps eventually Thomas would make enough money to buy it from us rather than rent it.'

'We could sell it to him at what we paid, less his rent and that way they would get a foot on the commercial property ladder.'

'That's a great idea Spencer, you must have been talking to Danielle.' I just laughed, my wife thought all my good ideas originated through Danielle including her birthday present. 'Do you think a gallery would go well there, only it's not in the high street?'

'His artwork is highly sought after both here and abroad, and many side and back streets in London house prominent art galleries. Thomas also does a lot of his business on line.' I gave it a few seconds to think. 'Yes, I believe he'd make a real success of it and it could be good for both the café and florist.'

'Can we afford it?' she asked.

'Yes, I think so.'

'I'll do the maths.'

I left it to Lola to check through the details. She had an eye for detail and she also read the small print. An hour later she called me back.

'The sale includes the shop and the flat above. I checked with the bank and we can afford both.'

I hadn't realised that Bartram owned the flat above as well as the shop, now it made sense how he was able to keep the book shop going

94

with few sales. A rental from the flat would give us a very good return. 'What do you think?' I replied.

'We should go for it Spencer. It would be an investment for the future, Amelia and Antonio's future.' I could hear Antonio babbling away in the background, not knowing if he was approving of the idea. 'Out back of the shop is a big space like you have the kitchen where Vera and Martyn prepare the food. Thomas would have a place for a studio and Mary has recently taken up pottery, she could share the space.'

'And the flat, is it big?' I asked.

'It has three good sized bedrooms, a family bathroom, a large kitchen diner and a lounge. It's bigger than what they have right now.'

I pictured the shop as an art gallery knowing Thomas would make it special. The three shops would sit ideally beside one another. As expected Lola arrived with Antonio less than half an hour later.

'Thomas loves the idea, but wants to see the shop and flat.'

'Of course, we'd do the same.' Antonio eyed me, but fortunately as chewing on something so I did receive his customary greeting.

'The estate agent is coming at two fifteen for us to have a viewing. It'll give us three quarters of an hour to explore before I need to collect Amelia from school. Mary said Thomas was very excited at the prospect of working next to the café and having his own gallery.'

'And Mary,' I asked, 'is she okay with Thomas being on the doorstep?'

'Yes, she loves the idea. He rents a small space at the present which is cramped and not ideal for an up and coming international artist.'

At ten past two the estate agent arrived to find the four of us waiting on the pavement with Vera and Danielle entertaining Antonio. I had expected to see Larry Lawrence arrive, but apparently he was on holiday. Poppy Perkins introduced herself and offered us each one of her business cards before producing the keys to the shop door. The moment that the shop door was opened Poppy had to stand aside to allow the escape of stale air.

'The vendor did warn me that the shop hadn't been open for a couple of weeks and might smell a little musty.' To evidence the fact she coughed the dust from her throat.

Stepping inside the shop was like stepping back in time. The shelves and various cupboard doors were all made of oak as was the counter top. It reminded me of the old curiosity shop in the Charles Dickens novel of the same name. I wondered, did Bartram's shop have a ghost like that of young Nell. With the sunshine shafting through the front window the dust inside was visible, but it did nothing to detract from the obvious opportunities that lie ahead.

'It's beautiful,' said Mary 'and like stepping into the page of a children's fairy-tale.' Thomas stood beside her as they stood centre of the shop to take it all in.'

'What do you think,' I asked Thomas, 'would it work for you?'

Thomas nodded. 'It sure would although with your approval I wouldn't change a thing. As Mary described, it has that magical feel to it, like some of the history of London had been captured and stored within the cupboards and later placed on the shelves. The light coming in through the window is amazing.'

Much the same layout as the café the rear stockroom had a toilet washroom and small kitchen. There was ideal room for both an art studio, a potter's wheel and even a kiln.

With satisfaction all round we went up the stairs to the flat above which was house on two floors. Again dated and like stepping into a time warp the accommodation just needed decorating along with a new bathroom and kitchen. Looking around I caught sight of Lola giving Mary an approving nod as they checked out the bedrooms.

'If your offer was accepted I could decorate both the flat and the shop, it would help save some of the cost.'

I patted Thomas's shoulder. 'Let's agree now that it would save you six months' rent if you did.' Lola smiled in agreement.

Poppy Perkins also has a smile on her face seeing a commission boosting her monthly salary. 'Does this mean that you're interested in buying the two properties?' Lola took Poppy to one side and as shrewd as ever reduced the asking price down by five percent along with the estate agent fee. The savings would pay for the new bathroom, kitchen and decorating materials. By the end of the week the arrangements were with our solicitor and a deed of legal transfer had been typed up.

Four weeks later allowing for the removal of any remaining stock we saw Bartram once, the day that he came to thank us for buying his shop and flat. Much more frail than I recall seeing him last he looked relieved.

'I've bought a little cottage by the sea where I'll be happy to see out my days.'

'And your books, what have you done with them?' I asked.

'I gave them to various charities. Some were limited editions which might fetch a good price at auction. I'll be sorry to walk away and leave the book shop as it has been in my family for several generations, but I am the last descendant and it needed a new occupant, somebody younger and with different ideas.'

I told him that Thomas was taking it over and would make it into an art gallery leaving the interior much the same.

'That's a marvellous idea Spencer. And the shelves they'll stay?'

'Yes, Mary has plans to utilize them and display her pottery for all to see.'

'That makes me very happy that the shop is being left in good hands. It'll please many I am sure.' He didn't say who and I didn't ask. Reaching into the deep pocket of his long overcoat he took out a small brown paper parcel. 'You would honour me by taking this as a parting gift. We've been neighbours now for a few years and always got on well.'

'Thank you Bartram, but I haven't got you a gift, I'm sorry.'

He shook my hand and surprisingly it was firmer than I had expected. 'You've already given me one by buying this shop and the flat. It has given me peace of mind. This shop was a boyhood dream that I had wished for and it became a reality when an elderly aunt left it to me in her will. Surrounded by books I felt safe and that a part of my childhood could never be lost hidden amongst the pages of some of the book lined up like soldiers on the shelves.

'I would spend days without a customer happy just reading a copy of Grimm's Tales or an almanac, perhaps even an encyclopaedia. Other day's young boys and girls would come with their mums and dad's and ask my advice on the purchase of a good book. I would find them something special, something interesting that I thought would engage their imagination, a book, a story that would become a memory in their mature years. Now I have my memories.'

I was sad to see him walk away, but Bartram was ready for his little cottage by the sea and he deserved his retirement. I never did find out his age. Going back into the café I opened the package. Oddly enough it was a copy of the old curiosity shop by Charles Dickens. It wasn't until we took over the premises that I learnt some very interesting facts about the man.

Born in Bulgaria to a father who was a musician and a mother a Romany Gypsy, Bartram hailed from a long line of Vaudeville Players who had toured across Europe entertaining crowds large or small in villages and towns.

With no formal education, Bartram had schooled himself with reading books. It seemed so apt that his passion and dream had become a reality and that he had owned a book emporium. There were rumours although not substantiated because of time that his father had royal connections. It would not have surprised me to learn that it was true. Putting Dickens copy alongside Alfie's travel guide I was proud to have known Bartram.

As promised Mary and Thomas gave the inside of the shop a thorough good spring clean and the upstairs flat was decorated throughout. Lola insisted on new carpets and a local firm installed a new kitchen and bathroom. Within weeks you would not have recognised the place.

Over an evening meal to celebrate their new adventure we collectively decided upon the name *The Rainbow Gallery* because it had been the image that had attracted us first to Thomas as he chalked away on the pavement outside.

Lola and Mary loved the named and said that it would attract people in the area, just to come see the paintings and pottery items inside. To make sure it was noticed Thomas painted a huge rainbow across the inside of the front window so that when the sun shone it threw a spectrum of colour across the far wall. To add the finishing touches Mary and Lola planted up tubs of seasonal plants to sit outside.

One quiet morning with Danielle in the kitchen chatting with Vera and Martyn I thumbed through the copy of *The Old Curiosity Shop* that Bartram had given me as a parting gift. Among the pages I found several foreign stamps from various European countries. I assumed that he had collected them travelling around different places with his parents and wherever the show took them. In a way the book had somewhat become Bartram's secret childhood passport.

It wasn't long before word got around about *The Rainbow Gallery* and even local tourist board in the high street had our three shops listed on their schedule of places to visit as an alternative attraction to Convent Garden. Amelia said that it was because now we had lots of colour for people to see with Uncle Thomas's window rainbow, our red façade and the florist shop that was always adorned with flowers.

Now the sceptics amongst you might not believe in spiritual influence, but long ago I gave up trying to fathom out how, why and when certain events took place. Owing all three properties we have secured the history and dignity of all three properties. If you don't believe me, why not pop along to the new art gallery and ask the tenant artist only he'll tell you that a friendly spirit roams freely throughout from the shop on the ground floor to the bedrooms at the top of the property. Mary will tell you that she is often inspired too when she is searching for ideas for her next pottery project.

Official records show that Bartram's shop had been a book emporium since the middle of the eighteenth century when Dickens was alive so it was conceivable that he might have paid the shop a visit and that some of his spirit did remain left behind, just like Bartram told me that some of his secrets had been hidden amongst the many books.

If after you visit *The Rainbow Gallery* you feel a certain presence, why not pop next door and have a calming coffee. Let me hear what you have to say and I might add an extra chapter to this book.

Vera's Darkest Day

For several weeks I had been on at Vera to make an appointment at the audiology clinic at the local hospital and have her hearing checked as it was getting worse and on the odd occasion she had made a mistake with a breakfast order having misheard Danielle. As stubborn as Vera could be she made excuses and point blank refused telling me that there was nothing wrong except a mild ringing in her ear which she blamed on a different shampoo.

Things came to a head and no pun intended, when Vera misunderstood Danielle just after she had opened the café. Danielle asked Vera if she wanted an extra slice of toast, Vera thought Danielle had said 'that she had just seen a ghost.' That was enough to demand that she call the surgery and make an appointment to see Doc Doland.

Replacing the receiver on the kitchen telephone Vera turned with a scowl, 'ten past five today, are you lot satisfied now.' The three of us nodded in response although it was difficult to hide our victory mirth.

'Look at you,' she said disdainfully 'you're like the three wise monkeys, hear no evil, speak no evil and see no evil. One day you'll be old like me and then you'll find out how difficult it is to keep up with your bodily changes.'

The kitchen echoed with laughter and Danielle didn't help when she mimed at Vera.

'What's that you say?'

Danielle grinned, 'I said, I'm glad that you're going at last.'

Vera turned away to add mushrooms to the frying pan. 'Time will catch up with you all soon, you especially Spencer Brand.' I'm not sure why she singled me out, but probably because I was closer her age than Danielle and Martyn. I thumbed a gesture that I was going back out front. Danielle followed my lead leaving Martyn to suffer the fallout of the appointment. We heard an *'ouch'* and guessed that Vera had slapped Martyn for not back her up.

'Will he be alright?' I asked.

'Yeah, he loves her like an adopted aunt, but he's used to her moans and groans. Do you think it's anything serious Spence?'

'No, probably an accumulation of wax that's all.'

With a swift whack of her plastic spatula she caught his arm, which made Martyn laugh all the more. Folding her arms across her ample chest Vera had her dander up.

'In my younger days I could hear the trains coming and going all night at Kings Cross. Nowadays you all walk around with something stuck in your ear blasting what little brain you have left. One day you'll suffer the consequences.'

Martyn mimicked Danielle by miming his reply. Vera used the spatula again only adding more emphasis. *'You didn't say anything, I heard you!'* She remonstrated by whacking him once again for his impertinence.

Danielle stood beside me watching the customers converse with one another their hearing unaffected. 'The other day I went into the kitchen and told Martyn that his flies were undone.'

Vera retaliated angrily raising her spatula accusing me of making fun of her predicament, stating that she already knew that Lola was due with Antonio at the café around one.'

Adding milk to our coffees I realised that Vera's hearing problems although funny were beginning to concern Vera. I made two extra coffees taking them through to the kitchen.

'A peace offering,' I proclaimed putting hers down beside the cooker. She looked at me with a frown.

'What are on about, I did degreased the oven last week.' I sighed and shrugged my shoulders at Martyn who did his best not to laugh again. 'Go back out with that dipstick and serve the customers. I know what I'm doing. Senility might be setting in with age Spencer Brand, but I've all my marbles still rolling around my head in one direction.'

'What's with all the commotion and laughter,' asked Shamus Mulligan, a builder and regular from the excavated site down in Argyle Mews.

'Vera,' replied Danielle 'the daffy old bat refuses to accept that she's going deaf.'

Shamus grinned. 'She's been that way ever since I've known her. Why only last week I arrived early and bumped into Vera coming out of the kitchen. I said 'hi and that it was nice outside,' the next thing you know she had sent young Martyn out with a slice of apple pie.'

I started to laugh so did Danielle and Shamus joined in. 'It was the first time that I'd had pie for breakfast instead of lunch. I've avoided coming in early when you're both not about.'

'Don't worry Shamus, Vera has an appointment later today with Doc Doland, maybe he can unblock the problem.'

'Maybe he can do something about her tongue as well. She's as sharp as a razor. I told me that later that day I had to go the vets with the cat. She told me that if I wanted a cigarette I'd have to go back outside. I wouldn't fancy being in Doc Doland's shoes.'

Danielle was almost beside herself with laughter as Vera poked her head through the kitchen door to see what was causing the noise. Seeing Shamus at the counter she shook her head before disappearing.

'She heard that alright,' he said.

Afternoon trade had been busier than usual and we didn't finish until almost four thirty five. I told Vera that I would finish clearing up and that she should get along to doc Doland's before she missed her appointment.

'Anybody would think I'm on the way out the way you three have been acting today,' with that she went.

'I hope she's okay, do you think that I should have gone with her?' Danielle asked.

'No, you know Vera and she hates to be fussed over. Doc will get one of the nurses to syringe the ears and after a wash through she'll be as right as rain.'

That evening I was playing with Amelia and Antonio before their bedtime when the phone rang in the hall. Lola took the call and moments later came back into the room looking somewhat concerned.

'What's wrong?'

'After visiting the doctor Vera went round to your mum, she is very upset.'

'Who mum?'

'No Vera. Apparently Doctor Doland told her some bad news.'

I felt my chest sink inward and my heart miss a beat.'

'I had best go round and see what I can do.'

I kissed the children and told Lola that I would be home again as soon as I had found out what was wrong. My mother's house was a short ten minute walk, but appeared much longer as my mind tormented my soul with the endless list of numerous complication. I arrived to find mum consoling Vera with a strong cup of tea and a tot of whiskey.

'Whatever's wrong?' I asked going over and putting a comforting arm around Vera.

'Doc Doland,' she replied, 'he checked everything. My head, my eyes, my ears, inside my mouth before going top to bottom.'

'But you only went about your hearing and the wax in your ears.'

'That's what he said and that'd not been for a long time. I didn't think it was that many years.'

'Did they syringe your ears?' I asked. My mother shook her head dubiously.

'The silly old sod kept on about my shears and that they needed oiling every so often.'

I suppressed the sigh. 'So what did Doc Doland say to you exactly?'

Vera looked up clutching her whiskey glass. 'That I had a lump on my chest.'

I thought about all the years that we had known one another. I hadn't expected the day to end like this and felt a dark cloud descend over my head.

'Is he sending you to the hospital for tests?'

'Yes, or least I think so.'

'It was definitely your chest?'

'You're as bad as that daft doctor. He said that I had a lump on my chest although I had nothing to fear. It's alright for a man to say that, but none of you understand what a chest means to us women and what we fear the most!'

Mum told me that Vera was going to stay the night and that she would probably take the following day off as there were important issues to be discussed. I left them promising that I would call in after work the next day.

I called Danielle and told her about Vera. Martyn told me that he could cope in the kitchen and I promised him extra help and Danielle said she would see if her sister was available.

'I didn't mean to laugh today Spence.' I detected the concern in her voice.

'We all laughed Danielle and when Vera is over the initial shock she'll laugh along with us, you'll see.'

That night I lay in bed with my arm around Lola as she slept, thinking about Vera. She had been my rock for so long watching me grow as a young lad into a man. Her words of wisdom had often been my guide and kept me on the straight and narrow. She had reached out and touched my arm when I had been sentenced by the judge telling me to bide my time, do my porridge and not get in any more trouble. She told me that she would be there when I came out of prison. That night I lay on a damp pillow.

The next morning the mood in the café was exceptionally sombre and although we each tried our best to smile along with the customers Vera's absence was a huge space we could not avoid. Danielle's younger sister Mary did a great job helping in the kitchen and her youthful dignity helped demonstrate how kind and unselfish people can be in a crisis.

It was a little after eleven and after the breakfast rush had died down that Michelle Mayes, the surgery nurse called in for a coffee.

'You're late starting today,' I enquired.

'We're running an evening session for the workers who cannot get to see us during the day.' It was a good idea and made sense. She placed an order for a ham and salad sandwich which I passed through to the kitchen before making her coffee.

'How's Vera today?' Michelle enquired as she watched me put the lid on her takeaway coffee.

'She's having the day off, the news from Doc Doland was upsetting and it's stolen all our smiles.'

Michelle looked at me puzzled. 'Why would she be upset?'

'The thought of going to the hospital and undergoing a series of tests frightens her. I'd be the same in her.'

Michelle had deep furrow etched across her forehead. 'It's only a quick test Spencer. It takes about ten minutes and is completely harmless.'

Now I had known Michelle for a long time having been at the same school together and she was full of kindness and all the patients opted to see her if they had a minor problem, but today I thought her approach a tads flippant all things considered.

'I thought it would take longer. I would have thought that a biopsy would be better investigated.'

Michelle stared at me. 'Biopsy, what biopsy. Vera came last night to have a build-up of wax in her ears removed, but such was the compact nature that Doc Doland is sending her to hospital clinic where they have better facilities than our own. We normally use a solution of warm oil, but it has been some time since Vera last visited the surgery.' She must have seen my shoulders sag. 'Why, what did Vera tell you?'

I had virtually cried myself to sleep the night before thinking the worst was going to happen. My only consolation in the possibility of losing Vera was that she would be with Cyril.

'That she had a lump on her chest.'

'Oh the daft woman. Doc Doland took the opportunity to give Vera a thorough check-up because it had been so long since her last visit. I was in the consulting room when he did it. She must have misheard.'

'But the lump, how did that come about?'

'As the doctor examined her Vera asked about his family and if they were well. Doc Doland said that his youngest son had the mumps which had affected his chest.'

I started to laugh rather than cry which surprised Danielle when she reappeared from the kitchen.

'What's so funny?' she asked.

'Vera,' replied Michelle. 'She has an appointment at the hospital for the audiology clinic. Her hearing really is bad.'

'So she's not going to die?' Danielle asked.

'Not unless they push the syringe in too which I very much doubt.'

'But the lump on her chest, she saw the doctor find one.'

'Oh that, it's only scar tissue from when she had a playground injury years back when she fell from the climbing frame. She has a small lump where the ribcage fractured, healed and protrudes a little. Vera I assure you is not going to die any day soon and she is as strong as an Ox.'

'I'll kill her when I see her next,' said Danielle the relief showing as much as my own, 'I hardly slept last night with worry.'

Afternoon trade was slack so I took an hour to visit my mum and Vera as I had some good news to relay to them both. I arrived to find them reading through insurance policies and a funeral plan.

'Have you burnt down the café?' Vera asked.

'I ought to do that and put you on top,' I replied.

Vera looked at my mother. 'Charming as ever.'

'I sat between them on the settee and close enough that Vera could hear.

'Doc Doland's young son has a bad chest and the mumps. You don't have anything wrong with your chest except an old scar injury. It's your ears that he's sending you to the hospital for so that they can syringe them.'

'So I'm not going to die?'

'You might if Danielle gets hold of you first.'

Vera burst into tears burying her head down on her chest as I held her tight just like she had done with me when I had been a young boy and frustrated with life. When she was done crying I told her to keep my handkerchief as I had a drawer full at home.

'I didn't sleep a wink last night neither. At one point my Cyril came to be with me and we sat talking for ages although I couldn't hear everything that he said to me. In a way I was disappointed come the dawn and that a white chariot had not come to collect me. Although Cyril did say that it was not my time.' I could see that my mum was also crying.

'Perhaps now in future when we say that you should go see Doc Doland or Michelle at the surgery you won't be so argumentative. It'll save us all, you included a lot of unnecessary heartache and the loss of a night's sleep.'

'I've learnt my lesson Spencer, really I have.'

'Good and when you have to go to the audiology clinic mum will come with you.'

She smiled, but there was a look of concern in her eyes that I didn't understand. 'Is there something else that you haven't told me?'

'I don't like going to the doctors because every time that I go Doc Doland asks me to lift my top and then he gives me the once over. Only my Cyril ever did that.'

Had Robert Styles been present he would have forgiven me for taking the good lords name in vain.

A Case of Mistaken Identity

Tom Shaw was a man who I had known since my misguided association with the police some years back. At the time Tom was a young policeman and although I generally made it a rule to avoid any connection with members of law enforcement I do however believe in justice and our legal system.

During the past decade working hard, both diligently and methodically Tom had risen quickly from the rank of constable to that of detective. Out of uniform and undertaking long hours, at times at short notice I had never known Tom Shaw to ever moan and like the formidable Canadian Mounties he nearly always got his man.

Mutually respectful of one another our paths only ever crossed when we saw one another at particular charitable events that we both supported, fundraising for children. I was therefore surprised to see his teenage daughter sitting in the café by herself one Saturday afternoon, looking remarkably pensive.

Now you can pass judgement and say that most teenagers are renowned for their odd behaviour, changeable moods and especially among young teenage girls where different biological changes can have an influence on their day. Gemma Shaw who I knew, had never struck me as the type to let such trivialities get in her way or indeed influence her day.

Taking across the order of coffee and a slice of cake Danielle engaged Gemma in a brief conversation before returning to the counter.

'That's Tom Shaw's eldest girl isn't it?' she asked.

I confirmed it was with a nod. 'I think this is only the second time that I have seen her in here. Did you by any chance ask why?'

'No, although I don't think she come in for just coffee and cake. She seems distracted.' Now for Danielle to notice, Gemma had to be.

I watched as she pushed the slice around the plate with her fork and letting her coffee go cold. There was definitely something troubling her as nobody ever left Vera's ginger and orange cake for very long on the plate. Staring at the street outside her thoughts were miles from here and the café.

'I'll see if I can help,' I said coming around from the counter. 'Would you like to change the cake?' I asked Gemma. Over a freckly button nose her eyes connected with mine as I interrupted her thoughts.

'No, thank you. The cake is nice, really nice, I was just thinking that's all.'

'Okay, but let me know if you want anything else.' I went to walk away, Gemma reached out and caught hold of my wrist.

'Actually Mr Brand would you have a few minutes spare to talk, I came here today to speak with you.' I took the seat opposite as she pushed the cake to one side.

'So can I help,' I asked. 'Whatever the problem you've been mulling it since you arrived.

'You know my dad, don't you?'

I nodded confirming that I did. 'I do, although we're not exactly friends Gemma.' It was important to get the common ground down before she went too far with the conversation.

'It doesn't matter. He doesn't know that I am here and I would rather that he never found out. Are you okay with that?' Gemma had certain characteristics of her father. One thing that I had admired about Tom Shaw was his direct honest approach. He was different to a lot of the coppers down at the station. A lot I wouldn't trust.

I smiled, raising both palms to help lighten the mood.

'I come clean, what have I done wrong?' I noticed that Danielle thought my gesture amusing.

'You've not done anything Mister Brand, it's my dad I am concerned about.'

I realised that whatever was troubling her young mind it was serious.

'Is your dad in trouble and has he done something wrong?'

'He's been accused of something that he didn't do.' There was that honesty in her eyes that I believed.

'Call me Spencer, it's easier than the formality and start at the beginning then perhaps we might both be on the same page.'

Gemma offered a half smile. 'Would you like my cake?'

'No, thank you, but I'm going to have a coffee, would you like another to replace the one that has gone cold?'

'Yes please.'

When I turned to look at the counter Danielle had already had the same thought as I watched her put two fresh cups under the Fracino Contempo.

'I will come straight to the point. My dad has been cited in a divorce by my mum. I know my dad Spencer and he is innocent. He loves my mum and he would never do anything to hurt her, nor me or my younger sister.'

'And how does this involve me?' I asked as Danielle arrived with our coffee.

Gemma waited until Danielle was behind the counter again before she continued. 'I know that you know some criminals in the area.'

She saw the alarm in my expression as I swallowed my mouthful of coffee.

'By that, I mean you do know of them not that you are associated. I think you know the Moffatt brothers who own the scrap yard over in Addleton Place, the one around back of the paper warehouse.'

Gerry Moffatt had been in prison when I had been her majesty's guest. He wasn't necessarily a nasty or violent villain, but shrewd Gerry was always an opportunist and looking for a way to make a fast buck.

'I know of the scrap yard and yes I have come across the brothers.'

Like her father Gemma didn't waste time with any niceties as she lay her cards on the table.

'Danny Moffatt is inside doing a three year stretch for assault, I know because my dad told me. That presents a problem and that Gerry relies on his brother to help run the business.'

Just like a detective conducting an interview she stopped explaining leaving the introduction hanging mid-air ing taking a piece of her cake. I wondered how many TV detective programmes she watched.

'I didn't know that Danny had been sent down. How would this implicate me Gemma?'

'You're innocent Spencer, but I had to tell you about the Moffatt brothers because they are the reason my mum is divorcing my dad.'

I was catching up fast.

'And not their sister Veronica?' I asked.

Gemma nodded slowly back.

'Three months back my mum started receiving anonymous mail stating my dad was having an affair with Veronica Moffatt. Dad denied everything, but mum can be stubborn and refused to believe him. Last week mum got the date of the divorce court hearing and it's this Tuesday. I know everything in the letters is a pack of lies and that they have been sent to mum as revenge for Danny going behind bars. I know people who have come to you for help. I have also heard that this café is special and it can make things right.'

It was a tall order and heavy reputation. 'We sell coffee and refreshments, sandwiches and cake mainly Gemma. Any problem solving is down to luck. There's no magic formula involved.'

'I heard that you were the man with all the answers.'

Gemma would have been good at tennis serving up ace shots. We sat in silence for a few seconds whilst I searched for an idea. Going up against the Moffatt family was not a favourable option. They were locally regarded even by the police as middle of the road criminals who dabbled in small goods, mainly this and that and that the scrap yard was their front, there so-called honest business.

'Did your dad put Danny behind bars?'

'No. My dad's been involved with a special squad over Lambeth way for the past six months. Danny got himself caught three and half months ago. My dad squad is targeting something else.' She didn't say what.

'So the Moffatt's think that he was behind Danny's arrest and so they've put the heat on him creating a false trail of evidence, namely saying that he's been over the side.' A case of mistaken identity.

'That's my theory.'

'Do you know where Danny was arrested?' I asked.

'Around back of the Horse and Wagon pub. He was involved in a brawl with some other men who he had been playing pool with. Somebody called the police and Danny got himself arrested. The injured man was taken to hospital and later pressed charges.'

'Okay, leave it with me Gemma and come back Monday afternoon. I might know somebody who can help, but I'm not making any promises. In the meantime don't tell anybody about this conversation and especially not your mum or dad.'

Gemma nodded. 'My lips are sealed. Thanks Spencer.'

I watched her leave and walk with a spring in her step. Gemma was no older than Danielle. Tom Shaw's daughter was an intelligent young woman and determined, she risked a lot coming to see me and I had to admire her pluck.

'Would you and Martyn mind locking up today, only there is something that I need to do?'

'Are you in trouble Spence, cos I can help if you are?'

'Not at the moment and thanks, you'd help by making sure that the café is locked.'

'Okay, but be careful Spence, the Moffatts are a bad lot.'

'I know, that's why I'll tread carefully.'

'So who you going to see?' Danielle had that look in her eyes that said I wasn't to lie.

'Stacey Stevens. She worked Billingsgate Market with me and she knows both the Moffatt brothers. Stacey is also a good friend of Gerry. She will know what's going on.' I could see Danielle was worried so I put a reassuring hand over hers.

'You know me, I'll be like the scarlet pimpernel, in and out before they know it making the right noises and then I'll disappear again for good. There is no way that I am jeopardising the café and you all because of a long standing feud between the law and the Moffatts. I will tread softly and anything above that and I'm gone.'

'Text me when you're on the way home so that I know you're safe.' I promised that I would.

When I knocked on Stacey's door she was getting ready to go out for the evening, dancing probably. Divorced twice, she was obviously looking for a third husband. She was surprised to see me.

'Blimey… hello Spencer… how's tricks. We don't see you much over this side of the estate.'

Stacey invited me in, filling and putting the kettle on the stove. She never trusted electric kettles saying that you couldn't mix water and electricity and I had never explained why or how they were safe.

'So what's with the social visit Spencer, you've not come all this way to check on my health?'

I came straight to the point and explained what I knew. We sat at the kitchen table sipping hot tea and nibbling sugary biscuits just like old times at the market.

'I did hear through Gerry that Veronica was seeing a copper, not that the family were keen on the idea as you can imagine, but Veronica is as hard as nails and will fist fight her brothers if she has too. When Danny got busted, Gerry was adamant that she finished the romance.'

Hearing that a policeman was involved I felt my heart suddenly sink as I thought of Gemma. Had her love and loyalty for her dad been blind.

'You wouldn't happen to know the name of the copper who was involved with Veronica would you?'

'I could find out if it was important.'

'It would help Stacey. Thanks.'

Looking over the top of her cup she studied me. 'Why are you helping Spencer, you were never keen on the police. Why the sudden change of heart?'

I shrugged my shoulders.

'I'm not sure Stacey, but I've turned the page. I have a café, a beautiful wife and two kids. I guess I'm trying to do the right thing.'

Stacey laughed. 'The next you'll be telling me is that you've found religion.'

I laughed too. 'I might walk the straight and narrow road, but there are limits.' I took another biscuit from the tin. 'Call it a moment of weakness on my part if you like, but when young Gemma Shaw came into the café, I saw an anxious young woman no older than Danielle and in need of help. She believes in her dad and Gemma is desperate to keep her family unit together.'

'And you believe that Tom Shaw is innocent?'

'Oddly enough I do.'

'As it's for you Spencer and for old time's sake I'll ask the question. I drop it into the conversation in passing and hope that that way you'll remain anonymous. Now tell me about your family.'

I told her about Lola, Amelia and Antonio. Stacey who had no children from any of her marriages seemed envious. I showed her a photo of them that I kept in my wallet.

'You've done well for yourself Spencer. We had ourselves some good times down at the market and I was sorry to hear that you got yourself banged up in prison. Bad breaks however can sort out your priorities. I am pleased that you settled down and found your niche in life.'

I remembered to text Danielle and tell her that I was safe.

Just prior to lunchtime Monday Stacey telephoned me I took the call outside of the café. I had been clock watching all morning knowing that Tuesday was creeping up fast. I had also expected Gerry Moffatt to walk into the café at any moment.

'Veronica was seeing a copper named Shaw, only he worked out of a station over Fulham way. The two met at a night club and all that she would tell me was that he was over six foot, good looking and had fair hair.'

I punched the air in triumph, the Tom Shaw that I knew was only five ten in height and had dark brown hair.

'You're a star Stacey and you've just rescued a marriage.'

'It's a pity that somebody didn't do the same for me.' I felt sorry for Stacey, but told her that somebody good would walk into her life one day and make the wait worthwhile. I invited her to the café and she promised to visit soon.

As arranged Gemma arrived late that Monday afternoon. She looked extremely apprehensive as she sat herself down at a vacant table. She was so nervous of my tentative enquires that she declined a coffee.

'How are things at home?' I asked.

'Not good. They're quiet and hardly say a word to each other. You could cut the atmosphere with a knife. I've hardly slept since I saw you.'

'I know, I can tell and you have dark lines under booth eyes.' I nodded Danielle's way. 'We'll have a coffee whether you want one or not and it will help calm your anxiety. I do have something to tell you.' Danielle arrived with the coffees then disappeared. I didn't keep Gemma waiting. 'Has your dad ever worked over Fulham way?'

Gemma shook her head. 'No, he's always been at Central, why?'

'Because Gemma, I think that I can prove that your dad is innocent and not guilty of adultery.'

She leaned into the table coming closer. 'Are you sure?'

'As sure as I can be.'

'So how do I go about proving his innocence?'

'I don't think you can, not because you're not smart and intelligent, but because you're involved, you're family. I think that I need to convince your mum that your dad hasn't been fooling around.'

'She's at home now and alone. Dad got called into work on something that was urgent. I think he was glad to get out of the house.'

'Right, come on drink up,' I said, 'let's go see her now.' I stood then held Gemma's wrist. 'I will go by myself if you would rather?'

'No, I'll come too Spencer. I need to hear what you have to say and defend dad.'

Marianne Shaw was as expected very surprised to see me standing on the hall mat when Gemma invited me in. Seeing a man twice the age of her daughter I think she thought that her day couldn't get any worse. I told her that I was there to help and she invited me through to the kitchen. Gemma insisted on being there as well.

I told Marianne Shaw everything that I knew although I would not disclose where my information had come from. I had to protect Stacey as well as Lola and the children. Hearing my explanation she collapsed onto a kitchen chair and began sobbing as Gemma rushed forward to console her mother. I wanted to leave, but Gemma asked that I stay. After several minutes of tearful relief she wiped her eyes with a tissue. Sitting herself up straight to show that she was alright she nodded at me.

'I won't cry again Mister Brand. How can I ever thank you. In my heart I never did really believe that my Tom could do anything so cruel to hurt me or the girls. The problem was that I kept getting letter after letter and after a while the mind accepts what is written. Love and loyalty is so easily replaced by doubt and uncertainty. Tom works hard and very long hours at times and there are so many divorces throughout the police community. I thought that I was just another statistic.'

She looked to the kitchen drawer. 'I kept them all, reading them when I was alone. They were so descriptive real.'

'They were sent to the wrong Shaw. Your husband has been working in Lambeth, not the Fulham area. I would take them outside and burn them if I was you, they have no place here.' I looked at the time on my watch. 'I had best go before Tom gets back home. You've some talking to do and hopefully tomorrow you'll wake up and the future will look that much brighter again.'

Before I left Gemma hugged me tight just like Amelia does before she goes to bed. 'Thanks Spencer, I will never forget this and what you've done to help.'

'You have an incredible daughter Mrs Shaw. She's a brave girl, beautiful and intelligent too. We see our children grow and yet at times we don't realise how they've made that sudden transition in adulthood.' I was thinking of Danielle.

Marianne Shaw put her hand on my forearm. 'And you're a very kind man Spencer. This family will be forever in your debt. Thank you!'

When I closed the front door on the way out I looked back to see mother and daughter holding one another. Right now all I wanted to do was see Lola, Amelia and Antonio, but I had to return to the café first.

The walk back was a thoughtful experience and I wondered why I had helped Tom Shaw. At one time he would have been regarded as the enemy. I reasoned that he was like any other man and just doing a job and that the Shaw's were like any other family. There are times when you have to sit on the fence and look upon the cracks below. It doesn't take a lot to mend them, but left untouched they quickly become a deep chasm. It was mine and nobody else's fault that I found myself arrested and in prison, and although I had not found religion a good friend of mine, Robert Styles had faith in me.

I was almost done cleaning the Fracino Contempo when the bell over the door rang and in walked Tom Shaw walked in. he came around back of the counter and immediately reached out to shake my hand.

'I owe you big time Spencer, thanks!'

I smiled. 'You owe me nothing detective, but you do Gemma. She is definitely a chip off the old block and you should be proud of that girl.'

'I would agree with you there. However, you looked at something that I never thought could happen and a case of mistaken identity. He nodded agreeing. We never stop learning do we.'

I was surprised when he accepted my offer of coffee although it felt good that he had.

'Let's get something straight, straight away Tom, the slate is clean and you don't owe me anything. I turned my back on crime several years back and nowadays I keep my nose clean. You won't ever need to come knocking on my door again.'

'Thanks and I am glad that you did. I am curious as to how you found your information, but the least amount that I know the better. There was a Shaw at Fulham, but he resigned before they threw out for being associated with a criminal family. I heard that he's already moved back up to the Midlands.'

I grinned.

'The thought of meeting the Moffatt's even by chance might have helped persuade his decision.'

'That would be my guess too.'

'A wise choice,' I added. Tom Shaw looked around the inside of the café.

'This is nice Spencer. You have done really well and Gemma tells me that you have a wife and two children, adopted. That's very creditable.'

'We would have adopted the whole home if we could and there's not much that doesn't get known around these parts.'

Tom held his hands up signifying that his knowing was nothing official. 'Robert Styles is a friend.'

'Ah Robert, the beacon of light on dark days.'

'I went to him for help and asked that he say a prayer for me, Marianne and the girls. It seemed that it was answered.'

We drank our coffee talked about family life, the state of the country never once mentioning anything unlawful. He told me that Gemma had ambition to go to university to study law it didn't surprise. I told him that she would make a first rate lawyer.

When he left, he shook my hand not as a policeman, but as a friend. As I watched Tom Shaw walk back up the road I didn't see a detective, but an ordinary man. A man who had almost lost everything and because of his chosen profession. Of course nobody ever heard from the Shaw, late of Fulham ever again and whether he had a visit from the Moffatt brothers when Danny was released from prison was none of my concern although I did hear a rumour that Danny had been arrested as a result of information that had been obtained because of his sisters romantic association with a police officer.

Two Fat Ladies

We could tell that something was not quite right when Robert Styles came running into the café mid-morning having obviously run all the way from Arbury Street and St Georges. Breathing heavy to invigorate his lungs Robert leaned on the counter top.

'Have you seen the devil?' asked Danielle as she looked to see if Robert was being chased.

'It's the church hall...' he gasped, but that was as much as he could offer until he had regained his composure. He sounded just like me when I had been a smoker.

'Why don't you take a seat,' I suggested, 'and Danielle will cut you a slice of ginger and orange cake while I make your normal coffee.'

Robert was in no condition to argue as he sat down. 'Bless you both.'

'So the church hall, what's the problem?'

He sipped his coffee. 'The kitchen toaster caught fire this morning in church hall. Every Wednesday we have an early breakfast session cooked by Mavis Whitworth and Cynthia Cookson. At the time I was studying for my sermon this coming Sunday when there was a calamitous bang followed by several screams. A second or two later the lights went out the toaster having short circuited the electrics.'

'And a toaster can do that?' asked Danielle bring over his cake.

'That and more,' I explained, 'we've a spare toaster if you need one.'

'Thank you, but not at present. The fire brigade arrived very quickly. They did their best to vent the church hall of smoke, but there still

122

remains a nasty smell that will not leave. My problem is that the insurers have to access the damage to the kitchen and they will not let us use the hall until at least the beginning of next week.

'So why run to see us?' I asked sensing that I already knew what was coming.

'We had arranged a bingo session at the hall late this afternoon. I would cancel, but the small group that attend look forward to the session so much and for one or two it is their only chance to meet with the others.'

If there was a god then he had funny way in making sure that Robert came to me for help. In the past we had held numerous events in the café, including a wedding celebration, an engagement party, a number of children's birthday parties and even a wake, but never a bingo session. I felt myself cornered.

'We could arrange the tables and if it's only a dozen we could accommodate the session here.' I saw Danielle grin, her smile an expression of respect for my decision and relief for Robert.

'The church funds will of course pay for any tea, coffee or biscuit provided.'

'I'll tell Vera that we've got a special party arriving after we close the door on business. She will no doubt knock up and extra cake or two if she hears that it's for the elderly residents in the area.'

'God will save you all a place in heaven.' Robert palmed his hands together in thanks. I watched as he finished off the ginger and orange slice. His eyes told me that there was more.

'And what else...?' I asked.

'Disaster is never alone Spencer and like Exodus and the ten plagues of Egypt poor Morris our bingo caller has been taken down with a bad stomach bug. I was wondering if you could do the honours.'

'He'll do it,' agreed Danielle on my behalf and I'll record the numbers called.

I turned to look at Danielle who was wearing one of her best *we'll have fun* smiles. 'The last time that I did any bingo calling was in prison on Christmas day. I warn you that almost ended up in a riot when Ernie Entwhistle mixed the numbers putting the nine in the six slot. '

'Have faith Spence, you have that air of authority that the oldies will respect.' Robert nodded agreeing with Danielle.

'People in the community respect you Spencer.'

'Okay, enough of the compliments I'll do it.' I looked at Robert. 'Tell me, why aren't you doing the calling?'

'Rules of the big house I'm afraid and thou' shalt not gamble in the house of the lord. As quoted by Mark 8:36, *'For what will profit a man, if he gains the whole world and loses his own soul.'*

'What about my soul?'

'The good lord has already recognised your humanity towards fellow man Spencer. You will be rewarded in heaven of that I am sure.'

'There is one condition,' I demanded. 'That you are present. I know what Sandra Ellingham's mum can be like when she attends the Mecca bingo. My mum tells me that Margaret takes the session very seriously.' Robert agreed that he would be available all afternoon to help keep the peace.

When the last customer left we locked the door and arranged the tables and chairs. Vera had baked two cakes, a fruity recipe with an extra portion of whiskey which she said would help keep the oldies warm and an extra ginger and orange cake. Just prior to four the regular group began arriving including Margaret Ellingham and surprisingly my mother.

'I didn't know that you were part of this group?'

'There are a lot of things that you don't know Spencer Brand and it's good that you've got Danielle to help with the balls, Margaret won't take kindly to any wrong calling.' With that she took her seat next to Gladys Turnbull.

Danielle nudged my arm as she closed and locked the door.

'Do you want me to pull down the blinds?'

'No leave them up, if the police drive past and see shadows they'll think we're running an illegal game in here.'

Settled at their respective tables all eyes watched as Danielle loaded the balls into the cylindrical tombola drum and I made sure that the slots were empty. Passing between the tables Martyn handed out tea and coffee.

'Got any cake young man?' asked a man with a scarf tightly wrapped about his neck.

'Vera's cutting some now, it'll be here in a minute.' The man sniffed although I was sure that he didn't have a cold, just a bad habit.

'Where's Morris,' Agnes Millar called out, 'he's our normal bingo caller?'

Robert who was sat at the table next to hers, leant back on his chair. 'Unfortunately poor Morris has been waylaid today Agnes, but Spencer has kindly offered to do the calling. He has previous experience so there's no need to worry and Danielle is on hand to make sure that the numbers called are recorded properly.' Agnes smiled at Robert, but looked at me then at Margaret Ellingham who was unusually quiet.

Jenny Soper and Agnes Millar arranged the cards on their table then whispered to one another. Sat snuggly between Harriet Haynes and Glenda Roberts, Leonard Williams the oldest man of the group gave me the thumbs up. 'You're doing a grand job lad, carry on.'

Dishing out the cake portions Vera and Martyn made sure that everyone had a pen that worked. With a spin of the drum the room went silent and all eyes fell upon me for when the spin stopped. Pulling open the wooden door I picked the first ball.

'Key of the door, forty four.'

'What,' remonstrated Agnes, *'that's droopy drawers, 'twenty one is the key of the door.'*

'Spencer is just being polite,' intervened Robert. We nodded at one another and I carried on.

'Eyes up...' I called as the drum went around again.

'Theresa's Den, number ten.'

We watched as pen's crossed through the number on the card.

'Go on Spence you've got their attention, 'keep going.' Whispered Danielle as I pulled another ball from the drum.

'A deck of cards, fifty two.'

I closed the door and Danielle spun the drum to show that there was no favouritism.

'Pick a mate, sixty eight.'

I noticed that Leonard had closed his left eye and had hold of his ear as he strained to hear me call. I repeated the number just for him, although instead of helping it only added to the confusion of the game.

'Is that sixty eight once or twice, only I've got it once.' It was Agnes Millar again.

Sitting beside Vera, Robert Styles had a smirk on his face.

'Sixty eight once.' Said Danielle. There was a muttering amongst the players. Bad hearing or not I was not going to repeat any of the numbers. Leonard sitting in the corner gave me the thumbs up and so I continued.

Danielle stopped the drum from spinning, handing me another numbered ball.

'Here,' called out a disgruntled and rather rounded Elizabeth Duke, 'only the caller can handle the balls at any given time.'

I put it back in the drum, gave the drum a quick spin drawing out another.

'The Brighton Line, number fifty nine.' How I wished I was on the train right now or at least at home with Lola and the children. When I told that I would be late because I had to help run a bingo session she just laughed.

A number of pink tongues protruded from lips as pens ticked off fifty nine.

'They look like a group of lizards,' Danielle muttered sitting beside me.

'A lounge,' I replied, 'it's a lounge of lizard's only this lot need locking up.'

'Two fat ladies, eighty eight.'

As the pens marked off the number there were a few in the room who would have benefitted from taking daily exercise. Looking around the tables I noticed that most of the cake had gone.

'Keep it going Spence, one of two like look they're about to nod off.' Danielle was trying not to laugh as she put the ball in her board.

Leaning in close to Danielle I had a question. 'Just out of interest what do they win, if they call house.'

'A small hamper of food for the first prize, a five pound supermarket voucher for the second game and the third prize Robert has yet to announce.' I looked to see that Robert was talking to Martyn and Vera.

'A free breakfast or afternoon tea by the looks of it.' I said.

'Robert was telling me that Morris normally sorts the prizes, but nobody felt inclined to go near him today to collect them, so Robert had to visit the supermarket on his way here. Martyn helped put the hamper together.'

I nodded my approval. I would have wanted to keep clear of Morris as well. It was time to move on as I withdrew another ball from the drum.

'Stairway to heaven, sixty seven.'

I resisted looking at Robert who was scanning the room. Leonard Williams looked from his corner table and winked sat between Harriet and Glenda. I didn't think that he would see heaven for a good few years yet.

'Number sixteen, lonely and never been kissed before.'

The number drummed up a fond memory in me of when I had been sixteen. I didn't have a girlfriend at the time, although I had been kissed and the girl who had stolen my innocence was none other than Vivienne Smith, the publican's daughter from the Barge and Rum Barrel. After the kiss I had plucked courage and asked Vivienne out on a date. A year older I also reckoned on her having some other good ideas. Being tall for my age I was able to meet with her lips head on. It was a nice memory and don't we all have them from time to time. An age of learning and innocence that we shared with others.

It was my guess that we were only two numbers away from somebody winning the first game, although I had known bingo sessions to go on longer, but that was in the pokey and there were so many thieves and villains under one roof that it wasn't just the thrill of calling *house* that excited them, but the side bets on who would win.

I gave the drum another quick spin hearing my stomach rumble. I wondered what was for supper when I eventually got home to Lola and the children.

'Thirty three, fish and chip with mushy peas.' The thought of that being served up on a plate for supper definitely caused a rumble from down below.

From out of the corner of my eye I saw a hand rising into the air, it was odd because the cards needed another number to be called before anybody would win. Vera realised the woman's error and helped by discreetly lowering her hand pointing out the blank spaces left to fill. Looking around the room the eyes had focused back on me. A group of vultures would have been a more apt term rather than lizards although the tongues were out in anticipation.

Sensing that the end was in sight Martyn went to refill the large teapot as I gave the drum a harder than normal spin. Inside the balls sounded like a lot of escaped ball-bearings. You could positively feel the charge in the air as I halted the spin and opened the wooden door.

'Life begins at forty.'' I held the ball up so that the whole room could see. Danielle and I were surprised that forty was met with a volley of

moans and groans with nobody needing the number. I proceeded with the game.

Poking his head through the kitchen door Martyn nodded to Vera that the tea was ready. Good lad and it would help calm the mood when somebody did win. The pens were once again poised ready.

'Dancing Queen, number seventeen.'

Danielle nudged me. 'That's me,' she whispered. 'Me and my moves on a Saturday night.

When I withdrew the next ball, I had to look twice to recheck the number believing that it had to be loaded by some divine intervention. I saw Robert smiling as though he knew.

'Well, what is...?' demanded a frustrated Agnes Millar, 'come on man, I'm waiting on one number.'

Did he load the ball knowing that it would be drawn every time, I shook my head not knowing. Having paid for the hamper and the voucher from his own pocket Robert was one of the most righteous and honest men that I had ever known, but quietly optimistic, he had to make sure that somebody did win and that the group enjoyed their Wednesday afternoon bingo session.

'The lord is my shepherd, number twenty three.'

And then it came, just as I had hoped it would. 'House, house!' somebody cried out. The excited shout had come from Roseanne Davies, an ordinary, quiet and unassuming widow sitting all alone. I was pleased that she had won. At the side of the room I saw Agnes drop her head dejectedly down onto her ample chest, just one number away she thought that she had been in with a chance. Sitting at the side Robert smiled at me, the winner a silent prayer answered no doubt.

We played the other two games with as much fervour as the first and on both occasions Agnes was unsuccessful, accepting that it just wasn't her day. Come the end of the session, in many ways it had been harder than the bingo session in the prison although much more rewarding and at some time soon we would see Leonard for one of Vera's special breakfasts.

The café closed later than usual that day although once again we had proved that we were there for every eventuality and occasion. I refused the offer of covering the cost of the tea, coffee, biscuits and cake telling Robert that any money saved could go towards the next hamper the following week.

'Morris has serious competition,' he said, thanking me.

'No, his weekly spot is safe I assure you. Twice in one lifetime is enough.'

Stephanie Steele reported on the fire at the church hall and mentioned the café in her article naming me as the stand-in bingo caller adding a small inset picture top right of the page. Danielle cut out the article and had it framed which then joined our photograph gallery. It was another bit of our history.

Watching Agnes and her friend Jenny Soper walk down the road that day after bingo I had asked if either had needed number eighty eight.

'We both ticked it off, why do you ask?' asked Agnes frowning.

'No reason, I was only curious that's all,' I replied smiling.

The Anniversary Mouse

Danielle named the mouse Keanu after her favourite movie star and sporting a thick set of whiskers when laden with dirt and dust having rummaged through our *unused* cupboard the rodent looked impressively like a mouse with a moustache. Unusually dappled in a reddish coat of gingery brown with a pale fawn tail Keanu came visiting the café one morning in the spring as Danielle unlocked the café early.

'Did you see that?' she said pointing to the corner of the coffee counter where we kept the recycling bin.

'See what?' enquired Vera as she stepped inside heading towards the kitchen. Vera looked, but saw nothing. 'You're seeing things my girl, probably too many late nights and not enough sleep. I've told you to get your eyes checked.' Danielle however wasn't so easily discouraged. A mouse she had seen and a mouse she was determined to find.

'I know what I saw Vera,' Danielle replied hanging up her coat, 'it was a little brown mouse, one of those field types, small and cute, only it had a moustache.'

Vera checked that the broom was handy by the back door. 'We've had them in here before. Pesky little devils and they can move fast too.'

'Well it was beside the counter near the recycling.' Vera took the broom to hunt for Keanu.

Tentatively pulling aside cartons and paper, there was nothing there, but a spider's web. She hunted around for another five minutes before giving up. 'I suggest you get an early night and make an appointment with the optician in the high street.'

Vera went back to the kitchen leaving Danielle to continue with the hunt. I arrived half an hour later. She told me about our latest visitor.

'I thought I caught a glimpse of one the other day, only when I looked around it had disappeared.'

'So you've seen Keanu as well. Did you mention it to Vera?'

'No. As I said it was what I thought I saw. One second it was there and gone the next. Almost in the matter of a blink of the eye it had vanished. You know what Vera's like and if she can't see it, it doesn't exist.'

We agreed not to mention it although Danielle said she would tell Martyn and that he should keep an eye out in case Keanu thought he had the freedom of the kitchen and the stock cupboard.

'I'll pop around to the hardware shop in the high street later this morning and buy some traps.'

'That's cruel Spence, can't we just catch him and find him a home?'

'What and advertise that we have a pet mouse looking for a good home. The food, hygiene and health inspector wouldn't agree to that.'

Danielle agreed that it would be a bad move.

Over the coming week it was only Danielle and I that ever saw the mouse. Keanu was fast and we could never follow him for long before he disappeared. We both began to wonder if it was a ghost mouse that we were seeing.

Martyn told Danielle at the end of every day that he had never seen Keanu in the kitchen. As an extra precaution, but more to convince Danielle and myself that we did have a furry resident I purchased an infra-red camera with a motion sensor. We put up on the shelf above the Fracino Contempo, angled down towards the recycling bin where we had both first seen the mouse.

The next morning with breakfast orders out of the way and Vera and Martyn busy in the kitchen we plugged the camera into the laptop viewing the overnight recording.

'There…' said Danielle pointing at the corner of the screen, 'do you see him Spence.'

We felt a presence standing behind and turned to see Vera looking.

'So we have got one,' she admitted. 'Where did he go?' she asked.

I pressed replay, but the recording was very short. We were joined by Martyn.

'There he is again,' said Vera as she pointed to the opposite corner, 'he must have wings to get from one side to the other so fast.'

We watched the creature emerge from behind the counter, run momentarily across the café floor then seemingly vanish into thin air. Danielle and I checked under the tables and chairs in case the mouse had died during the night, but as expected we found no trace of Keanu.

This coming and going went on for two weeks and every morning we would check the camera recording, see Keanu foraging about then vanish. There was no evidence of stolen scraps of food, no mouse droppings or trail to suggest where he slept during the day.

When the café was shut we searched for holes in the skirting boards, that walls and around back of the cupboards finding nothing out of the ordinary. Keanu always seemed to make his entrance next to the recycling bin and vanished somewhere around middle of the floor of the café. We showed the video to Thomas in the gallery next door in case it was coming in from Bartram's old book emporium and then to Mary in the florist, but neither had ever seen a mouse.

'Are you sure that it's not a ghost mouse,' asked Thomas, 'I have heard that they can exist?'

Ordinarily we would laughed and mocked his theory, but we had to admit that it was definitely looking like Thomas was right. Before we called in the experts to be doubly sure I bought another camera so that we could angle an image down from the wooden beam which would capture the entire café floor below. Vera and Martyn added gorgonzola cheese the various traps that we placed out at night.

Come the next morning and to our surprise every trap had been sprung, the cheese was missing, but we didn't have a mouse. Now there was six of us around the laptop to watch the recording of the nightly events.

'There...' cried Danielle, 'do you see him, Keanu's over by the front door!'

And sure enough he was. Sitting on the chair as large as life Keanu was staring up at the camera. I had to grin at his cheek. Lying at his feet were the small pieces of gorgonzola that Vera and Martyn had left as bait. I had to admit our furry little friend was clever and not easily fooled. We watched as he devoured the cheese then vanish.

'Where'd he go?' asked Vera as she looked up at the camera to check that the red light was active to indicate that it was working properly. Danielle went and checked the chair that we had seen Keanu sitting on. It was clean and there wasn't the tiniest morsel of gorgonzola left behind.

'How come it sprung the traps, took the cheese and didn't get caught?' asked Martyn.

We watched the video recording several times, but each time there were no answers.

'I am beginning to believe in Thomas's theory and that our mouse is a ghost.'

'So it can't be killed then?' Danielle exclaimed.

'Not if the mouse is already dead.'

Danielle looked at me before looking back at the screen. 'But ghosts, even mice ghosts surely don't eat and especially not gorgonzola cheese.'

'Why not?' asked Mary.

'Not unless Keanu is an Italian mouse.' Added Thomas. We all looked his way our expressions demanding an explanation.

'Before Lola took over the florist it had been owned by her aunt and she was born in Italy. There is no physical evidence found to say how the mouse gets in and out of the café, but logically it could come from the florist shop. Maybe Lola could ring her aunt and find out if she ever saw or had a mouse.'

Danielle piped in somewhat dejected, 'I still like the name Keanu, Giuseppe wouldn't sound right.'

An hour later, after a call to Florence Lola arrived with Antonio.

'Yes, auntie did have a pet mouse. She called him Giuseppe after an uncle of hers. She described the mouse as reddish brown with a thick set of whiskers.'

Danielle looked downhearted. 'I still prefer Keanu.' She said picking up Antonio and showing him the image of the mouse on the screen.

'And did the mouse escape?' I asked.

'Not exactly, it died. She kept it at the shop because the children who came in with adults to buy flowers liked to bring him seed and small pieces of cheese.'

'Don't tell me... gorgonzola?'

'Yes, how did you know?' Lola watched the recording from overnight. 'Oh, I see,' she looked at Danielle. 'He is cute, in a cuddly sort of way, isn't he.'

'Cute,' I remarked. 'If the public food and hygiene inspector calls in and sees this recording we'd lose our licence to sell food.'

'But, it's a ghost Spencer.' We looked at Thomas, he was right.

'Proving that could be difficult. The inspectors see the evidence and don't concern themselves with the niceties of how cute our resident ghost is or was, they would demand that the problem is eradicated, resolved and as soon as possible.'

'The previous owner of the café was a Muriel Smith and she had a cat,' said Vera. I could almost hear what was coming next.

'A cat to catch a mouse?'

135

'Not exactly, you see the cat would be left in the café overnight as she had encountered problems with a mouse, but the cat was never fast enough to catch the offending rodent. She had tried traps, poison and even cheese, but none of it worked.'

'What happened to the cat?' asked Danielle.

Vera explained. 'Muriel would arrive to open the café early to find chairs overturned and cups and saucers broken lying on the floor where the cat, a large tabby had given chase. This nightly event went on for a month until Muriel found the cat dead one morning. She took it along to the vet who performed an autopsy. The vet found undigested fish pieces in the cat's stomach which had been laced with rodent poison. There was a rumour that Muriel had asked the local paranormal society to visit the café, but their investigation amounted to nothing.'

'So we could have a ghostly cat too,' Danielle suggested.

'Yes,' I replied looking at the screen,' the original Tom and Jerry. So what was the outcome?'

'That's just it, nobody really knows. The interest in the story of the mysterious mouse and dead cat boosted the café sales, but soon after the visit by the paranormal society the mouse was no longer a problem. It seemed to have disappeared, until very recently.'

'So why reappear now after almost ten years?' asked Lola.

'Maybe it's coming back marks a special event.' Suggested Martyn.

'Is Muriel still alive?' I asked Vera.

'Yes, although she's a little dotty. The incident with the cat didn't do her any good. Neighbours say that she still leaves out a saucer of milk at night for *Cuddles*, that's what she called the tabby, only Muriel never had another cat.'

'That might explain why Cuddles doesn't visit the café, it doesn't need too!' I had to agree that Thomas had a good point and one pet ghost was enough.

136

Vera said that she would call in on the way home and visit Muriel and mention our mouse. The next morning as we gathered around the laptop she explained. She checked the calendar where Danielle had drawn the tiny silhouette of a mouse against the day and date.

'The day that Danielle first saw the mouse was the tenth of April.' Said Vera. 'That was when Muriel had first seen the mouse as well.'

I could see a sequence materialising. 'Today is the twenty third of April and yesterday was the twenty second. Don't tell me... that was the date when Cuddles was found dead?' Vera nodded.

'Muriel told me that the cat had looked shocked when she had found it. The autopsy had suggested that poison had killed the tabby, but she reckoned it had initially died of shock.'

'How?' asked Martyn.

'She found an overturned jar near the counter, a large jar. She believed that in the chase the night before the mouse had hidden behind the jar. When cuddles came upon the upturned jar the face of the mouse was magnified, the shock and the poison killed the cat. She said it was just too much for cuddles to take.'

To prove that it could be true Martyn picked up an empty jar magnifying his eyes through the rounded glass.

'So last night was the showdown of that anniversary.'

'More or less,' said Vera. 'Muriel was a bit hazy about what happened next, but she remembered Lola's aunt having a pet mouse. She said that her grandchildren would visit her in the café then go next door to take it pieces of cheese.'

'But the café, its' been renovated and decorated since Muriel. There isn't a mouse hole in sight nor one to be found.'

'Tell me Spencer what ghost needs to use a door?' She replied. Danielle tenderly touched the screen where Keanu was looking back at her. 'Do you think that we will have to wait a whole year before we see him again?'

137

'I reckon that could be the case.' I saved the image and shut down the recording.

'I'll miss Keanu.' She turned and went to the kitchen with some dirty crockery. Martyn followed leaving Vera and myself alone.

'She's as daft as a brush at times, but her heart is the right place.' Vera said she had baking to do and left me at the counter alone.

I decided to leave the cameras in situ just in case Keanu or Giuseppe, whatever his name decided to make another appearance only I had a funny feeling that he would be back long before the spring.

No Way Back

Gerald Dabbs was a generally happy-go-lucky man. Always smiley, a passionate church goer and member of the choir he saw the good in everybody, irrespective of their race, the colour of their skin or religious beliefs. A print worker for a good majority of his sixty four years he had helped produce fashion magazines, fiction and non-fiction books, almanacs and children's story books sold in this country and overseas. A family man through and through Gerald was proud of his life, his loyal wife, children and grandchildren. Married for almost forty years to Mavis his childhood sweetheart he had every right to feel a deep sense of pleasure and satisfaction in his life's achievements.

Not regarded as one of our regular customer I was therefore surprised to see Gerald in the café shortly after lunch when he was normally at home with Mavis or the grandchildren.

Having retired early with the offer of a good pension package Gerald had graciously agreed and never looked back. With his home built and furnished to their liking Gerald tended to his allotment most days come rain or shine and Saturday he would listen to the cricket on the radio, whereas Mavis would take the grandchildren over the park in the afternoon. Through Robert Styles I had been told that Gerald was on the church committee at St Georges and one of his responsibilities was looking after the welfare of the church and grounds.

I watched as Danielle went over to Gerald's table to take his order. He wanted only a cup of tea, nothing else.

'You know Gerald doesn't seem right to me,' she whispered. 'He seems vacant as though his mind is wandering.' I had to agree as Gerald continued to gaze out of the café window where the odd bus and delivery van went by. 'I asked him if he was okay, but he responded with a shrug and something that looked like a smile.'

'He certainly looks like he has the weight of the world's problems on his shoulders.'

We decided to leave Gerald to his private thoughts as there were times when a customer came to the café for some peace and quiet, to take a refreshment and just muse with the world outside. Danielle went about her normal business fliting between the tables, but I knew that she was keeping an eye on Gerald. After half an hour of serving and clearing away dirty dishes she came back to the counter.

'He's not touched his tea... its stone cold I shouldn't wonder.' I took it upon myself to find out why.

'Hello Gerald, we haven't seen you in here for a little while, I hope that everything is well with Mavis and the family?' he looked up at me with eyes that seemed almost lifeless as though somebody had switched off the light behind.

'Oh hello Spencer, forgive me my friend, my thoughts were travelling elsewhere. Can you tell me, have I been in here long?'

'Long enough that your tea's gone cold, but don't worry about that as Danielle is pouring you a fresh cup.'

'Thank you, 'I'll pay for the two.'

'Don't worry about. Is everything okay?'

With his eyes turning moist he suddenly need to talk, opening up to someone who wanted to know. I took the seat opposite.

'They came and took Mavis away this morning Spencer. I've spent the morning at the Mary Grace old people's home in Tatlock Street.'

'And you missed lunch?' I asked.

'Hunger was the last of my concerns.'

Danielle brought Gerald's tea over. She was about to leave when I caught her arm.

'Do you like pasties?'

He nodded. 'Ask Vera or Martyn to warm one will you for Gerald and add a portion of chips on the side.'

'That's very kind of you both, but I am okay. I'll make myself some supper later.'

'No you won't.' Danielle looked surprised that I had replied so firm, but I knew that in his present state of mind Gerald wouldn't care for his diet and he would forego meals thinking about Mavis. 'It's important that you keep going Gerald, you keep up your strength for Mavis and the family.' I let go of Danielle's arm and she went straight to the kitchen.

'Mavis, she's younger than you isn't she?'

He smiled, it was a good sign. 'Four years, not that you'd know it.' I could see that his thoughts were beginning to open up a photograph album in the recesses of his mind. 'We were eleven and seven when we met. I didn't like her at first and thought that she was all airs and graces, but over the coming weeks we would play out in the street, laugh and joke with one another. We've been inseparable ever since, until today. I thought that my chest would burst when I walked away from the home just after lunch. I'm not sure that I want to go on by myself Spencer.'

Looking at the countertop we had a charity box to help support patients suffering from dementia, alzeihers or other neurological disorders and conditions. The box was due to be collected and was quite full of coins.

'I am really sorry to hear about Mavis, I had no idea.' There was no reason why I would know, but to give up somebody that you loved knowing that part of them was still alive physically must have been soul destroying. It made me think of my mum.

'I never saw the signs Spencer, not until they began creeping up like a dark shadow. First to go was Mavis's memory. She would forget where she had put things, her comb, her hairbrush, lipstick and pieces of

141

jewellery. Then she would have difficulty telling the time or she didn't know what day of the week it was. Worst of all and what upset Mavis the most was when she couldn't tell me the names of our grandchildren, even our own children. It must be like walking down a long narrow dark tunnel and the lights begin to dim.

'Who noticed the changes?'

'Doctor Doland. Mavis went along for something else, but he rang me after the appointment and asked that go along and see him. It was quite a shock at the time.'

'How long ago was that?'

'Middle of last summer. The deterioration has been quite rapid, faster than what the medical profession expected.'

Danielle arrived with the pasty and chips, bring me a coffee as well.

'And Mavis, how is she in herself?' it might have seemed to some like a ridiculous question to ask, but my reason for asking was to help Gerald. I think he knew it.

'She has good and bad days although the bad ones seem to outweigh the good. Most of the time she lives in a bubble of safety, almost like dream like state, walking through the day oblivious of her surroundings, time and the problems shared by many beyond our doors and windows. I don't think she fully appreciates what's happening Spencer. However, walking away from Mary Grace today I had to come to somewhere where I knew that there would be people only I just couldn't face walking into an empty house.' Gerald tucked into his pasty and chips not realising how hungry he was.

From time to time we all forget things, we lose track of time and we mislay objects, especially car keys, but Mavis had a real genuine excuse not that she had asked for the condition, side effects or complications. I was glad that this afternoon Gerald had opted to come to the café instead of standing on a rail bridge and watching the trains pass underneath.

'I'm a deeply religious man Spencer and I always have been, but what's happening to Mavis doesn't seem right. We've never done anything wrong our entire lives and her getting dementia doesn't seem fair.'

'Life throws a low ball when you least expect it Gerald.' I knew that he would grasp my meaning being a fan of cricket.

'Yes, but this damnation of a syndrome has knocked my poor Mavis for six and left me floundering about in the slips.' Gerald shook his head disbelievingly as he cut through the end of his pasty.

'And the family, how are they taking it?' I asked.

'Not great. Our children feel like a big part of our family has suddenly just disappeared and the grandchildren don't understand why nanny and grandad can't live together anymore.'

'How was Mavis when you left her today?'

He swallowed the chips in his mouth before answering. I thought that it also gave him time to consider his reply.

'There were moments when she didn't know me Spencer. She looked through me as though I were a ghost.'

Again I thought about my mum and how she had begun to mislay things about the house, phoning at odd times during the day and asking if I had seen them when I went visiting.

'Besides the very bad days are there good days?'

'Yes and no at the same time. Lucid moments when she realises what is happening, but Mavis is no fool Spencer. She knows the outcome and there is no cure for dementia. I'm her bad day because I want to be strong for her and the children, but I admit that I struggle.'

'That's not a bad thing to admit Gerald. A man without feelings and afraid to show that he has emotions is without compassion. Whether you realise it or not you are still the rock upon which your family depend upon. You've shouldered responsibility all your life and now you've shown just how strong you are.'

143

'How's that exactly?'

'By accepting that you cannot cope and placing Mavis in the one place where she will receive twenty four hour professional help and in some odd way find her dignity.'

'Her dignity, I don't understand?'

'She can arrange her room as she likes, she can do what she likes and without you watching over her and making sure that she is okay every waking hour of the day. Mavis needs to find her own level by which she can make mistakes and then put them right. The dementia will inevitably steal more of her every day, but Mavis has always been a strong woman, a fighter and she won't give in so easily, you'll see.'

'If I didn't know you better, I would say that you've been a fly on the wall for the past year. Yes, my Mavis is a fighter and she won't give in, not until the end.'

'And she would want you to fight as well Gerald. She would want you to still be that rock that you have always been.' Gerald nodded, but I knew that he wasn't entirely convinced. I tried a different approach.

'Robert always tells me that god works his magic in mysterious ways. He might think different when I turn up at the gates and convince St Peter to let me in.'

'Robert is full of praise for what you do for this community Spencer and some of my friends have walked away from the café feeling better than when they arrived.' He didn't say which friends.

'It was Anna, John and Clare who persuaded me to approach social services and start the ball rolling. They were right of course and they didn't want to see their mother suffer any longer. It's the feeling inside of me that is eating away at my insides. I feel that I have let Mavis down and that I could have done more.' He pushed his plate to one side leaving only a few chips.

'Nobody that knows you Gerald would ever think anything bad of you. You have earned your respect around here and whenever you feel the walls falling in, you're always welcome here.' I let my proposal sink in before continuing. 'It takes a very brave man to let his wife go to a nursing home. I know that I would struggle and need help. Not every man can go through what you did today.'

Gerald took a photograph out of his wallet and showed me it. It was slightly worn around the edges where it had very rarely seen the light of day. It was a black and white image of Mavis and Gerald on their wedding day. They both looked so happy.

'We got married in Hampstead. It was a beautiful sunny day and everything seemed right with the world. To our surprise Anna was born a year later. We had wanted children, only perhaps planned better, Anna was god's choice so we prepared ourselves for the happy event.' He produced another photograph of their three children. 'John came next and Clare wasn't that far behind.' Gerald chuckled as he stared at the images. 'You never know what's going to happen Spencer, none of us do.'

'The lord made sure that you and Mavis started life together by surprising you with Anna, then John and finally Clare. He was telling you that he approved of your union Gerald and whatever you feel right now he still approves and he'll continue to walk beside you, perhaps even more when you visit Mavis.' I surprised myself that I was sounding a lot like Robert.

When the bell over the door echoed out its customary ring I turned to see Robert Styles walk in. I couldn't help, but look up at the sky beyond the window. Did he really hear me and approve of everything that I did no doubt one day I'd get the opportunity to ask. Robert smiled at Danielle then walked over to our table.

'I've been looking for you Gerald.' I took my cue to stand and offer my seat.

'Here, it's still warm and I'll get you a coffee sent over.' Robert thanked me as he sat down.

'I was making my rounds at Mary Grace and I heard that you had brought Mavis in. I wanted so much to see you both, but another resident wouldn't let me go until we had recited the Lord's Prayer together. I thought that I would find you here.' I wasn't sure how Robert knew, but I guessed that he would tell me later and that it would involve some mysterious ways.

'Did you see Mavis?' Gerald asked.

'I did and although a little confused she looked happy, at peace with her new surroundings.' I saw Gerald's shoulders sag with relief. Robert noticed too. 'We had a conversation about you and the children, all the children.'

'She didn't know me today, it was like I was a ghost.'

'She talked about the day that you married and giving birth to Anna saying that it was a surprise, but a happy one. She remembered that John followed and lastly Clare.' I saw Gerald swallow hard and understood why. God did work in mysterious ways. 'She hoped that you would be at church this coming Sunday and that you would take the children too.'

Gerald nodded that he would be there. 'I'll speak to the others later.'

'There'll be a special prayer for Mavis and all like her in the service this Sunday.' The thought made Gerald smile. 'I told Mavis that we would go and see her the next time together, would that be okay with you?'

'I would like that vicar, thank you!'

Gerald offered to pay for his pasty, chips and teas, but I told him that it was on the house and that we would put the money in the charity box instead. Danielle would make sure that we did.

'Thank you Spencer, the café was my salvation today.'

Gerald would come and visit the café once, if not twice a week and when time allowed he would be accompanied by Robert where they would enjoy and afternoon together. Each visit was with news of Mavis, good and bad days, but through it all we felt that we were there for one another.

The weeks turned into months and Gerald would bring a different photograph on each occasion, a memory from the past that Danielle and I were happy to see. I showed him pictures of Lola and the children and Danielle reciprocated with her photographic memories of Paris.

146

Every time that Gerald said goodbye and thanked us for our hospitality my heart went out to the members of the Dabb family. Since Gerald had arrived that afternoon and told me about Mavis, I had made sure that I kept every available moment that I had free for Lola, the children and my mum.

What we don't realise until it happens is how precious life is to each and every one of us. Each memory that we make in the past or present and we store can so easily be stolen by debilitating illnesses such as dementia, alzheimer's and other mental health issues.

There were times when Mavis recognised Gerald and other days when he was nothing but a ghost. It was the same when her children and her grandchildren went to visit, but the nurses told Gerald that at some time later the visit did register a memory so none were wasted time.

It was Gerald visiting the café that afternoon and Robert arriving soon after uninvited, having been out looking for Gerald that made me seriously think about his religion and that there had to be something special that made everything happen.

Time could not go in reverse and neither could we, and there was no way back for Mavis and the many like her. I felt too that we had a duty to our loved ones to make sure that the memories we shared together were never lost and like the photograph that Gerald carried around in his wallet of their wedding day, a small black and white image could well be the one necessary lifeline in an ocean of uncertainty and hopeless despair.

The Cake Competition

Come the last week of April the mood in the café kitchen had changed and tensions were riding high as Vera psyched herself mentally in preparation for the annual cake competition.

Why exactly Vera got herself so inexplicably anxious was a surprise to us all. The cake competition had become a regular event on the annual calendar and our ever capable cook had been a contestant every year of the tournament. What Vera didn't know wasn't worth knowing. A deserving winner on many occasion she had added her successful recipes to our cake cabinet and each slice was a delight to all who came to visit the little red cafe. Many's the time that I had seen Robert Styles blessing our cake selection.

However, a competition it was and there was one miniscule chink in Vera's otherwise impenetrable armour and that was her fiercest rival Betty Brunswick. Once good friends the competition had driven a wedge between their friendship and they were like two feral cats who would size one another up turning into snarling, untamed rivals. Other bakers who knew of the rivalry gave them both a wide berth come the day of judging.

'So what are you going to put in as your entry?' I asked Vera.

'My classic lemon drizzle cake.'

I smiled nodding in agreement. 'Good choice, a tried and tested recipe.' Vera was unusually quiet. Danielle and Martyn had already left to head off home. 'And Betty,' I asked, 'do you know what she will be producing on the day?'

Vera shot me a disparaging look that needed no explanation. 'I'm not sure, although it will something underhand as usual.'

'That's not very sporting. How can you be so sure?'

'Because Jane Barton is my eyes and ears on the inside.'

I shook my head. 'This all sounds remarkably dishonest Vera. I would say that you and Betty Brunswick are serious about standing up there on the winner's rostrum this year.'

Vera looked at me her eyes focused. 'It's called upping the ante Spencer and keeping ahead of the competition. The cake contest means a lot to me and the café. A lot of people around here follow the event and expect a new recipe to come from the competition. It's not just my reputation on the line, but the little red café.'

'Then what can I do to help?'

Vera closed her recipe book leaving a page marked for later. 'Nothing, this is something that I have to do. Cyril always said to me that is was better to meet challenges head on than shy away from controversy. This book is my ammo for the battle ahead.'

None of us start out as sinners although growing up with Alfie Wilson I did occasionally deviate from the path of righteousness and like Vera found that the odd irregularity could prove fruitful. For example, I would give my money to an older boy on the estate to buy cigarettes because I was underage. We would split the packet on a ratio of seventy thirty and that way we both took advantage of the circumstances. Watching as she finished off in the kitchen Vera was doing nothing wrong really.

Midday the next day Jane Barton walked into the café, she asked to see Vera.

'You have the look of a bearer of bad tidings.'

Jane sighed. 'I'm afraid the worst kind Spencer.'

I asked Danielle to watch the counter while I accompanied Jane through to the kitchen. Seeing Jane arrive, Vera handed the receiver to Martyn to complete the order.

'You know something, don't you?' she said, looking at Jane then me.

'I had to come straight away Vera. This comes straight from the horse's mouth.'

'Well don't dilly dally about, tell me.' Vera wiped her hands down her pinny.

'Betty Brunswick got her card marked before yours. The judges accepted her application as the first entrant and as such she gets first choice of cake. She's making a classic lemon drizzle.'

I thought the roof was going to come off the building when Vera heard the news, instead she paced back and forth thinking. Several times she cracked her knuckles and flexed her fingers like a boxer would about to spar. When she stopped pacing I felt the relief drained down through me.

'I had a sneaky feeling that the slime bag would do something like that this year. It doesn't matter only last night I spent the evening going through my recipe book. I'll enter my ginger and orange with a splash of plantation rum.'

'That's a forty percent rum Vera. Remember that most of the judges at the cake competition are in their dotage. You'll have them rolling about the aisles.'

With a glint in her eye Vera grinned. 'I have only ever made it once before and that was for Cyril on his birthday.'

'And he survived the day?'

'And the night.' Vera replied. Neither Jane nor I felt inclined to ask how or what took place. 'I'll show that conniving Betty Brunswick that when you play poker having four of a kind is a winning hand, but a royal flush tops the lot. My cake will knock the competitors for six.' With the addition of the plantation rum it was certainly going to do that.

I left them sorting the list of ingredients that Jane said she would source before the shops ran out, neither wanted any other hiccups in the run up to the baking. Before she left the café I had a question for Jane.

'This vendetta between Vera and Betty is getting worse. Do you know what caused it to get so bad?'

Jane checked first to make sure that Vera wasn't around. 'You know Spencer, they were the best of friends at one time, but when the cake competition was launched their competitiveness became like a drug, that and Jim.'

'Jim...' I repeated, 'who exactly is Jim?'

'He was Betty's husband.'

'That's past tense Jane, is Jim dead?'

'Well he might as well be. You see Betty accused Vera of making eyes at Jim at one of the events. Betty believed that Vera was using her large chest and sexuality to win over Jim's favour in the voting. It was poppycock of course and as we both know Vera only ever loved one man and that was Cyril.'

'And is Jim still around?'

'No, rumour was that he went to the pet shop early one morning to buy the budgie some seed and only he never went back home. Betty being Betty blamed Vera for Jim's unusual vanishing act telling everybody that Vera and Jim had a lover's tryst.'

'Surely Betty knew about Cyril?'

'Yes she knew, but love is a very funny thing Spencer and can set the mind in a lather when things are not good at home. Betty and Jim were always at one another and their relationship was tempestuous to say the least. None of us was surprised when Jim disappeared. The accusation left a bitter taste in both their mouths.'

Vera had good reason to dislike Betty. When Jane left I would go through and talk to her.

'What about the other entrants, are they okay this year?'

'Yes, the normal bunch. Although there are a few oddballs here and there, but that's only senility taking hold of their mind and baking skills. It

151

does make for a few laughs on the day, especially if a cake has a sudden meltdown before the judges can scrutinise each entry.'

'I don't get much chance to be there on a Saturday when the event is in full swing, but I might come along this year as Danielle can hold the reins here.'

'Vera would like that.' Jane clicked her forefinger and thumb together having a sudden thought. Abigail MacDonald... now there was a lady who raised an eyebrow or two. There were rumours going around that Abigail had been seen with quite a few of the boys in the school rugby team, only when she got bored with rugby she averted her attention to the cricket eleven. She could have scotched the rumours as she got older, but the year Betty accused Vera of flirting with Jim, Abigail made a cake in the shape of a rugby ball. She's missed the last few competitions although nobody knows why, but this year I saw her name on the list of competitors. She could be the fly in the ointment.' I was definitely going along this year. Abigail MacDonald I had to see.

'And her cake is what...?'

'A carrot cake.' I wondered about the shape.

'Does Vera know about Abigail?'

'No, not yet. She's already stewing over Betty, so I would let her find out about Abigail on the day.'

Come the day of the actual competition you could feel the nervous tension inside the church hall as bakers added the finishing touches to their masterpieces. With deft precision they would tighten a bow or add sugar glazing to the petal of a leaf.

The children were with Lola's mother which meant that we could both go along and show our support for Vera and if needs be step in a separate the two main rivals. Fortunately the judges in their infinite wisdom had put their exhibits either side of the room. I introduced Jane to Lola.

'Vera was surprised to see that Abigail was here and of course Betty believes that it's another underhand trick of Vera's to influence the result.'

'Is Abigail's cake ready for viewing?'

'Not yet. She still has it hidden under a sheet. I must say that it does look an impressive size although an odd shape.' The thought of what it could be made me grin.

'To make matters worse Abigail MacDonald knows of the rivalry between Vera and Betty, she is quite happy to fuel the fire.'

'Have you had a whiff of Vera's cake?' Lola asked Jane.

'Yes, it's rather potent to say the least. Several of the judges are men and they like their drink. I think Vera's used a trump card this year.' I hoped that Vera hadn't over gone overboard lacing the cake with rum. Her Christmas pudding were a big hit especially when lit. Last year's blue glow over the pudding had Amelia and Antonio clapping for joy. I thought that it was time that I went over and found out how she was coping.

'How are you holding up?'

Vera looked very flushed. Her neck was red and there was a bead of sweat on her brow, it was so unlike her. 'If it weren't bad enough that the slime ball is here again, this year Abigail Macdonald has put in an appearance as well.'

I leaned over and smelt the cake, it was strong. 'Your cake smells grand. I take it from your tone that Abigail isn't a friend neither?'

'We were all friends one time and we didn't mind that Abi was all lipstick, frilly knickers and wandering hands. Shameless MacDonald we used to call her. If she weren't pulling up her underwear she's be taking down some boy's rugby shorts or cricket whites.' Vera pointed to the shapely blonde at the end of the hall, her table almost next to where the judges would make their deliberations.

'Shameless...' I repeated. 'That's quite a reputation. Are her cakes any good?'

Vera scoffed. 'Anything in trousers and she begins to quiver like an uncontrollable jelly. Yes, Abi was always good as domestic science. She could have been a celebrity chef, but her desires took her elsewhere.'

I could feel the burning of eyes penetrating my skull as I turned and saw a woman looking our way. A large woman with forearms that some of our building trade customers would have been proud to own.

'That's the enemy,' said Vera, she grimaced making Betty turned around to put her back to us. 'The unmistakable Betty Brunswick.'

I noticed that in a box under the table Vera had hidden her bottle of rum. 'Please tell me that you're not going to add any more rum to the cake?'

'No, that's for me and when the judges go back to their table to discuss their findings. It helps steady my nerves.'

'When did you add the rum?' I asked.

Vera turned to look, first at the cake then me, why?' she asked.

'It smells very nice, intoxicating...' I quickly added, 'which should attract the judge's attention. Why do you think I've overdone it?'

I took another sniff. 'No, it's about right. It could kick a stubborn mule into walking on with a lame leg.'

The cake was still wrapped around the edges in greaseproof paper. I asked why.

'It helps keep the cake moist and when you peel it off it adds a certain sheen to the bake. An old trick of the trade. Our cookery teacher taught us that.' Vera suddenly felt the need to sit down.

'Are you okay?'

'Yes, don't fuss I'm alright. You could cut the atmosphere in here with a knife. It's just getting a little warm in the hall that's all.' I thought that the hall could have done with a few radiators on as there was a slight chill in the air.

'Do you want me to get you a tea or coffee?'

'A coffee, black would be good.' It then occurred to me what might be wrong.

'When did you add the rum to the cake?'

'When I made the mix. A little last night to help and some more this morning to give the top of the cake a rich brown texture.'

'And did you have a tipple on the side?'

Vera grinned. 'Naturally, all good cooks sample their ingredients.'

'I'll get you your black coffee.'

'Is Vera alright?' asked Lola as she joined me at the refreshments table.

'Let's just say that she's under the influence of her cake.'

'The rum...' exclaimed Lola. I nodded. 'Hence the coffee, black and strong!' We added some sugar.

'If there was a canteen open here I'd get her a nice greasy bacon sandwich, it would help soak up the alcohol.'

'Have you seen the lady at the end of the hall,' asked Lola, 'the blonde with the funny shaped cake?'

'Yes, she also was a friend of Vera's at one time. Her name is Shameless MacDonald.'

'That's unusual?'

'Not if you knew the history as to how she acquired the name.'

We took the coffee over to where Vera was still sat on the chair scowling at the back of Betty Brunswick.

'Strike first and where it hurts the most, that's my motto.' Said Vera.

I looked at Lola and then around the hall to see if I could see Jane, but she was nowhere to be seen. Neither of us had a clue as to what Vera was on about.

'Here drink your coffee only the judging is about to start and they might ask you questions.' At that moment I saw my mum arrive to lend her support to Vera.

'What have you done to her,' my mother asked as she hugged and kissed Lola.

'It's the cakes fault…' I explained.

Mum's shoulder dropped. 'I told you last night not to add any rum this morning. Did you have any more?'

'You was with Vera last night?'

'Yes. Vera called me over to see that I approved of the cake. We injected some rum into the bake and had a glass ourselves.'

'But you don't drink!'

'There are some things Spencer Marlon Brand that I do, that I keep secret from you because you're always telling me what is good or bad for me. Living dangerously is fun.' Behind me Lola was smiling.

Vera didn't help sitting there with a silly grin on her face. 'Brunswick and MacDonald are here, the gruesome twosome.' She said to my mother.

'You'll win hands down this year. I felt it in my water when I got up this morning.'

Instinct or a feeling in my water had me look in the box under the table. I was surprised to see pushing the bottle aside a large plastic catering syringe. There was also a bottle with just a drop of liquid left at the bottom.

'What's with the syringe?' I asked.

Vera put her index finger to her lips. *'Sccchh Spencer, keep your voice down. They happen to be our contingency plan. The royal flush.'*

'What contingency plan?'

'When po-face opposite and knickers down here I come at the end of the hall went to get a coffee, I paid their exhibit tables a visit. A dose of amaretto will make their cakes smell like a hoard of kernel nuts that have gone to seed.'

156

I could not believe what I was hearing. I turned to look at my mother.

'Did you aid and abet in this crime?'

'When we heard that Abigail MacDonald was also an entrant we came up with plan B.'

Vera suddenly pulled me down by my shirt front. 'That rat Betty Brunswick nicked my cake recipe and Abigail MacDonald once nobbled my cake in the domestic science exam. Revenge was mine for the taking, but I've waited years to exact that revenge. Today was the day. If it wasn't for your mum swapping her cake for mine that day of the exam I would never have passed or become a cook.'

Vera's face was less than few inches from mine. I could smell the rum. *'There are times Spencer when being a little devious gets results. The deed is done and now we can't do a thing about it!'* She let go of my shirt.

Lola gently pulled me back up.

'Women do things sometimes that men don't always agree with Spence,' she said, 'my mama and auntie would do the same when they were young girls. The world of a female is vastly different to that of a male. Watch your daughter and son grow, you'll see the difference.'

'How much did you put in Betty Brunswick's cake?'

'Enough to entice the squirrels to the church hall when the judges cut a slice.'

We all watched as the judges walked around the hall visiting each table. After the first they arrived at Abigail MacDonald's table where she had pulled back the sheet protecting her exhibit underneath.

'A rather usual perfume of almonds for a carrot cake?' the judge implied.

Abigail MacDonald looked surprised. 'There's no almonds in my recipe.' She bent over to sniff her cake that looked like a braided twist of hair. They cut a slice and each judge forked a small piece into their mouth. They thanked Abigail for taking part in the competition and the judge with the clipboard marked up his sheet accordingly before they moved to the next table.

'That was one of my designs,' whispered Vera, 'serves her right.'

Eventually the panel of judges moved along the various tables until they arrived at Betty Brunswick's cake. A lady judge with thick lensed spectacles moved in closer to the table to view the Lemon Drizzle, sniffing loudly.

'You can smell the lemons.' She sniffed again like a squirrel with his nose amongst the autumn leaves, 'almond again. That's an odd ingredient.' She cut a slice and the plate handed around between the judges with a bewildered Betty not understanding how the female judge had detected almond.

When they arrived at Vera's table a good ten minutes later the coffee had done wonders along with an extra strong mint. Standing back from his visual and aroma inspection the judge looked impressed. He cut through the cake and forked a decent amount into his mouth. We watched as he closed his eyes letting the rum infuse his nostrils and taste buds.

'As moist as it looks with a taste of ginger and orange, although not overpowering.' His jaw rotated as he macerated the cake. 'The rum is delicious, a good planation variety I'd say.' He opened his eyes and smiled at Vera. 'Forty percent?'

'Nothing less.' She showed him the bottle from the box to prove that it was.

'I would another piece after the judging if that's okay?'

'I'll be here,' she replied.

Standing opposite with her arms folded across her chest Betty Brunswick was fuming. Half an hour later the judges announced that Vera's cake had won first prize with no placings for Betty or Abigail. She gratefully accepted her certificate and offered the rest of the cake to the judges table. Standing next to me my mum was cheering and clapping louder than anybody else.

When the applause ceased I congratulated Vera.

'You would have won without cheating,' I said. I was surprised when Vera laughed.

'I was certain of winning whatever happened Spencer only you see I wasn't the only entrant to tamper with Betty Brunswick's cake. Joyce Althorpe suffered at the hands of Betty when we were at school. I've no idea what she added to the lemon drizzle, but I doubt that the end product endeared the judge's favour or their taste buds.'

There was a sudden flurry of activity from the end of the hall as we turned to see Betty Brunswick and Abigail MacDonald arguing with clenched fists threatening one another being held back by the male judges. Somehow Betty managed to pick up the ceramic base of a potted plant and smash it over Abigail's head. Others came to the rescue of the judges. Voices were raised so we didn't have to move closer.

Slightly dazed, with murderous thoughts in her eyes and head Abigail retaliated angrily. *'You old dragon Brunswick. My darling Jim told me that you had a bad temper and an equally bad breath to match. No doubt the judges have suffered the same tasting your cake today!'*

At my side Vera was grinning. Not only had she won the contest, but any dishonest intervention on her part had quickly vanished with the smashing of the flower pot base.

'So it was Abigail MacDonald that Jim ran too when he left for the pet shop that morning.'

Vera nodded as she continued to watch. 'I knew that, but I wanted to have Betty Brunswick suffer. She was not the same girl that I had known at school Spencer. Time changes some people and she was never nice to Jim. That's why he left her.'

A flushed, although apologetic Robert Styles arrived in time to see Abigail being escorted to a waiting ambulance and the police talk to Betty Brunswick.

'What have I missed?' he asked joining our group.

'Vera winning the cake competition. Justice being served and the police being called.' I replied.

An hour later as we helped to clear up the hall I watched as the police having spoken to Betty for some considerable time left the building without taking Betty with them. Even more unexpected was when she came across to Vera's table.

'I owe you an apology Vera, can you ever find it in your heart to forgive me for being so stupid.'

To my surprise Vera graciously accepted the apology even suggesting that they have tea one afternoon and with Betty agreeing that the best cake had won.

'How did she find out that Jim was with Abigail?' I asked.

'She was wearing a necklace that Jim had once given to Betty. It was his mother's necklace and unique as it had been specially made. Betty saw the necklace today and quickly did the sums, the rest we all witnessed.

Lola had been right about women walking a different path to men and this year's cake competition had certainly opened my eyes. From dishonesty had come truth, and a friendship had been reborn with justice being served. Robert had said that he would visit Abigail when she returned home from the hospital to make sure that she was alright, but Vera advised against the visit telling Robert that his faith would be sorely tested if he did.

When we were alone he asked me why, to which I had but one explanation.

'Shame hath no mercy within the underwear of a woman without morals or scruples Robert and God works in mysterious ways.'

Four and Eight

Now I have always considered Thursday as a rather unusual day of the week. Sitting unevenly middle of the seven days and not Wednesday as many consider, Monday starts with the blues having reluctantly let go of the fun that we had at the weekend, we begin all over again.

Tuesday is like a hangover from Monday and it means we need to get back in the groove. Wednesday is the middle of the normal working week, although now we have Saturday and Sunday to consider and Robert would tell you that Sunday is one of his busy days.

Friday has always been considered a good day, a fish eating experience although if you born on a Friday you were deemed to work hard for a living. Whereas Saturday and Sunday, well the weekend is what you make of it. A time to visit family and friends, to generally unwind.

This particular Thursday however was the day after the dog racing at Stamford Hills Greyhound Track which always took place every other Wednesday in the month starting with the first race at seven fifteen. Come four thirty we had said goodbye to Danielle who had an appointment to her hair done. Having changed out of his kitchen shirt and trousers Martyn emerged from the cloakroom in a smart shirt and clean jeans.

'And where are you going all spruced up?' asked Vera.

'To the dogs.'

Vera eyed him suspiciously. 'You sure it's the dogs and not elsewhere. Does Danielle know?'

'No, she thinks I'm going to the snooker club with some mates.'

Vera shook her head disapprovingly. 'You know that's a serious gamble that you're taking Martyn. That girl lives and breathes you.'

'I've a reason for going Vera, trust me.'

'I hope so my lad because if she finds out you lied to her, they'll be hell to play.'

Martyn passed me at the kitchen door, saying goodnight to which I wished him luck. We heard the bell over the door chime then go silent. 'I'll lock up and put the kettle on, do you fancy a coffee?'

'Yes please, it's been one of those days. I could kill a cuppa.' Vera who had been vigorously cleaning the inside of the oven reversed herself out arching her back. 'I'm getting too old for this...' she said hunching her shoulders together.

'You should get Martyn to do it. He has youth on his side.' I helped Vera stand.

'The dogs is a mugs game.' I filled the kettle flicking the switch. 'You never recoup what you put down as a bet.'

'He's a sensible lad and he would never hurt Danielle, not knowingly.' I smiled to show that I had every faith in his reasons for going to the dog track.

'They are made for one another,' Vera replied sitting down on the kitchen stool, 'but I'm worried Spencer. When I send Martyn to the high street shop for additional supplies, I know that he's slipping into the betting shop and placing a bet.'

'He's over eighteen, there's really not a lot that we can do about it Vera and he'd have every right to tell us to mind our own business.'

'I know, but it's the deceit that worries me. Danielle doesn't know.'

My loyalties were divided. Danielle was like a daughter to me and Martyn a son. Together we had been through so much. I could see that Vera as concerned. 'I'll slip the subject into a morning conversation when were alone and having a coffee together.

'He listens to you.' She added milk to the clean cups. 'You might want to mention the horses, the weekend football pools and the lottery on a Friday night.' I switched off the boiling kettle. It sounded like he had got the bug.

'Maybe it's just a phase that he's going through. I remember being his age and doing the same. When the money ran out I realised that it was a mugs game.'

'For all her bravado and streetwise mannerisms Danielle is a sensitive girl at heart. I'm worried that if she finds out it could drive a wedge between them. Deceit in a relationship is a wound that never really heals. When Cyril was around we would tell each other everything.' I had to agree and I had no secrets that I kept from Lola or the children. I filled the cups with hot water.

'I'll make sure that I get the opportunity to catch Martyn alone, maybe when he takes the rubbish out.'

Vera seemed satisfied that I would. We ended the day with our customary coffee and chat mainly about Amelia and Antonio, Lola and my mum.

That evening the hours seemed to drag by and annoyingly like a father expecting his errant son anytime soon I found myself watching the clock, wondering what race was running and how Martyn was doing. I wondered if he was up or losing.

'You've been clock watching all evening, are you expecting something to happen?' I told her about Martyn. 'That's not good,' she replied. 'I have an uncle who still go to the horse race. My auntie has told him to stop, but he tells her that he would lose face with the other men in the village if he did stop. He tells her it is a man thing. He spends many a night in the barn with the chickens and cows when he loses. I'm so glad that you don't bet Spencer.' Looking at the framed photograph of Lola, myself and the children I too was glad that I no longer felt the urge to have a flutter.

'I promised Vera that I would talk to Martyn tomorrow. I feel there has to be a good reason for his current obsession.' I wanted to text Danielle to see if they were both okay, but Lola said that would only make her worry

163

all the more if he wasn't home. It was almost one in the morning when the phone beside the bed rang waking Lola and myself. I reached for the receiver, yawning and checking the clock beside the bed to make sure that I had the time right.

'Spence, it's me,' said Danielle, her voice full of alarm as it shocked my subconscious into responsive mode, *'I am really worried as Martyn has not come home!'*

I rolled from the bed searching in the dark for my slippers, putting my hand over the microphone I told Lola that the call was from Danielle. Within an instant she had flicked on the bedside lamp and was going for her dressing gown.

'Maybe he decided to stay over at one of his mates, rather than disturb you by coming back this late.'

'Or maybe he's with some bird.' Concern had turned quickly to anger and doubt.

Inside my head I saw a red light go on, a warning sign of danger. Vera was right.

'Oh come on Danielle,' I was trying the gentle approach and aware that the children were asleep in the next rooms. 'You know that's not true. Martyn idolises you and he would never cheat on you.'

'Does he Spence, I'm not so sure.' She was suddenly calmer. 'I've been dropping hints all over the place recently about us getting married only he never really gives me a reply. I think Martyn's getting cold feet.'

If I didn't find my slippers soon, I'd be the one getting cold feet whereas Lola was heading for the door to check on Amelia and Antonio. She stopped at the door to turn and face me. *'I'll put the kettle on,'* she whispered.

'Maybe you're reading a lot more into this situation than what there is and Martyn has a reason why he's not forthcoming with his commitment.' It didn't sound right, but my head felt heavy and I had never liked being disturbed from my sleep. There was a few seconds silence as Danielle mulled over the possibility.

'Will you talk to him in the morning Spence and get to the bottom of what's going on. He's also acquired a bloody annoying habit of taping the side of his nose when I ask him a question. If I don't some straight answers soon, I'll bash the side he keeps tapping and put it permanently out of alignment.'

'Alright, I promise that I'll talk to him. Did you want to spend the night here rather than be there by yourself?'

Ten minutes later I knocked on the door of her flat.

'He still not here?' Danielle crushed me as she fell against my chest throwing her arms about my back.

'I just know that he's with somebody else Spence, I can sense it. Women have an inbuilt radar for these things.' Her sobs were heavy and wet. I tried to soothe her pain by patting the back of her shoulder.

'There'll be a good reason why he's not come home yet, you'll see.' I looked down to see her overnight bag was already packed.

After a coffee and a long cuddle with Lola, we gave Danielle the spare room. Ten minutes later when Lola checked Danielle was already asleep, exhausted and no doubt content that she was safely tucked up under our roof.

'Amelia and Antonio will be thrilled when they wake and find Danielle sleeping in the next room.'

Lola smiled. 'The only trouble is they'll both want her to stay home and Amelia has school.'

We had just lay our heads back down on the pillows when my mobile phone announced that I had a text message. Lying beside me I felt Lola shake the mattress as she tried not to laugh. I activated the text screen knowing that it would be from Martyn.

'Late night and I am just home. Thanks for looking after Danielle, I found your note. Would you mind if I was an hour late in the morning, as there's something that I need to do urgently.' I replied and agreed to the

hour, but warned Martyn that Danielle would almost certainly be on the war path upon his arrival. He didn't reply.

That morning the three of them sat at the kitchen table playing games with Lola and myself watching. Amelia and Antonio looked upon Danielle as their older sister rather than an auntie and she loved every moment with them.

Walking to work we talked about anything other than Martyn. I was hoping that Vera would be there at the café waiting when we arrived. She was there and told me that she could cope until Martyn arrived.

'You're sometimes too soft,' she said when Danielle was sorting the tables and chairs out front. 'You need to have a firm hand and deal with him good and proper when he does arrive.'

'Well let's hear his side of the story first.'

Ten o'clock the bell over the door chimed and Martyn appeared. Danielle glared at him from the table in the corner, but luck would have it she was busy taking an order.

'You had better have your story straight,' I warned, 'only she's been stewing nicely waiting for you to show.'

'Thanks Spencer, I'll make up the hour.'

I don't know why I asked, but I did. 'How'd it go last night?'

'I lost the first three races, won on the fourth only my mum always said that four was a lucky number. I didn't do so well on the fifth, sixth and seventh, and lost out on the ninth and tenth.'

'But what about the eighth?'

Martyn was about to answer my question when Danielle appeared at the counter. Her face was as black as thunder.

'Your story had better be good otherwise you're going to need plastic surgery and I'm talking about your boat race.'

I cringed as Martyn tried to kiss her cheek, but she pushed him away.

'You've got to be joking. For all I know you could have been kissing another woman last night.'

The clatter of knives and forks on plates instantly stopped as all eyes looked at the counter. I wanted to help Martyn, but I saw Vera standing in the open doorway of the kitchen. Man to man I could only hope that he said the right thing. When he grinned and tapped the side of his nose I shut my eyes waiting for the crunch of bone. It was only the gasp coming from some of the women at the tables that made me open them again. I had to look over the counter top to see Martyn bent down on one knee.

'The only lady that I was with last night was lady luck.'

But a cloud of red mist had descended and clouded Danielle's patience. I could see that her fists were clenched. 'I don't care what her bloody name was, I'll kill you first and then her when I catch up with her.'

Martyn reached inside his jacket pocket withdrawing a small square box. He looked at me and answered my question. 'The eighth race came in Spencer, with bigger odds than the fourth!' With that he opened the lid of the box. Somebody sucked all the air from within the café as Danielle put a hand over her open mouth.

'I should have told you that I was going to the dogs last night instead of the snooker hall with the lads, but I needed to find lady luck at the dog track.' He took hold of her free hand. 'Will you marry me?' he asked.

Danielle looked at me, then Vera, at the faces staring at her around the café before looking back at Martyn. 'And that's why you didn't come home last night and you're late in work this morning?'

'That's why,' he replied, 'so what's it to be, yes or no?'

Danielle leant down to look at the diamond as it sparkled in the sunlight. 'Is it the right size?'

'It's the right size.' Martyn took the ring from the box and showed it to Danielle. 'So will you marry me?'

Suddenly all the worry, doubt and heartache left her body as the tears streamed down her cheeks as she announced that she would marry him.

The café erupted with a tumultuous cheer and at the door to the kitchen I saw Vera wipe the tears with her pinny. She saw me looking and nodded. Danielle slipped the ring over Danielle's ring finger and sure enough it did fit. Vera was the first person that she showed it to and that pleased me immensely.

'It's beautiful, really beautiful,' said Vera, 'and I am so happy for you both.' Danielle hugged Vera then proudly showed her ring to all in the café. I congratulated Martyn and would get my turn with Danielle when she had finished going between the tables.

Going over to Vera I put my arm about her shoulder as she was still crying. 'I won't be needing that conversation with Martyn after all.'

She sniffed into her pinny. 'They'll be other times.'

I offered my clean handkerchief. 'The only advice I think I'll be giving is how to go about arranging the wedding with Robert.'

Vera blew hard into my handkerchief. 'I just wish that Cyril had asked me to marry him before he got killed.'

'He'll be waiting for you and then when the time is right Cyril will go down on bended knee and make your heart fill with joy.'

'Are you sure?'

'Trust me, a man knows these things!' I was beginning to sound more like Robert every day. It was a little disconcerting.

I never did get the chance to ask Martyn just how much he had won on the eighth race, but whatever the prize it paid for the cost of the engagement and wedding rings, the ceremony and their honeymoon. And over coffee one morning when Danielle was discussing a wedding cake I did get the opportunity to talk to Martyn about gambling, but as expected he had it all covered.

'I am no gambler Spencer and I only went through that phase to help secure our future. My gambling days are well and truly behind me now.'

So that is why we refer to every Thursday as our four and eight day because it was when Danielle accepted Martyn's proposal of marriage and without her knowing it, Norse legend deemed that Thursday was the day when Thor arrived on a fiery chariot with an accompaniment of thunder and lightning. Had Martyn not won at the dog track and arrived the next morning at his normal time he would have walked into a storm like no other from Danielle.

To end this chapter I should really tell those of you who are interested or wondering, that I was born on a Friday.

Following a Shadow

Wee Archie was how I was introduced to the ventriloquist's dummy which was sat on the man's lap occupying the table next to the wall mural. Down by the man's side was a large suitcase. I guessed by the way that he and the dummy were dressed that together they would be heading off soon to one of the West End's most celebrated theatres.

I was about to shake the hand of Wee Archie when the hand shot back and palm up as a warning. With its big saucer eyes the dummy dropped its smile. 'I'm sorry, but I only shake hands with royalty or a successful agent wanting me to sign a lucrative deal.'

Instead the ventriloquist offered his hand. 'Don't take any notice of Archie, he can be somewhat abrupt and rude at times. I'm Donald to friends.'

The dummy sat there staring back at me, then quite by sudden it opened its mouth. 'Know any good jokes mate?' Archie asked.

Now I had never been good at telling jokes and only one came to mind. 'Would a knock-knock joke do?'

'I suppose so.' Archie sat himself upright to take part. *'Knock-knock, who's there?'* he asked.

'An old lady,' I replied.

'An old lady who?'

'See you can yodel, yodelay hee hoo.'

He looked at me, then at Donald before his head fell forward in laughter. Stood behind the counter Danielle was shaking her head although she did have a smile on her face. Suddenly another verse came to mind.

'I once fell in love with a blonde

Of whose name I have forget

But she called me up late one night

To ask if I was free

Only I let her down lightly

Declining the invite because I was only four'

This time Wee Archie just sat there, his mouth slightly open and shaking his head from side to side. 'The steam from the coffee machine has started to affect your brain. Maybe you need to get it serviced.'

I wanted to tell him what a cheeky bugger he was, but several eyes were watching from the other tables. I needed something stronger so racked my memory cells. *'What has a wooden leg, a head and a claw, is as strong as iron, but cannot move unless pushed back and forth?'*

Wee Archie pondered the conundrum for several moments putting a hand to his chin where over the years he had rubbed it clean of paint.

'Your mother...' he replied.

'Don't be impertinent,' said Donald, so the dummy kept on rubbing thoughtfully. Seconds later he raised a hand.

'A hammer.'

I nodded agreeing, Wee Archie was good.

'My turn now,' the dummy cried. The café was almost silent with only the sound of passing traffic going by outside.

'A ten year old girl came home from playing in the park to be told that her grandfather had died that morning. So being considerate of her grandmothers loss she went straight round to see that grandma was alright. 'Why he had a heart attack darling,' said the grandmother responding to the little girl's question as to why he had died. 'We were

making love at the time.' Now the granddaughter who was very astute for her age wanted to know how at ninety they could still be participating in sex. 'Well darling grandpa went to see the doctor for some advice and he told grandpa that he should have sex in time with the sound of the church bell as it went back and forth, dinging one way, then donging the other.' The girl thought about what the doctor had said for a moment before asking another question. 'Well if grandpa was doing it slowly, how come he had a heart attack?' Grandma smiled back at her granddaughter. 'Everything was going just dandy until the ice cream van arrived.'

The café erupted into a fit of laughter, bringing Vera and Martyn out from the kitchen. 'Whatever is going on?' she asked seeing the ventriloquists dummy sat on Donald's knee.

It was Danielle who explained. 'The dummy was just explaining to Spencer how dangerous it can be having sex when you're old and the ice cream van arrives outside.'

Vera looked back at Danielle curiously. 'And how exactly will buying an ice-cream kill him?'

'No, not the ice-cream, the sound of the jingles.' To help Martyn mimicked the ding-dong, ding-dong chime increasing in tempo. The penny dropped into place.

'Oh, I see,' replied Vera. 'Mavis at the women's institute told a similar joke, but it didn't make sense because she got her jingles mixed.'

Seeing Vera appear from the kitchen the dummy spun its head around. *'Gawd preserve us,'* it said, *'who let her out.'*

'Bloody cheek,' Vera responded. She turned about and went back into the kitchen, leaving Martyn and the café laughing.

'Here,' said Wee Archie recognising that it had the attention of the customers, *'have you heard the one about the removal firm that employed an Englishman, a Scotsman and an Irishman?'*

'No,' cried a man at a nearby table, 'tell us.'

'Well,' Archie started, *'everything had been going well and the three of them had cleared the ground floor together, when going up to the bedrooms on the floor above the Englishman and Scotsman were struggling to get the wardrobe down the stairs.'* Archie checked that everybody was listening. *'Where's Paddy?' asked the Englishman, to which a voice came from inside the wardrobe calling out, 'I'm in here to stop the clothes from moving from side to side and getting damaged.'*

With tears running down the cheeks of some they asked for more, so Archie obliged.

'Having been in a fight at the rugby match and arrested by the police the judge sentenced the offenders, an Englishman, a Scotsman and an Irishman to six months in jail. Arriving at the prison they were immediately confined to solitary, but were granted one wish to see them through the six months inside. Paddy asked for six months' worth of Murphy's stout. The Scotsman, six crates of good highland whiskey and the Englishman a supply of cigarettes that would see him through the solitary period. With the six months completed the guards opened up the doors of the cells and let the three of them go free. To their surprise they found the Scotsman had died as a result of alcoholic poisoning and the Irishman the same, his liver giving out. The only man to survive had been the Englishman. 'I thought that he would at least have had a lung condition smoking all those cigarettes,' said one of the warders as the Englishmen stepped from the cell breathing in the healthy fresh air. The Englishman having overheard the remark, responded. 'I probably would have died had I asked for a box of matches as well.'

Danielle arrived at the table with the ventriloquist breakfast order, two rounds of toast and a pot of tea. Donald thanked Danielle as Wee Archie sat on his knee looking up and down at Danielle. *'Who squeezed you inside that dress?'* the dummy asked.

Danielle went in close so that she was only inches from Wee Archie's face. 'If I told you that, it would no longer be a secret would it.' For once the dummy was silent. Donald put the dummy on the chair next to him while he ate his toast. He gestured that I sit down at the next table which was free.

'Some places where we have breakfast don't invite us back, but the little red café, why it has a friendly atmosphere.' He looked around taking it all in. 'You feel it the moment you walk in through the door.'

'We never refuse paying customers. How long is your stint at the theatre?' I asked.

'We're booked for the initial three weeks. It's a new comedy show and the producers want to see how it is received by the audience before they commit to a longer contract. With comedy you only survive if the audience laughs. Hit a brick wall of silence and suddenly you become part of history, not that anybody will remember you.'

I looked at the dummy sitting on the chair. His head was forward with his chin resting on his chest. 'And Wee Archie, has he been with you long?'

'We've been together since I was a boy. He once belonged to my late uncle who travelled all across Europe with a troupe of dancers, musicians and comedians until tuberculosis ended his tour. As part of my uncles Will, Wee Archie was left to me. As a young benefactor I did think it an odd bequest, but we've been inseparable ever since. So far it has been good, but comedy is a fickle subject and nowadays too political. A wrong word here or there could change your fortune forever.'

He looked around again nodding to himself. Donald Archibald Campbell struck me as a man who had seen and done a lot, visiting many places and meeting many audiences. He told me that he had ancestral connections to a twelfth century Scottish titled landowner although for himself he wasn't interested in titles. Comedy was his sword and shield.

'Are you married?' I asked although there was no ring on his left hand.

'No never. Maybe close on occasions, but my lifestyle and Wee Archie put paid to any concrete plans of settling down.' Donald sounded like Alfie Wilson and I wondered if their paths had ever crossed.

'You must enjoy what you do?'

It surprised me when Donald shrugged his shoulders. 'Most of the time I do, although there are times when being alone can get very lonely. I very

174

rarely get the chance to visit my beloved Scotland and if I do, it is only to perform overnight in a show before I am back on the road again. This suitcase and the worn leather can probably tell many a story better than myself. It's been two years since I have seen my family.'

Having finished his toast Donald hoisted the dummy up onto his knee. I could see that they were inseparable. Almost immediately the dummy came to life, smiling and swivelling his head left and right interested in his surroundings. He looked at me, then at Donald. 'Did you miss me?' the dummy asked.

Donald smiled. 'Did you miss me is more important?'

Wee Archie nodded gently. He then swivelled his head my way again. 'I dreamt about you,' it said.

I pointed to my chest playing along. 'I hope you saw me as a warrior or adventurer.'

'Neither. You were walking through a park holding onto the hands of two children.' Wee Archie swung his head around to look at the photo gallery on the wall near the counter. 'The little one, the boy he's almost as tall as me.'

'That's Antonio, my son and the little girl she's Amelia, our daughter.'

Archie nodded thoughtfully. 'Nice family, pretty wife.'

'Thank you. After you leave here, where exactly are you heading next?'

Wee Archie replied. 'Some dusty old stage in a not so famous west end theatre then catching the train to the south coast if this show doesn't run for the entire season. 'I'll have you know that it's no fun being cooped up in a suitcase.'

'Claustrophobic I should imagine.'

'It affects my arthritis.' The dummy replied. 'It can get mighty damp and cold standing about on train stations. I much prefer a cruise ship, warm sunshine and lots to see, especially the women in their bikinis. After the last cruise my eyes needed repainting.'

It wasn't long after that that Donald decided it was time to leave as they had rehearsals to attend. He was about to put Wee Archie back in the suitcase when Danielle came over to say goodbye.

'Was that your handsome young man your fiancée who came out of the kitchen with the old dragon?'

Danielle nodded back at Wee Archie. 'Yes, that's Martyn.'

The dummy looked Danielle up and down once again. 'Lucky man, but if he ever dumps you, you'll find my name in the showbiz columns under comedy.'

'I'll remember that,' replied Danielle.

The dummy gestured with his hand. 'Here, come forward,' he said, 'I've one last request before I get shoved in the suitcase.'

'What's that?'

'You're as hot as a rocket going to the moon, can I have a kiss to help with my dreams.' We watched as Danielle kissed the tips of her fingers then placed them on the dummy's lips. Wee Archie sighed then flopped, crossing both hands across his chest. He then closed his eyes and whispered *'goodbye'*.

Before he left the café Donald gave us tickets for the show and we promised to go along. I took a photograph of Danielle with Wee Archie on her knee and his head resting on her chest. Later at home I would download the image and put it amongst the others on our wall.

A week later Vera and my mum went along to see the show. They said it was very good, very entertaining and loved the spot with Donald and Wee Archie.

'Apparently, he insults most of the women that he meets,' said Vera.

'Unless you just happen to be Danielle. I think the dummy had a soft spot for our young, attractive assistant manager.'

Spirits, Unusual Vibes and the Future

It was a strange request and one that I had to consider very carefully. The local spiritualist group who normally held their monthly meetings at a local hall had the venue cancelled because of redecoration. They had approached me as a last resort having tried nearby hotels, other sizeable venues and even a pub, but none of the proprietors could accommodate their needs at such short notice. I was assured that all they would need was tables and chairs, and somewhere where they could make tea or coffee.

'Go on Spence, it's only a one off and it'll be a lot of fun. I will cover the evening if you would rather not and Martyn will be there also, he'll make sure that there's no funny business. Besides it's only a bunch of ladies, not the international wizards and witches convention.'

'It is not the ladies that worry me so much Danielle, but what harm their vibes might do to the little red café. We have a friendly ambience here, a welcoming spirit that is our resident spook. I don't want them insulting our ghost's integrity or stealing their spot. A good many of our customers come to the café hoping that his or her spirit will rub off on them.'

'Okay Spence, if any call up a dead uncle or aunt who owe money, I'll keep my eye on the till.'

'And what about Vera, she might want to be involved.'

Danielle cottoned on quick. 'You mean Cyril.'

My nod was emphatic. 'You know that she goes regularly to see a medium hoping he'll come through.'

'I don't know why she doesn't come with me and my mum. We go to my aunties and she don't let any old bugger through, only the important ones. First off they have to state why they want to come through before their granted access back into our world. You have to think of the other side as the social services, the spirits have to queue like they do at Marks and Spencer otherwise they get shown the back door.'

I could see why Vera had never opted to go with Danielle and her mum. Danielle had a special way of describing things that few could match. I agreed hesitantly to the spiritual evening although I said that I would come along, not necessarily to help run the event, but solely as a bystander I wanted to ensure that our friendly spirit wasn't frightened away.

Since the day of my wedding when I had sat alone in the café and spoke with my late father seeking his advice I had felt his presence around often and especially when I had a difficult decision to make. I know that he looked over my mother, Lola and the children, but I had hoped also that he was proud of my achievements. It was his spiritual presence, plus others that I didn't want to lose.

On the odd occasion that I had seen Antonio looking up at the beam in the café when Lola had brought him in after lunch, I had wondered if his childlike innocence saw something that we could not as adults. Sometimes Antonio would gurgle away incomprehensibly to himself and other times he would just sit, watch and smile.

When I told Lola about the booking, she too had her reservations.

'You will have to be careful Spencer, the café is like a backbone in the community. Many of the elderly customers who visit morning or late afternoon come because they feel safe in the café. They come to meditate.'

Neither of us had noticed the little face which had appeared in the kitchen doorway. 'Does that mean that there will be ghost's daddy, only Antonio and I saw one on the telly the other day and they had a dog like Scooby.'

I looked at Lola mouthing *Scooby?* She pulled Amelia into her hip. 'Silly daddy doesn't know Scooby Doo and the gang.' Amelia seemed satisfied that I had failed the telly test. 'It's a children's programme.' Lola told me when she went to find her brother. A minute they both came back.

'Antonio's seen a ghost.'

'Really,' I replied, 'where?'

'At the café.' I felt my skin creep.

'Auntie Danielle told us that Vera scares away any nasty ones.' I would have to talk to Danielle. Lola didn't help by laughing.

'Any ghosts that we have at the café come to help the customers.' I said trying to allay any fears in their young minds, although neither my daughter nor my son seemed the least perturbed by the prospect of seeing a spirit float around the ceiling of the café.

'And Auntie Mary has told us about the Angels. They sit on the end of the bed as we sleep and if we get cold they cover us with their wings of feathers.' Antonio had his tongue protruding between his lips, but he was just watching me, awaiting my response. Lola gently flicked the tip of his tongue, but he giggled assuming that it was part of the game. Now if there was a spirit that had come back to haunt me, it had materialised itself in the body of my son.

Tuesday night around seven the ladies started arriving and piling into the café, some passing me by without so much as a hello or even asking why I was there, others seemed oblivious to my presence. Calling the gathering to order Myrtle Moncrieff raised her arms high into the air before slowly bringing them down like a descending pair of wings until they came to rest on her generous hips. I looked across at Danielle who had expanded her own hips with her hands to mimic Myrtle.

'We should thank Danielle and Martyn for allowing us to use the facilities of the little red café tonight.' She quivered her wings. 'The vibes here are strong, can you feel them ladies.' There were several *oohs* and *aahs* along with the odd acknowledgement. As Danielle had said this was no wizard and witches convention, it was a bunch of ladies hoping that Myrtle would produce at least one decent spirit.

I felt my apprehension drifting away as I arranged the cups for tea and coffee on the counter. To add atmosphere Martyn had draped dark blue cotton strips over the ceiling lights, it made the inside look like a tanning studio. I did catch myself looking up at the wooden beam wondering if anybody was sitting up there wondering about the gathering below. I couldn't blame them if they did.

'Now are there any questions before I begin?' asked Myrtle. Waiting two seconds without a murmur to be heard she sat herself down at the centre table. 'Good then I will start.' On cue Martyn dropped the blinds down over the windows. Fascinated I watched as the expressions changed on their faces. I did have a wicked thought and almost prayed behind the counter that my father would make a sudden appearance.

No sooner had they settled and began holding hands, apparently to strengthen the circle engagement did the candlelight on the centre table begin to flicker. I checked, looking at the doors and windows detecting no draughts. I caught Danielle look my way. I responded with a shrug and upturned palms.

'The spirits, they're coming through ladies,' Myrtle sounded excited as eyes around the circle went left and right, 'be strong now and don't break the circle, let them through so that we can communicate.'

I was so tempted to call out *'boo'* but doing so would have probably given half the participants a bad turn.

'I feel Fred coming,' one of the women suddenly cried. I spied a big lady with a purple highlight streak in her hair. She looked like an older version of a female superhero. I could only surmise that if Fred had come through and he noticed the streak, he would soon depart.

'That's it Agnes,' Myrtle replied encouragingly, 'keep the channel of communication open, it will help others in the room call upon their loved ones.'

Stepping silently around the outside of the circle Martyn cynically arrived at my side. 'How much has she charged for this cobblers?' he whispered.

'I'm not sure, but perhaps we should consider getting Danielle's auntie down here every week. This is more amusing than watching the television.' Danielle who was stood on the far side of the room raised her eyebrows indicating auntie's sessions were much better. It added credence to my suggestion.

Myrtle was now in full swing. 'Fred, are you there Fred... if so give us a sign.'

When the voice, a little muffled at first came through even I jumped. 'Where the hell did that come from?' asked Martyn as our eyes scanned every part of the room although we saw nothing out of the ordinary. Even Danielle the other side looked.

'I'm here Agnes, how are you doing girl?'

Agnes obviously exhilarated by the experience of hearing her beloved Fred was almost beside herself with excitement. Whether the voice sounded like or belonged to Fred, Agnes didn't care. A mythical troll could have come through instead and she would have believed him when he told her that he had a sore throat. Agnes had come along this evening to hear from Fred and here he was.

'I'm missing you Fred, I really wish you were here!' she cried.

There followed a moment of silence before the spirit replied. 'Perhaps Fred is happier where he is on the other side...' whispered Martyn.

Looking again at Agnes with her purple streak it would have concerned me to have woken alongside at night. I was pleased that Lola wasn't into colouring her hair.

'I've not got long Agnes,' Fred replied, *'is there anything that you need to know before I go?'*

I focused my attention solely on Myrtle wondering if she was working some kind of voice box hidden under the table supported by her knees, but like the others around the table her lace gloved hands were joined with the two women on either side.

'Fred my darling, I can't find the password to release the money in the building society, do you know where you put it?'

Several more seconds passed before the voice coughed, giving up the reply. *'It's inside the cuckoo clock. I'm sorry but I must go Agnes as others are pushing me aside and wanting to come through. Goodbye.'* Danielle was right, it did give me the impression of the queue at the social services office.

Agnes begrudgingly said goodbye. She turned to the lady to her left. 'I knew my Fred wouldn't let me down.'

All around the table there was silence as eyes focused on Myrtle once again. Suddenly the lady with whom Agnes had held a conversation, Felicity Parnell cried out making the table shake. 'I don't have a cuckoo clock.' she cried.

'You might not, but I do.' Replied Agnes. All eyes turned to look at Felicity. 'Did you know my Fred?' Agnes asked.

'This is getting interesting,' muttered Martyn.

'Fred did pop around once or twice to help change a lightbulb or fix my headboard when it had rattled itself loose.'

The thought of her husband being another woman's bedroom horrified Agnes, especially one such as Felicity who was fast approaching ninety one.

'Keeping the mind active, keeps the body parts working just as well Agnes. You should remember that. Now concentrate on the meeting otherwise you'll interfere with the lines of communication.'

I looked at Martyn. He was enjoying this as much as the participants sat around the table. I saw Danielle raise her eyebrows agreeing with my thoughts.

'Spirits,' Myrtle again invited, 'is there anybody there, does anybody else want to come through?'

When the spirit replied it made even Myrtle sit up straight.

'Myrtle Moncrieff this is your mother.'

The look of horror on Myrtle's face made the coming along that evening worthwhile. She had not expected her own mother to push to the front of the queue. Myrtle realising that she had an audience answered rather meekly. 'I'm here mother!'

'I know you are you fool otherwise I wouldn't be.'

Undoing the front of her shawl to allow extra air to her chest Myrtle was clearly uneasy. Martyn was right, this was fun.

'Is there a reason why you have come through mother?'

The reply was curt. *'To teach you a lesson child.'*

Flushed with embarrassment having been upstaged in front of her ladies Myrtle broke hands with the lady on the right to fan her face. 'A lesson dear, what kind of lesson of would that be?'

'That meddling with what you do not understand is a dangerous undertaking.'

Myrtle gulped.

'Here it comes,' whispered Martyn, 'look at the guilt in her eyes.'

'Meddling mother, I can assure you that I have not seen Gerald Arandrake in weeks.'

'Not men you foolish girl. I am talking about the other side, the spiritual world.'

Like two bags of uneven cement Myrtle's shoulders sagged. The voice belonging to her mother continued.

'We take things over this side very seriously and fraudulent shows to entice a mixed group for conversation are bad for our reputation. You have got to stop it and stop it now Myrtle, otherwise I warn you girl, I will not be able to get you an entry pass when your time comes to join us.'

'Does she collect two hundred as well?' Martyn muttered.

The lady nearest the counter hard his comment. She turned to face us both. What came next surprised us both.

'And tell that pretty young girl standing all alone that I have a message for her as well.' I watched as Danielle's expression changed and her jaw fell open.

'Remove that shawl Myrtle and come clean,' her mother demanded, but Myrtle was reluctant to oblige knowing the outcome if she did.

'Now,' boomed the voice.

Myrtle reluctantly pulled the shawl over her head to reveal as I suspected a small voice box. Around the table there were gasps and mutterings of disappointment.

'No wonder my Fred sounded funny,' said Agnes. She lowered her head in frustration. 'I was so sure that he'd come through to me at last.'

Myrtle's mother intervened.

'Fred is standing beside me now Agnes, he says you to check inside that pair of white shoes that you hate wearing. The password to the account is hidden inside.'

Agnes thanked the spirit yet she refused to look at Myrtle. It was at this point that I expected the circle to be broken and the participants to begin drifting away, but they remained sitting around the table looking up at the ceiling above.

The voice was once again profound. *'And you will return these dear ladies their money that they paid you and after tonight you will not dabble again in this sham practice. Is that understood Myrtle Moncrieff.'*

Myrtle removed the voice box before reaching down into her handbag for her money bag.

'I'm watching you Myrtle, remember every penny is to be returned.' There was a flurry of activity as the ladies opened and closed their purses. The voice suddenly changed direction. *'And now to you young lady. Danielle I have a message from your grandfather who tells me that you*

might want to bring the date of the wedding forward by several months. He is smiling and hopes that you'll understand.'

Quite a few heads turned to look at Danielle, whose hands covered her belly. She looked at Martyn as a big smile creased her face. She understood the message alright. Danielle looked up at the wooden beam overhead. 'Will tell grandad that I said hello and that I love him.'

The woman's voice chuckled. *'He heard you and he sends his love back, saying that he be there for the happy event.'*

'Christ...' was how Martyn greeted the news. 'I'd better have a word with Robert as soon as possible.'

Then unexpectedly the voice crossed the room once again.

'You think I would let the evening pass without coming to you Spencer Brand. You might stand there silent and amused by the events unfolding, but maybe it's time to get that spare room decorated only your father tells me that you too will have another addition to your family soon.'

'Rock on Spencer,' said Martyn as he congratulated me, 'it would seem that we both have an event to celebrate soon.'

I gave Danielle a congratulatory hug. 'You must have had inside information about wanting this evening to go ahead.'

'I'm not sure it was inside info, but quite possibly from the other side. I was always close to my grandad. Lola's going to be surprised.'

'Not as much as I am.' I replied. 'I had better get in touch with Thomas and make the necessary arrangements to have the bedroom decorated soon.'

The voice from Myrtle's mother had vanished without any of us realising and soon after that the ladies did disperse in two's and three's. If anything the evening proved that it didn't pay to meddle with the spirit world, they know and see all from wherever they watch us.

I volunteered to tidy and lock up the café having watched a very happy Danielle and Martyn walk up the road arm in arm. They certainly had a lot to discuss as did I when I got back home. Before switching off the lights I looked up at the beam where I found myself saying thank you to my father. The next time that Antonio looked up, I would know why. I liked that he did.

Unrequited Love

It wasn't so much a book about love, but the usual collection of letters that had been bundled together with the main subject love. Reading through this accumulation of emotion one particular letter clearly questioned the man's intentions.

That morning strolling into work knowing that by the time I arrived Danielle would have everything organised at the café the walk through the park with the birds singing as company was very enjoyable. It was the brown package sticking out of the waste bin that attracted me across. Torn down one side I could see that the contents included a number of different sized and coloured envelopes.

Not normally given to foraging down waste bins I did consider leaving the package in situ, but there something about the contents that had me remove the package from the waste bin. Taking a closer look at the envelopes they had each been handwritten and addressed to the same person – Hannah Phillips of Ashbourne Grove, London. Pulling the damage edges together I tucked the package under my arm, nodded at a lady walking her dog and continued with my walk.

Standing behind the counter of the café with the contents spread across the countertop I was surprised to see that all, but one of the letters had been marked as *return to sender – addressee unknown*. I say all except the last envelope which had been left unfranked having not gone through the sorting process at the post office. There had been an address on the back of the envelope, but somebody, presumably the author of the letters had inked over the details making the address illegible.

'You getting fan mail now Spence,' Danielle inquired as she put two mugs under the hot water pipe.

'No, I found this package and envelopes on the way into work. It's an odd collection because the recipient sent them all back without opening a single letter.'

'Unrequited love,' Danielle replied as the hot water discharged from the pipe into the mugs.

I stared at her as she casually went about making us a coffee each. She had aptly addressed the matter in her usual feminine *life happens Spence* manner.

'When I was at school there was this boy in the year below who had a crush on me. It was sweet at the time until he started writing down what he felt. Dirty little sod got all suggestive and it had nothing to do with love. It shocked me to read the letters and I soon realised that I could not encourage his fantasies, so I went round to see his mother. Whenever I saw him in the playground or we passed in the corridor he ignored me. In a way that hurt more than his sending me the letters. I should have spoken to him about it rather than his mum.'

'Did you keep the letters?' I asked.

'Of course, they were the first that I had ever got from a boy. In a way and when I looked at them months later they were kinda sexy.'

She turned away adding a froth to the top of our coffee. That was Danielle all over. Meet a problem head on and deal with it. I felt sorry for the young boy who had plucked up courage to write to her. Maybe if he had sought the advice of somebody older and wiser he might not have had to stop writing. A rebuke from his mother could have had serious repercussions and put back his romantic endeavours by a good couple of years.

'Were they really that graphic?'

She blew out her cheeks. 'What he suggested we do behind the boating shed down at the park lake bordered on pornographic.'

I laughed letting my imagination envisage the struggle that would have ensued had Danielle gone along with the idea. The young Romeo didn't know what a lucky escape he'd had.

'Beyond school, have you ever seen him again?'

'Believe it or not I happened to be walking through Covent Garden and he was suited and booted. He looked like he was waiting to meet someone so I didn't go across and talk to him. I wish I had. He'd grown, got taller and he was alright, quite handsome. It was one of those moments I regret not doing.'

Putting down our mugs either side of the counter Danielle picked up an envelope where the seal had been slightly damaged. Peeling back the flap she carefully withdrew the letter from within and read the contents.

Dear Hannah

It has been almost six months now since we last met and although the pain of your rejection stings my heart like that of a thorn bush, I am willing to overlook the disappointment of your anger towards me and give our relationship another chance.

Without elaborating upon our last conversation, my proposal of marriage was genuine. Perhaps time has given you the opportunity to reflect and I am confident that we can consolidate the bond that we initially felt towards one another in the office.

Always yours

Henry

Danielle scornfully put the letter back in the envelope before putting it to one side. 'His sentiments hardly demonstrate his love for her, it's no wonder she rejected him. I'd have kicked him into touch long before he'd written half of this lot.'

I read the letter and agreed. There was no feeling in the author's intentions and the letter was more like the kind that you would expect from the power company about an unpaid account. There was one that we kept as a reminder when we had first opened the café:

Dear Mr Brand

Owing to an oversight in our digital accounting system, we have miscalculated your annual usage and although we realise that this additional cost might cause you some immediate financial hardship, we are willing to have the outstanding amount paid by monthly instalments to meet the terms and conditions of the contract between us.

We are as ever, endeavouring to fulfil our promise to our customers and provide the best possible service to which they have come to expect. Should you encounter any problems with the proposed arrangement, please do not hesitate to contact my office.

Yours sincerely

Augusta Johnson, Customer Services Manager.

Although the contents of the brown envelope belonged to both Henry and Hannah we wanted to know more. We would of course blame the post office if the question ever arose as to why some of the envelopes had been opened. The next letter had been penned with the same amount of passion as the last.

Dear Hannah

I wish I could stop the dreams at night, but without them I just know that I wouldn't sleep as I constantly think about you and of the places that we would have visited together had we stayed together. Adding up the cost of the four photographs taken in a station booth at Kings Cross and a new passport, I had pinned my hopes on us taking in some of the remaining wonders of this world, as depicted on the map in my study. Places where the stars would have looked down favourably upon us and bore witness to our love.

I have however kept the travel brochures, in anticipation that you do reconsider rekindling our relationship and the travel company have kindly said that they would hold onto the deposit for a twelve month period before the tour operators increase their price regime.

Just say the word my princess and the world could be all yours!

With love

Henry

When I passed the letter over to Danielle I saw the white of her knuckles tighten. 'He needs locking up and them throwing away the key. He's a danger to women.' I did wonder myself if they had been penned by a stalker.

We opened another looking for any other clues. Holding the envelope up to the light Danielle could just about make out the address of the sender through the scribbled out ink: one hundred and fifty seven Wandsworth Terrace, Notting Hill. She did an internet search on her mobile phone and the resident of that property belonged to a Henry Lafasche. She did another internet search and found that he was a professor of archaeology. It might account for his eccentricity.

'I get this mental picture of Doctor Doolittle, only not surrounded by animals, but dead mummies.' We read the letter together.

My Dear Hannah

Time is now of the essence and I need an answer as prices are rising and the rocks beneath my feet are crumbling, as is my heart. The world nor time cannot stand by and wait any longer. I am due to visit Egypt again soon and I beseech you one last time to reconsider my proposal.

I have spoken to the college and they are willing to part-fund an assistant programme, providing the right candidate applies. You are that person Hannah and together we could make new discoveries together, taking the expectation of modern archaeology to new heights.

I am packing my travel bag as I write this letter and I have added your toothbrush to my toiletry bag, the pink coloured.

With fond love

Henry

As Danielle laughed I shook my head left and right.

'No wonder Lara Croft threw his letters away, he's hardly the passionate type and I know where I would have stuck that pink toothbrush!'

We could have carried on reading, but I think we had both seen enough. Instead we put back the letters making sure that each was sealed. Notting Hill wasn't that far away and I could have delivered the parcel to the home of Henry Lafasche, but to have done so would have possibly meant me becoming entangled in the affair. I was about to seal the damaged side with a strip of masking tape when Danielle held up the one envelope that was unfranked.

'We owe it to ourselves to at least know how it ended.' She was right, we did.

'Okay the last one.'

My Dearest Hannah

You will have noticed that I have not recorded my address on the seal of the envelope as I intend leaving London today at midday, departing from Southampton to Cairo. My ship leaves around five this afternoon. I have to say that I am somewhat disappointed not to have had at least one reply from you in the past six months.

Harsh words, said in haste cut deep and although I have forgiven you many times for what you said on our last encounter, I had hoped that there would have been a moment when we could have pitched our forks alongside one another again and uncovered rare treasures.

Egypt beckons and with so much to offer, I am excited at the prospects and of the opportunities that lie ahead and just like Howard Carter, my destiny might mean that I never return. If you do reconsider, you'll know exactly where to find me.

Yours

Henry

And that as they say, was that. We both felt a bit flat. There were no answers to questions that had formed in our minds. Henry was seeking pastures new, ignoring the dangers of mosquitoes, the snakes, crocodiles, scorpions, spiders and scarab beetles. He had ditched his last hope of love on one final letter.

'I wonder why he never sent it,' Danielle pondered as she carefully folded the creases of the letter before resealing the envelope.

'It'll probably remain one of life's mysteries like the unfound mummies that Henry so desperately seeks. The fact that the package with the letters ended up in a waste bin in the park suggests his hopes had turned to anger.'

'Martyn and me could take the bus over to Notting Hill and deliver the package. That way we would see who opens the door.' We agreed it was a good idea. I sealed the parcel with the masking tape. Danielle could detach herself from emotion much more quickly than myself so it was better that she took the letters back. Later that evening she called me at home.

'Well, did Henry answer the door?'

'No, but his sister did.'

'Was she surprised to receive the package and the letters?'

'Very. The night before you found the parcel in the waste bin she had reported Henry as missing to the police. So far he's not been found. He never did arrive at Southampton, board a boat or arrive in Egypt.' She paused. 'And there's more to this mystery Spence. Hannah, his one true love died sometime last year according to the sister. She had contacted a bad case of pneumonia whilst excavating a lost tomb somewhere in England of all places. Apparently the shock of losing her sent poor Henry round the twist. His sister said that he had kept all her letters in his study bureau, but when the police looked they were missing. At least the police now know that he visited the park. The sister will contact them and have their teams search the area.'

Listening to Danielle my emotions were a jumble of mixed thoughts. I felt guilty having delved into Henry's private life, his love and now his disappearance. With his present state of mind he could so easily have been wandering about, alive and in need of help.

'Did his sister mention how old Henry was?'

'Sixty eight. He's been an archaeologist for the past forty eight years. Henry is a renowned scholar in his field and before the death of Hannah he had been invited on many digs around the world. He blames himself for Hannah's death. I left the sister my details Spence and she promised to get in touch if they hear any news, good or bad.'

It was just before midnight when Danielle sent me a text message.

'The police found Henry at a village called Upper Folsworth. It was the dig where he and Hannah had been working when she had contracted pneumonia. He was wandering the field when the police found him. He's at the local hospital and expected to be kept in for observation and a psychiatric evaluation. When released he will come back home to live with his sister.'

That night I didn't sleep very well and around four in the morning I went downstairs to the kitchen to make a coffee. Although I had slipped from the bed without disturbing Lola she padded down after me some ten minutes later.

'Are you still wondering why you were meant to find those letters?' she asked. I filled her mug with coffee, sugar and hot water.

'I know it's daft, but I feel connected, like I was meant to find the package and the letters, and that I was meant to take them back to the café.'

Lola laid her head on my shoulder as she yawned.

'Maybe that's the magic pull of the little red café and that it does attract all kinds of problems and people. At times I believe it is a sort of psychic centre where lost souls can find help. Maybe you're the link Spencer only you don't recognise it as such.' It was an interesting thought. Maybe my father had something to do with helping as well.

'At least Henry is somewhere safe now.'

'Without your intervention in the park the poor man might still be wandering the field and it is a cold night outside. You saved his life Spencer.'

Looking at it like that, it did make sense and Lola could always be relied upon to see through the fog like Danielle. They had that practical, logical approach. It was nice to think that the café was a hub for lost souls to meet up and it was somewhere where they felt safe.

A nephew of Alice Lafasche went with her to collect her brother Henry from the hospital in Yorkshire where the psychiatric doctors had assessed his mental trauma as being only a temporary state of shock albeit that it had lasted for over a year. In time his mind would settle as he laid the memory of his beloved Hannah to rest.

The psychiatrists recommended that he receive bereavement counselling to help deal with the loss of Hannah. With the sister's permission the café commissioned Thomas to paint a portrait picture of Hannah from a photograph which Henry could hang in his study and hopefully not feel as alone as he worked.

Before I locked up at the end of a busy day I ran my hand along the counter top where Danielle and I had read Henry's letter's to Hannah. A highly respected academic Henry might not have been so adept with his words or the pen, but his heart had been grieving and his pain could only be felt by Henry himself. I hoped that in time he would remember the good times that he and Hannah had shared together and that she had managed to read his letters albeit without him knowing.

Looking up at the wooden beam where Jake had caused pandemonium in the café, I smiled to myself, silently telling Hannah through my thoughts that one day she and Henry would be together again. Perhaps they could make that trip to Egypt and work on another dig.

The Bonfire Party

The phone rang early that Saturday morning not that it really mattered as Lola, Amelia and Antonio were already up, all excited that the children's home was having a bonfire supper to celebrate Guy Fawkes Night and that we had all been invited, that was the extended Brand family which included Mary and Thomas, Danielle and Martyn, Vera and my mother, and not forgetting of course Stephanie and Robert.

All week Vera and Martyn had been busy making sausage rolls, homemade beef burgers and cakes. Stephanie, being Stephanie had been using her journalistic influence around town with certain stores cajoling and promising reduced rate advertising in exchange for masks, costumes and gifts for the children of the home. The bonfire was an annual event that everyone looked forward to, only without knowing it this year was going to be extra special.

When the phone rang Lola got to the receiver before I did, sensing that it would be for her.

'*Mary,*' she whispered to me.

'Are you okay?' Lola asked, her expression becoming tight with concern that Mary had been was feeling understandably down.

It had now been just over two weeks since Mary had been rushed into hospital and sadly suffered a miscarriage, an event that had not only distressed understandably both Mary and Thomas very badly, but each and every one of us closely associated with our lovely friends. Lola had told me that for some time now they had been trying for a child of their own, but Mary had been experiencing problems with her chromosomes.

Mary had been to see the consultant gynaecologist at the hospital clinic the day before and although Lola had talked with Mary that evening she had been expecting the call this morning.

I had been married to Lola long enough to know that if she turned and looked out of the window she was instinctively concealing her feelings from the children. There was something soothing about looking out at the garden.

'Is mummy crying?' asked Amelia as she passed a soft biscuit to her brother.

'No darling, she sniffed some flowers this morning and the pollen has got up her nose. It's making mummy's eyes water a lot this morning.' Lola remained looking out at the garden. She could have gone to another room, but she wanted to be within the hub of her family.

'I am here all day until we dress and get ready for this evening, why don't you come over and have a coffee this morning. Get Lizzie to cover in the shop. The orders are all complete and she is more than capable of coping on her own.'

Lola replaced smiled into the receiver and quietly said goodbye.

'Is she coming?' I asked.

'She will be here between nine and half past. Mary just wants to make sure that Lizzie doesn't need anything else before she leaves the shop.'

The birth of Antonio had changed many things, especially time or the lack of it. Our son was a demanding little boy who could not be left alone for a second as his inquisitive mind wanted to go exploring. He was so much like Alfie. The flower shop was doing well, but Lola felt guilty about leaving Mary to do so much more and she blamed herself partly for adding more stress on Mary resulting in the miscarriage. We had talked about this, but I would be the first to tell you that I am no expert.

Six months back we both acknowledged the valuable contribution that Mary had made in making *Florrie's Flowers* so successful. As a co-partner now with Lola the pair worked very well together and they shared one another's secrets. Recognising that Lola and Mary would want to share the same over coffee alone I opted for my alternate plan.

'Shall we go to the shops this morning kids,' I asked. They both looked up from their cereal bowls and then at one another surprised that it was me who had offered. 'I could give Auntie Danielle a call and see if she will consent to giving me the morning off?'

Amelia watched Antonio look at me before looking back at her. I am sure that the pair of them had mastered mental telepathy. 'Yes please daddy, although Antonio doesn't like the old furniture shops, he only the toy shops.'

Lola grinned as she bent over and kissed Amelia's forehead, then Antonio's. 'You walked right into that one.'

Lifting Antonio from his chair she took him through to the front room to put on his trainers. Amelia was quick to gather together their coats, hats and scarves. 'I don't know what I would do without you,' she said helping Amelia slip on her coat.

'You wait until the next one arrives.' I answered. It was a happy household and the children had settled in without any problems. With Amelia keeping Antonio amused I took the opportunity to enquire about Mary.

'Are you okay?'

'No, not particularly. Mary had the tests back from the clinic. They show a hormonal imbalance that will make having children difficult.' She touched my cheek tenderly. 'Not impossible, but it won't be easy. The consultant at the hospital wants to do some more tests before they can say anything conclusively.'

'Perhaps tonight will help and have forget their troubles for at least an evening.'

'Maybe, although Mary wasn't sure that they were up to going.'

'The children will miss them both.'

Amelia brought Antonio into the kitchen holding his hand. I could tell from the look on their faces that they had been discussing the coming trip to the shops. 'My brother told me a little secret in the front room daddy and that we would especially like a fire-engine, one with flashing lights, a siren, big ladder. The one that he saw the other day when he was out with mummy. The one with the men and ladies that sit in the back.' It made Lola giggle.

'Would he,' I replied, 'and he would know about such a fire-engine?'

Amelia nodded confidently. 'Oh yes, Antonio told me which one he likes.'

'And he told you this, when you were both in the front room?'

Crossing her arms just like her mother when she was talking to me sometimes, Amelia looked at Antonio then back at us both smiling.

'Of course, we talk a lot.' Lola picked up my wallet on the kitchen worktop and handed it to me.'

'Never question the magic that exists between children. They possess something that we lost long ago.' I looked at Antonio who had the tip of his tongue between his lips. Lola flipped the end and made him laugh. 'Put it away darling only it's a little cold outside and it might drop off.'

Antonio continued to stare at me pulling the tip of his tongue back. He looked like a lizard who had sniffed the air and detected its prey. Lola put Antonio in the buggy and we left heading for the toyshop. I had yet to find out what Amelia had seen in the shop window.

It was almost lunchtime by the time that we retuned armed with two big bags and Mary had already been and gone back to the flower shop to be with Lizzie. Antonio was busy knelt on the floor with Lola showing her his new fire-engine and Amelia was happy to sit on the settee with a new story book and doll. I was a happy man because my family were happy, but I was in need of a drink. Several minutes later I was joined by Lola.

'They're both thrilled with their visit to the toy shop.'

'We would have been home sooner, but Amelia couldn't make up her mind whether it was a reading book or a new doll. In the end I got both. I'm not sure how he knows, but as soon as we were in the shop Antonio pointed at the red fire-engine.'

Lola smiled. 'Trust me, he knows and Amelia is fast learning the art of shopping. A little hesitation is all part of the shopping experience for a woman. There is never an instant decision, but when she buys, it is the right one.' I think what Lola was trying to tell me was that there would be other occasions to come with Amelia and Antonio.

'How was Mary?'

'As expected, putting on a brave face. We talked, she cried, I cried and then we prayed for a miracle to happen. Thomas believes that if it's meant to happen it will. He told Mary that there were alternatives.'

'You mean adopt?'

'Yes. They've discussed the subject at length. You know that they adore Amelia and Antonio. Mary say's that they're financially sound and Thomas is doing well at the Rainbow Gallery. If they can't have children naturally they would like to share their home with little ones.'

'From Saxon House.'

'Yes... look at the love and precious moments that Amelia has brought to this family.'

That evening we made our way to the children's home where the bonfire had been built up high in the grounds around the back garden with a safety fence erected to keep everyone safe. Thanks to the efforts of Stephanie Steele there was also a marquee supplied free from a local camping shop. As the technicians set up the fireworks there was a buzz going around that the evening was going to be extra special. With Antonio holding onto her hand Amelia went in search of her friends.

'She's a different girl, extremely happy,' said a familiar voice. In the glow of the flames as they leapt skyward we turned to see Carolyn Johnson standing alongside. An exchange of hugs and greetings we were happy to see her. Carolyn noticed the bump under the long coat worn by

Lola. 'And by the looks of things, Amelia and Antonio will be celebrating a new brother or sister soon.'

'Antonio follows her everywhere. And they have secret conversations.' I replied.

'That's a must Spencer. Many of the children here live in a secret world, a safe world where the creatures are magical and the fairies dance in the garden at night. We actively encourage them to believe in such things.'

I liked coming to Saxon House and seeing Carolyn, but it would always tug heavily on my heart strings to see all the other children running about, so happy, often smiling and laughing. I hoped the magic lasted forever in their world.

It was as we were talking to Carolyn that I noticed that Mary had focused her attention on a little boy who wasn't running about but standing near to the safety rope where he was mesmerised by the flames rising skyward. Mary went alongside and knelt down to watch as well. The boy turned and smiled. 'Hello, my name is Mary, do you like the bonfire?' she asked.

The little boy with long ringlets of blonde hair smiled and pointed to the darkened sky.

'I like it when the fire explodes and the sparks reach the stars!' he replied.

'What's your name?' asked Mary.

'Guy,' the boy replied. It was just Guy with no surname.

Mary retuned his smile. Little Guy was like an angel and the amber glow from the fire made his eyes light up.

'How long have you been at the home?' Mary asked.

The boy momentarily turned away from the bonfire long enough to see that she was pretty. 'A long time.' His remark didn't go unnoticed by Carolyn.

'That's Guy Wither's. He is a strong will little boy and he knows his own mind. He can be quite headstrong at times, but he is fiercely protective of his younger sister.'

'He has a sister?' asked Lola.

'Yes, Guy's almost six and Skye has not long turned three. They came to Saxon House about three months ago. The father died whilst working abroad and the shock sent their mother into a deep recess of depression. She committed suicide four months back. At first they wouldn't talk to anybody except with each other. Gradually it was the other children who got them to open up. Skye relies upon her brother for almost everything.'

'We love coming here and seeing you Carolyn,' said Lola, 'but why is that every time we do, you manage to break our hearts in two.' I could see that Lola had to wipe the tears from her eyes.

Carolyn John pursed her lips together as she gently held Lola's hand. 'My heart lives permanently in two pieces, but I try to shelve my emotions otherwise I would go under like Guy and Skye's poor mother. I guess in the end the poor woman just couldn't cope.'

Mary stayed a long time with Guy and was surprised when a little girl with identical hair arrived promptly holding onto her brother's hand. I saw Mary smile at the little girl and she made sure that the front of her coat was properly buttoned up. Moments later they were joined by Thomas.

'I think they've acquired some new friends,' said Carolyn. We watched as the four of them talked, even little Skye was talking which surprised Carolyn.

'That is so unusual as Skye is normally wary of strangers.'

'Mary isn't a stranger,' replied Lola, 'she is an angel sent down from heaven.'

We watched the four of them interact with one another and Lola told Carolyn about Mary's recent upset.

'I am pleased that she came,' said Carolyn, 'the decision was a brave one, but perhaps talking with Guy and Skye might show that there is always hope.'

'Are they up for adoption?' Lola asked.

Carolyn appeared surprised. 'You would take on another two?'

The reply made Lola chuckle. 'I wasn't thinking of me!' Carolyn nodded understanding.

'Mary and Thomas have been talking over adopting.'

'They wouldn't be daunted by two children.'

Lola and I watched Mary and Thomas with Guy and little Skye. Outlined by the glow from the burning bonfire, they looked just right.

'Nothing daunts Mary or Thomas,' I replied, 'they are by far the gentlest couple that we have ever known. They would make ideal parents.'

'Maybe I should spend some time with the four of them.' Carolyn hugged Lola and touched my forearm. 'If they're anything like you both, then we're halfway there.'

We went to find Amelia and Antonio knowing that they were safe. We found them huddled together with a group of Amelia's friends. Pulling on Lola's arm Amelia whispered in her ear. 'Some of the children who were here have new mummies and daddies now.'

Lola whispered back. 'Let's hope that one day all the children here find new mummies and daddies.'

'Does that mean that there'd be no more bonfire party's?'

Lola gave a shake of her head. 'No darling. I am sure that Carolyn will always invite us every November fifth.'

I turned to see Carolyn with Mary and Thomas surprised to see that Skye had moved around and was standing very close to Mary. I found myself looking up at the night sky where the burning embers from the fire were dancing high against the backdrop of the stars and dark blue. In my mind I was saying a prayer.

When the technicians setting up the fireworks launched the first rocket the children whooped with delight. It climbed high before exploding into a kaleidoscope of colour before fizzing out and disappearing, quickly replaced by and another, then another. I met with Thomas in the marquee where he was getting food for himself, Mary and the two children.

'They look nice kids.'

'They're amazing,' replied Thomas. He looked at me and I could almost read his thoughts.

'If it's right Thomas, it feels right!' I clamped the palm of my right hand over my chest. 'It felt like that when I first catch sight of Amelia and now the love has grown stronger every day since.'

'It's going to be a wrench tearing Mary away from here tonight.'

I could only nod and agree. 'You can come back you know. I'm sure that Carolyn would let you.'

We were joined in the tent by Danielle. I asked where Martyn was.

'Outside watching the fireworks. He's like a big kid.'

With Antonio on my shoulder and Amelia yawning we headed back to the car after the display. As expected Mary struggled with her emotions and Lola helped as they said goodnight to Guy and little Skye. Coming back to our house for coffee Lola told them about the formalities ahead and seemingly endless catalogue of forms and interviews. The one positive note was that they had Carolyn Johnson unequivocally on their side, and as a friend.

Later as we readied ourselves for bed, I pulled the duvet over Lola, but I wasn't at all sleepy with too many thoughts racing around inside my head.

'I know how they feel. Will they cope with the wait?' I asked.

'Yes,' Lola replied confident that they would. 'Mary told me that she can't face many more tests at the hospital.'

'And financially. I know Thomas is doing well. We could help.'

Lola snuggled down beside me.

'I already told Mary you would and that's why I love you Spencer Brand.' And I loved Lola for having the confidence to know that I would. 'Did the toys cost you a lot?'

'An arm and a leg, but what the hell. They are only children once.'

We went to sleep that night both thinking about Mary and Thomas, a young blonde boy and his sister. Going to Saxon House always left us with a sleepless night.

A Resurrection at the Wake

Now we have held some rather unusual bookings at the café over the years and some that perhaps were considered maybe peculiar. Some events held a memorable significance like the children's party where I handed over Angus to Amelia, but one day in particular stands out more than the others, not because it was any more interesting or important, because is concerned the wake of the recently departed Lawrence Morris from Albert Street.

Ordinarily wakes in memory of our dearly departed are held either at home, in a privately rented restaurant or in the nearest public house, but quite by coincidence in the case of poor Lawrence none were available and two were stuck in the middle of a decorating project so with some apprehension I took the booking providing that it was held after three in the afternoon and when trade went generally slack.

'That'll bring a black cloud overhead,' Vera replied as she washed down the preparation bench.

'I know, but Gladys Morris was in a tight spot and as Larry had been a regular I felt it was our duty to oblige and help out.'

Adding more cleansing agent to the sink, she swished the wet cloth back and forth over the stainless steel top. 'As long as word don't get around that we've added wakes to our list of services.' She stopped swishing. 'We've all worked hard to build up the reputation of this café and I wouldn't want to see it damaged in just one afternoon by several cars arriving outside loaded with mourners with long faces and attired in black suits, black hats and dresses to match. The next thing you know you'll be taking a booking for the local witch doctor's convention.'

'Don't be ridiculous, it's Larry's send off and anyway it'll be nothing outrageous other than a few plates of sandwiches, tea and coffee with cake or biscuits.'

It was unusual for Vera to be so reluctant about a booking. Ordinarily she saw the opportunity to make some extra cash. She had gone back to cleaning the sink and I sensed that it would be futile to push her as to why she was so unenthusiastic. Danielle also had mentioned earlier that she thought Vera was quiet and pensive.

'I think my mum went to school with Lawrence Morris.'

With a final wash down of warm water the bench was once again meticulously clean. 'Me and your mum. We went on a date as well although only the once. I saw the signs back then and they weren't in no stars.'

'You mean it was dark or overcast that night?'

Vera turned to face me squeezing the excess water from the wet cloth as though wringing my neck.

'Don't be impertinent, it doesn't become you Spencer Brand. The signs that I refer too were about Lawrence. He was flash, thought himself a regular spiv, a teenage black marketeer who could lay his hands on virtually anything and as long as somebody had the ready cash he would do business with you. How, where it came from or went was of no interest to me. His lifestyle left me as cold as a dead fish down at Billingsgate Market.'

'So where was your one night of passion?'

Vera sniffed. 'The cinema over Holloway. Like a bloody octopus he was. I didn't know a young man could have so many hands all at once. Walking out halfway through the film I told Lawrence Morris that I didn't want to see him ever again.'

Her memory of Larry didn't match the quiet man that had come to our café two, perhaps three times a week for a peaceful afternoon read of the paper, a cup of fruit tea and slice of fruit cake.

'Mum didn't go out with him then?'

'Not bloody likely. After my encounter with squiddly diddly I warned her about his intentions. Some of the other girls in our year group did go out with him and rumour was that one had to leave school because she got herself pregnant, although nobody would outright say it was Lawrence's lovechild.'

Knowing Larry in the prime of his life he didn't seem like the kind of man to have left a lady, young or old in the lurch and as far as I had known, he had always worshipped the ground on which Gladys walked.

We left the conversation about Lawrence there and two weeks later the afternoon had arrived. First to arrive was the highly polished black limousine that had conveyed Gladys and her two sisters there and back to the cemetery. Following behind was a small convoy of vehicles, including an ice-cream van.

Vera had prepared a spread of cold meats, sandwiches and cakes with tea and coffee, which Danielle and Martyn had volunteered to serve. Wearing a white shirt and black tie, Martyn looked quite smart from his kitchen scrubs.

'He likes it out front sometimes Spence,' Danielle whispered as Martyn happily went between the arriving guests offering refreshments.

'I see Vera made Larry's favourite fruit cake.' I whispered back. The night in the cinema could not have been that bad. I hoped that Martyn didn't get too attached to being out front of house only he was a very valuable asset in the kitchen and Vera for one wouldn't want to lose his help.

Wearing a white shirt and tie especially picked by Lola for the occasion I blended in quite nicely recognising some of Larry's family. Danielle too looked very elegant despite her bump, but Vera had advised on a long smock type black dress and matching shoes. She looked every inch corporate management and had come a long way in the few years that we had worked together.

I was talking with Gladys Morris and she was saying what a beautiful spread Vera had laid on for the mourners when we both noticed a woman about Gladys age arrived accompanied by two younger women.

'They must have got stuck in traffic,' I said. Al three were wearing black.

'I have no idea who they could be, they're not family?' said Gladys as she made eye contact with the older woman. Seconds later we found out when Vera appeared from the kitchen.

'Oh my goodness,' exclaimed Vera as she quickly stepped forward with her right hand raised as though warding off an evil spirit. 'Blanche this is hardly the right time or the place, not now!' The conversations around instantly ceased.

'Hello Vera, long time no see. You know that I have every right to be here.' The latest arrival looked around at the faces staring at her. 'And when exactly is a good time, certainly not now that Lawrence has gone.'

Although I had no idea who the trio were I sensed an underlying tension building in the atmosphere as Danielle went and stood beside Vera to show her support. They were joined by Gladys.

'What's going on,' she demanded, 'this is a private affair in memory of my late husband.'

Very quietly Vera suggested that Gladys sit down. Danielle sensing that something startling was about to come forth patted Gladys shoulder as the woman waited. Vera continued.

'This woman is Blanche Tilbury and her daughters. Lawrence had a double life Gladys. Blanche is his other wife.'

You could have heard a pin drop in the silence that followed. I saw the colour drain from Gladys face. 'And you were his girls,' she said pointing at the two young women?' they each nodded back. In less than a second I was around from behind the counter and supporting

Gladys as she slumped on the chair. Danielle immediately went for the smelling salts from the first aid box.

Although they wanted to stay and hear the gossip Vera suggested that the other mourners take some sandwiches and cake and leave. Remorsefully they took their paper bags of goodies and left. Sitting one side of the table with Vera sat beside her Gladys glared at the three women opposite. I took across a tray of coffee's and a small brandy for Gladys.

'We would have made the funeral if it hadn't been for the bus breaking down.'

Gladys didn't reply, instead she looked at Vera. 'You knew about Lawrence having another family. How long have you known?'

'At first they were rumours Gladys, then I saw Blanche at the market where she introduced her girls to me. There could be no denying that they weren't Larry's girls. They had his eyes, nose and mouth, even his colour hair. Blanche and me, we went to school together.'

I looked at Blanche wondering, could she be the girl who had to leave school because she was pregnant. I'm no good at gauging ages, but the eldest of the two women sat either side of Blanche would be about the right age.

Gladys took in a deep breathe. 'My Larry, a bigamist... I can't believe it.'

'Me neither,' said Blanche. She opened her black handbag and produced a photograph. I didn't need to see it to know what the image represented. 'I'm sorry Gladys, but as I told Vera, when was the right time. Maybe you and I need to talk.'

I thought Gladys might explode, but a member of Robert Styles congregation she breathed in deep again and dished out the tray of coffees to Blanche and her two daughters. 'I guess one way or another we have a common interest, albeit the bugger has taken the easy way out.' It was the first time that I had ever heard Gladys swear.

I had not noticed the man standing at the back of the room, although I had seen him talking with Martyn. I found out later that he had been in the bathroom when the revelation was announced. Douglas Morris stepped up and stood alongside where his mother sat. He looked at the two younger women shaking his head.

'We do have similar redeeming features.' He used the tips of his fingers to point them out. 'The eyes, nose and mouth. Funny how he had that upturned little kink at the end of his nose.'

I felt the atmosphere become less icy as the two women grinned back.

'I'm Sandra, 'said the older woman, 'and this is Louise, my younger sister.'

Louise took up the reins to explain. 'We wouldn't have known about today, had we not seen the obituary that you had put in the paper. You see our train was delayed outside of Waterloo and then the bus broke down.'

Gladys whose heart had not stopped beating fast felt her son's hand rest on her shoulder. She covered it with her own.

'You missed a nice ceremony. Lawrence was given a good send off.'

'How far have you come?' asked Doug as we knew him.

'We live in a small village outside of Bournemouth called Upton-leigh-Burton.'

Gladys looked at Doug. 'That's where Arnold Morris, your dad's cousin lives. He used to have a large flat in Bournemouth overlooking the sea. He would have come today, but he's recovering from a bad bout of influenza.'

'We know, it was Arnie who told us where to find the café.'

'You must be starving,' said Gladys, much to everyone's surprise. She turned to look at Martyn who brought over a tray of sandwiches.

'Thank you,' replied Blanche, 'we missed lunch too.' Doug took a seat next to Louise and his mother.

'Please help yourself, we should have offered you something when you arrived.'

'So where do we go from here?' asked Blanche as she took a small bite from the corner of her quarter cheese sandwich.

'I don't know, this is quite a shock. My insides are still doing a tango on my late husband's grave. I'm trying to hold it together for the sake of the children.' I saw Doug lower his head as he breathed out silently.

'We're hardly children mum. And my half-sisters are grown women. As adults we can sort this situation peacefully.' I liked Doug's approach and Vera was right, this would be our last wake.

When the bell over the door chimed I almost burst into a fit of laughter as I saw Robert Styles arrive.

'I am so sorry that I am late, I did expect there to be more here!'

'There's been a revelation from the other side vicar,' said Gladys. She gestured with her hand at Blanche, Sandra and Louise. 'And these ladies are Lawrence's other family. Why Robert looked at me I didn't know, but I responded with a nod as much to say that it was true.

'Oh...' was all Robert said and for the time ever he appeared lost for words.

'Have the grave diggers filled in the grave only I would like to have had a final word with my, our husband.'

'Me too,' said Blanche in agreement.

'I am afraid that they've not long finished. I stayed behind to make sure that Lawrence's journey to heaven was as it should be.'

'I hope St Peter has the day off,' Gladys muttered. Her remark made Blanche smile.

'I could go if you wish,' Robert offered, 'or I could stay and bring about a union of souls in this situation.' Gladys removed her handbag from the chair next to her where Vera had sat.

Standing beside me Vera whispered. 'He's going to have his work cut out on this occasion.'

'I will begin with the truth,' said Robert, as Danielle arrived with another coffee. 'I saw Lawrence at the church only days before he passed away. He came to confess his sins and ask for forgiveness. I think he knew that his time was coming. We spoke that afternoon nearly all afternoon about life, family life and of actions that could not be undone. We prayed and I believe Lawrence left the church with a clearer conscience than when he had arrived.'

'Did he tell you about his other family in Bournemouth?' asked Gladys.

'It was part of our discussion that afternoon... yes. Lawrence confessed to being a rogue for most of his life. He told me about Blanche, Sandra and Louise.'

'Did he tell you about the other rogue in the family, Arnold Morris?'

Robert grinned. 'Yes, he mentioned Arnold. Robert looked at Blanche. 'You once owned a furniture shop with antiques.'

'Yes, that's right vicar.'

'And that was how you met?'

Blanche shook her head. 'No, we went to school together. I had to leave when I found that I was pregnant with Sandra. Lawrence set me up in a flat near to his cousin in Bournemouth. He came to live with for a while, but Lawrence had a restless spirit and yearned for the bright lights of London again. He would come down whenever he could. Louise was born two years after Sandra.'

'That's about the time that Lawrence asked me to marry him.' Everybody looked at Gladys. So it's me who is the bigamist.' I reached for the smelling salts, but Doug was quick with an extra spoonful of sugar in her tea.

'Not necessarily,' said Robert. 'Lawrence and Blanche were never married.' Gladys sighed.

'I still hope that he turns in his grave and faces down with the devil looking up. I always used to say that he sat on his shoulder on more than one occasion. Two by the looks of it.'

'How did you meet dad?' asked Sandra.

'I was the usherette at the local cinema in Holloway Road.' I saw Vera shake her head with contempt. Lawrence Morris had been a lucky escape.

Nodding Gladys remembered back. 'He had a way with words, could roll them off his tongue. Like Blanche, I soon fell under his spell and one thing led to another and he moved in with me. We rented a small top floor flat in a pokey house north of the city, but we were happy. After a year I found myself pregnant with Douglas.'

Sandra pushed her plate to one side, picking up her cup of coffee. 'I always used to wonder how he would come and go so often, before the visits stopped completely. How did he manage to flit between London and Bournemouth without either of you knowing that the other existed?'

Gladys took up the story. 'Lawrence joined the army reserves. Every so often they would go away for weekends, overnight manoeuvres he would tell me that lasted a week. He'd tell me that an attack on the mainland was imminent and the government had ordered his unit to a secret location. I never questioned his loyalty to his country as he was always so happy when he came back.'

Blanche nodded as she also remembered. 'He told me that he worked for the government in the secret service division. His missions were always overseas.'

'Dad a spy,' said Douglas, 'why he didn't know how to tell the time on the twenty four hour clock let alone work through an encryption.'

214

'That had me puzzled too,' said Gladys, 'but he had a certain way of telling things that always seemed plausible.'

Robert intervened smiling at the faces sat around the table, three that looked very similar.

'Lawrence played the fool, but in reality his life wasn't a complete lie. He did serve his country and he was in the army reserves, but his skills and quick thinking brain was spotted by officers who put him into intelligence. There were times when he did put his life on the line for his country.'

'My dad was a spy,' said a surprised Louise, 'wow!'

Gladys and Blanche stared at one another across the table before their expressions creased and they began laughing.

'He certainly knew how to keep us fooled,' admitted Blanche. I recalled the times that Larry had sat by himself sipping his fruit tea and slowly eating his way through his cake while doing the crossword in the newspaper. Was he, I wondered a spy to the end and decoding a message rather than solve the crossword clues. When the laughter died away there were a few sighs as each accepted the situation for what is was.

'So where do we go from here?' asked Blanche.

It was Robert who once again saved the moment.

'Lawrence came to see me because living a lie for so many years he didn't know how to heal the pain that would come once he was no longer around and he knew that eventually the truth would be revealed. He was a tormented soul who had lived his life by the skin of his teeth in so many ways, but his heart I felt was genuine and in the right place. He loved you all. You Gladys and Douglas, and you Blanche with Sandra and Louise. Somehow he managed to divide his love and provide for you all.'

Robert focused on Douglas, Sandra and Louise. 'You three especially have a lot to talk about and your father hoped that in time you would find that special bond that exists in siblings. Whatever your father, he was brave and a Christian.' Opening the pages of his bible Robert removed an envelope. On the front was written their five names. He handed the envelope to Douglas. 'As the man of the family, perhaps you should read it, but when you five are alone. I would suspect that there are some very personal messages contained within.'

'Thank you vicar.' Robert put the envelope in his jacket pocket patting the exterior of the cloth to denote that it was safe. He looked at Blanche and his mother 'I think the ideal thing is for us to all go home where we can read the contents of the letter.' There were agreeable nods all round. Thanking us for the use of the café and for the buffet spread they left. Halfway up the road I saw Blanche put her arm through Gladys. Breathing a sigh of relief I sat down with Robert.

'You pick your moments to arrive, but boy Robert do you get it right!'

'Had I arrived earlier it might not have gone so well. It's not often that I get to play the messenger, but whatever my feelings about the situation I had promised Lawrence that I would come and hopefully keep the peace.'

'Do you know what's written in the letter?'

'No, but having heard his confession I should think that Lawrence had quite a bit to explain. Perhaps his words will help settle any doubt that they as a family may have. Whatever their feelings he did know them all and he has through death brought them together.'

I raised my hands. 'I know and god works in mysterious ways.'

Robert laughed. 'Indeed and remember that he is all seeing Spencer and he walks besides us all every day.' I was beginning to believe it too. 'Do you know,' Robert complimented,' this fruit cake that Vera made is exceptionally good.'

I nodded agreeing. 'I guess in a way Larry resurrected himself to make sure that no stone was left unturned. I suppose we have to admire him for that.'

'I feel that he went to heaven a much happier man.'

I thanked Robert and watched him leave going next door to talk with Thomas. I found Vera, Danielle and Martyn clearing up in the kitchen.

'That was a turn up for the book,' I said as I grabbed a spare tea towel.

'It was a fortuitous escape I would say,' replied Vera. 'I could have been sitting down reading the contents of that envelope as well.'

That Red Bicycle Again

Now the last time that we had talked about a certain red bike the owner, a very generous man named Ambati Sharma Kumar had agreed that the bicycle should remain with the café. Skilfully sign written along the length of the frame by Thomas it was there for anybody who had a need to use it. Martyn had taken it upon himself to regularly check over the bike making sure that the tyres were sufficiently inflated, the brakes worked and moving parts were oiled.

The familiar sight of the bike parked against the wall outside between several large potted plants and our red painted window frame had in many ways become a symbol of local interest. All that we asked was that anybody who had use of the bicycle would tell us why and where it had been. We had a box tucked under the counter that contained various scraps of paper, an odd assorted history and every so often I would revisit the box remembering the people who had been involved in certain journeys.

An icon of our café we had had the bike professionally resprayed in the spring to stop it from rusting and keep up the bright, shiny red appearance. Danielle had suggested adding a shopping basket for any lady users which Martyn fitted. Recent notes that had been left included:

Hello the Café

My need of your little bike was to say the least, most urgent. You see I was on my way to a rather important evening appointment when I realised that in my haste I had forgotten my wallet and bus pass. Yes, I could have walked across town to see the person waiting at the other end, but as this was my first time with a clairvoyant, I didn't want to disappoint her or keep the spirits that might have been waiting hanging around.

Madame Arabella as she likes to be known to her customers was recommended to me by a friend who told me that her power of communication with the other side were legendary. That being the case I felt compelled to not be late for the appointment and without the use of your bike I would not have arrived in time.

'That's a nice bicycle,' said Madame Arabella, upon my arrival, 'please put it down the side path behind the gate where it will be safe.' She then took me through to a conservatory at the rear of the house where the birds were singing and the early evening sun was settling across the tops of the chimney tops opposite. 'I am so pleased that you have arrived on time, only I have an impatient spirit waiting to come through. I was advised that you were on your way and that the embankment this evening was especially busy.'

How did she know I had cycled along the embankment? I was already impressed. Amazed. We sat ourselves down at a small round table upon which were stacked a deck of tarot cards, two full glasses of water and a candle alongside a box of matches. Lighting the candle Madame Arabella had to tell the spirit to be patient.

'She is very insistent that I begin straight away.'

She momentarily closed her eyes, breathed in deep and outstretched her hands. 'Please take hold of mine,' she asked, 'it will help make the link.'

I did as she asked.

'The impatient spirit is your grandmother.' Yes that was grandmother and her patience levels had always been low. 'She is standing beside you!' My head turned so fast to look Madame Arabella heard the crack in my neck. She opened one eye, smiled then closed it again.

'Your grandmother tells me that she has been waiting a long time to talk to you and you should have come sooner because there's something important that you need to know.'

Now it is at moments like this when your brain goes suddenly in reverse and you try to think of all the things that you might have done or indeed done wrong, not done right because they rarely get a mention. Try as hard as I could, I couldn't think of anything that was particularly bad.

'She tells me that you have been searching for something of late, something that you believe links you with the past.' It jogged a memory and yes I had. I had been searching the internet for any information about a woman with whom I had worked with. We had worked in the same office and yet when I had left for another chapter in my life we had lost touch. The years had passed, but I felt that my destiny had been with this woman. I was about to say her name when Madame Arabella opened both eyes to tell me that a name was not important. 'This person she also thinks about you.'

I felt the relief wash through me although I was still at a loss as to how to find her as she no longer worked at the hospital where we had both worked.

'Does she still work at the same place?' I asked.

Madame Arabella opened her eyes and smiled.

'Your grandmother tells me that you should think harder and about what you did together when you were at work, only therein lies the answer.'

That was the riddle that I had been trying to solve for some time. 'And that's it, there's nothing else?'

Madame Arabella shook her head. 'No, nothing else. She reiterated that you need to look again and the answer will present itself. She has to go now, but she sends her love.'

And that was it, grandma was gone. I looked around, but naturally saw nothing.

'Don't dwell on it right now,' Madame Arabella advised turning over my right hand. 'Let us see what the palm lines tell us instead.

Tracing the lines with the tip of her index finger she kept on nodding giving the odd ooh and aah.

'You have a good, healthy long life line.'

'That's reassuring.'

'And your headline is strong as well…' she checked once again, 'although I see a little confusion emerging, mostly around your thoughts.'

I had never studied my hand before and especially not my palm lines, they were kinda interesting now that she mentioned it. It was a patchwork of mystery.

'You tend to fall in and out of love, and yet you search for just one woman.' She traced my heart line. 'Listen to what your grandmother told you. The answer will reveal itself soon.' Somehow I knew that she was right.

Madame Arabella read my thoughts as she picked up the cards. 'Believe in yourself first and then let down your guard. Living is as easy as the wind that blows through the branches of a tree.'

She shuffled the cards spreading them across the table top. I was asked to pick ten cards. With deftness of hand she arranged them into a specific pattern. 'Your past, present and future. With the card facing up or down the significance changes. Most were up, it looked favourable.

Turning over the cards one by one Madame Arabella predicted what the cards told her. My living on a roller coaster ride, going between jobs without any thought about settling in a career. My trouble was I could never get the tall, leggy blonde out of my mind. Turning over the last card she gave me the girl's name.

She had one last piece of advice before I paid for the session. 'Clouds come and go all the time, but every so often you see one that you think you saw before. Let the sunshine show you the way.' In the hallway the grandfather clock chimed away announcing that the hour was almost up. 'That's the thing with time, it never lets you know when the right moment has arrived. Take the red bicycle home and do the rest of the journey on foot.'

Looking back I was no further forward only the name I already knew, a location would have been more useful. I was really grateful for the loan of the bike. I will keep you posted should any of tonight's predictions come true.

Gratefully yours

Alfred

That was one of our longest explanations ever and most definitely missing a definitive ending. Danielle and I discussed the possibilities that were open to Alfred coming to the conclusion that he had to start at the beginning of his journey to find his true love and where best, but return to his previous place of work only there had to be someone still working there who knew them both.

'I've a feeling that she's also been looking for him,' said Danielle. I think she was right and that soon the clouds would part and let the sun shine through. Maybe one day Alfred would call in and let us know, bringing with him the mystery lady.

I unfolded the next explanation for using the red bicycle.

Hi and many thanks!

I had use of your red bike tonight to assist with an emergency as the wife burnt the evening dinner. To cool down the contents along with the dish it was put outside where the dog scoffed the lot and an hour later was violently ill.

Thank goodness for the addition of the basket on the front of the bike as I had to take the dog to the vet and Fetchum, as he is affectionately known was too heavy to carry.

After the Vets examination it turned out to be a bad case of canine indigestion, together with the ping pong ball that the kid's had left out in the garden earlier. It made my wife feel better too knowing that it had not been her cooking.

Cheers

Ray

That made me laugh as I continued to flick through some of the others, short and to the point, but each time the bike had been used it had saved somebody time and helped resolve a problem. I was reading with interest the next about a lady who had used the red bicycle to visit a friend, telling us that cycling through the streets of London was safer than walking alone when the bell over the door chimed. Standing before me was a young couple holding hands.

'Good morning, are you the owner of the café?' the man asked.

I wiped my hands dry where I had been cleaning the Fracino Contempo. 'Yes, that's me. I'm Spencer. How can I help?'

Together they smiled.

'You already have,' replied the young lady, although I doubt you knew it.'

Instinctively there was something about the man that I thought I knew. I took a wild stab that I was right.

'Don't tell, you must be Alfred.'

He reached across the counter and shook my hand. 'And this is Rebecca,'

'Ah the future,' I said.

'Most definitely,' he replied. The woman raised her left hand to show me a new engagement ring.

'Would you both like a coffee?'

'We would and we hear that the cake here is exceptionally good.'

There was nobody else in the café so they asked me to join them

'The bike, it is well maintained and had a recent paint job, I could tell,' said Alfred as he settled himself down beside Rebecca. 'Has it been many places?

'As far as the Czech Republic.'

Rebecca looked surprised. 'And it came back?

'It always does. There's something about the bicycle that is special.'

Danielle obliged by cutting two generous slices of Vera's homemade ginger and orange with a splash of rum. She brought them over where I introduced Alfred and Rebecca.

'The mystery lady... wow... at last.' Danielle's surprise made them laugh. 'How did you find one another?'

Danielle had got there before me in asking. 'Did your grandmother help?' I asked Alfred.

It was Rebecca who told us how.

'On special days, birthdays, saint's days and at Christmas Alfred would take me to the coffee bar in the park, the one near to the band stand. We always had the same lunch, laughing and joking until it was time to go back to work. I was standing by the band stand looking across at the coffee bar when I felt a presence come and stand beside me...'

Alfred took up the story.

'I was lying in bed one night and thinking about the spiritual session with Madame Arabella when I remembered her turning over one of the cards. It was the picture of a star with a naked woman standing beside the water. The woman reminded me of Rebecca and the times that we had sat beside the lake in the park talking.'

'I was never naked,' grinned Rebecca.

'No, but you were always so beautiful,' replied Alfred. 'That Sunday I felt drawn to the park and unbelievably Rebecca was there beside the band stand. It was like a miracle had happened.'

Rebecca showed Danielle her ring. 'We're to be married next spring.'

We congratulated them both. I told them about Joe long and how using the red bicycle he had avoided capture and escaped the long arm of the law. How another user, Tiffany had used it to have tea at Claridge's. They wanted to know more so Danielle and I obliged bringing over the box from under the counter. I offered the letter back to Alfred thinking that they might to keep it and show their children one day, but Rebecca had another idea.

224

'Alfred's letter should stay here only it belongs here along with the other letters and notes. The red bicycle, the café and all the users, they're all part of the magic. One day when we tell our children the story about what brought us together perhaps you'll still have the bicycle so that they can come see it for themselves.'

Danielle was confident that we would still be here and so would the red bicycle. So far the bicycle had always come back after every use and never been misused, damaged or stolen. Even Stephanie Steele had done a full page article in the local newspaper on the mysterious travels of the bicycle and every so often we saw children come just to see the bike sitting outside.

As for me the coming together of Alfred and Rebecca epitomised just how special the café and the red bicycle was to us, together with all the other wonderful stories.

After Alfred and Rebecca's visit I purchased an identical red bicycle which we kept out back in the yard store just in case it did ever go missing. We had to have a reverse in the event that they did bring their children along to see the bicycle and tell their amazing story.

Miracles Do Happen

Christmas had arrived with all the joy of the occasion that it always was, only this particular season's festivities was made even more special because the adoption forms had been eagerly completed and submitted by Mary and Thomas two days after the bonfire party and now we were all praying had that very soon they would have two additions in their life.

And Christmas is a truly wondrous, magical time for children and this year all our prayers were answered including Robert's when Carolyn Johnson telephoned Mary and Thomas a week before Christmas inviting them along to the Saxon House Children's Home where she had made the necessary arrangement to have little Guy and his younger sister Skye collected. I think Lola was as nervous as Mary that day.

Come Christmas Day our large front room was full of adults and children. As I watched them playing happily together I found it quite amazing how the mind of a young child can process and departmentalise events, places and people so easily accepting change. In the hubbub of noise and giggles from Amelia and Antonio, Guy and Skye I saw Lola take Mary to the kitchen.

With tears streaming down their faces they were both attacking the tissue box.

'I can't believe it Lola,' cried Mary, desperate to not let her tears be heard. 'They are simply beautiful and they belong to me and Thomas now. This morning, seeing the joy in their little faces as they saw the presents stacked up under the Christmas tree is a memory that will live inside of me forever.'

Lola hugged Mary knowing how she felt.

'Believe in miracles Mary. I do and they happen when you least expect them. My two miracles are happily playing with Skye and Guy.'

Mary smiled and nodded. 'Since receiving the call from Carolyn I have been living in a sort of haze and I'm waiting for the bubble to burst. I keep waking in the middle of the night and I have to go and check on them both, just to make sure that nobody has taken them away.'

'That's only natural and I did the same when Amelia came home with us the first night. We hardly got any sleep that night and yet she slept soundly. Children adapt fast and they accept more quickly than adults.'

'Thomas is so proud and he already has plans for the future. A bigger place so that the children have space to run and he's already begun building them a small table so that they can sit and paint on. I think he's looking ahead and hoping that one day they will share his studio at the back of the gallery.'

Lola laughed. 'Spencer hopes that one of the children at least will want to continue with the café. I've a feeling it might be Antonio. He seems to already have a strange affiliation with the place. He's a boisterous, inquisitive little boy, but when he arrives at the café he is calmer and he's very much at home there.'

Mary wiped her cheeks dry. 'The magic of the little red café no doubt.'

'That's what Spencer say's. He thinks our son has a secret conversation with his grandfather when nobody is listening.'

'You know that your priority now is the children and not the florist,' Lola insisted. 'Why don't you take some of that holiday that you're owed and spend it with your family. I am sure that your mum and dad would want to see you all.'

'But what about the shop and the orders, there are so many things happening around the New Year?'

Lola however was always on hand with a solution. 'How about Anna, could she help?'

'I could ask and she's always happy to earning some extra money.'

'She'll need it, only now she has a nephew and a niece who will gladly take her shopping making a beeline to the nearest toy shop.'

'Anna is already in her element and she spends as much spare time as she has coming round and playing with them both.' Taking a deep breath she exhaled slowly. 'It all had happened so fast Lola. I'm not complaining, I am just saying that it took the wind out of my sails. It seemed like I wasn't fully prepared.'

'You'll find that as time goes on there will be moments when they suddenly get thrust upon you and no amount of planning will help. Antonio has become a master of surprises. In any one day I can normally gauge his mood or interpret his thoughts whereas Spencer still doesn't know how or what Antonio is thinking. His son, he said is like a disciple of the devil.'

'He's lovely,' Mary quickly defended.

'Yes, but he already has the measure of his father. His sister is adept at manipulating her father too. She knows how her father's mind ticks.'

'Promise that you'll be there when I need help?'

Lola grinned as she topped up Mary's wine glass.

'Always and you have your parents. Thomas's mum and dad too, plus Vera, Danielle and Martyn around to help. I know that you and Robert are close. He is amazing and thinks things through. Spencer and I, we value his wisdom and you will have no shortage of baby-sitters.'

'It will be a long time yet before I need anybody to baby-sit.' Replied Mary. 'I don't want to let little Skye and Guy out of my sight.'

Lola grinned. 'Trust me Mary however much you love your family there will still be days when you need an hour to yourself, doing something different. Soon you will all settle into a routine and things will become easier.

'If it wasn't for you and Spencer, we might never have met the children!'

'No Mary, you made it happen. The moment that you made the conscientious decision to leave the convent, you broadened your horizons finding love with Thomas, taking on *Florrie's Flowers* and now adopting your son and daughter. God has been with you all the way, but it was you who pushed all the right buttons to make it work.'

'Coincidentally I spoke to Mother Superior the other day and she has invited us all to go see her at the convent. She is so excited about meeting Guy and Skye. Naturally I said that I would although I can't help feeling a little apprehensive.'

'Why,' replied Lola, 'surely by taking Guy and Skye the sisters will see that you made the right decision and now taking on the responsibility of two young souls you have continued doing the lord's work.'

'That's what Robert told me. You both have a way of putting things into perspective.'

Lola laughed. 'Living around Spencer, I have too.'

Walking from the lounge to the kitchen I overheard my name being mentioned.

'My ears are burning.' I said as I entered the kitchen.

'And so they should be,' replied Lola as she topped up my glass. 'We were just discussing Mary taking a holiday and spending more time with the children. Anna might look after the flower shop.'

'Great idea.' It was obvious that Mary had been crying and so had Lola, but they looked happy. The recent lines of tension had also disappeared from Mary's face replaced with a healthy glow. I could not remember the last time that she had taken a holiday. 'So how was I mentioned in the conversation?'

'We would tell Anna that you are only next door in the café in case she needed help.'

Mary was about to call Anna to see if she was available where there was an unexpected knock at the door. 'Have you invited anybody else?' asked Lola.

'No.'

Leaving the kitchen I was closely followed by Antonio who always liked to see visitors. I felt my jaw fall to the floor with astonishment as I pulled the door open.

'Hello little man,' our visitor greeted, 'I had heard through the grapevine that you had your mothers good looks, her brains and hair colour. Thank goodness there's not a lot on top surface that resembles your father!' Antonio was scooped from my side and hoisted high.

I stood aside as Alfie Harrison 'Arris' Wilson stepped into our hallway. With his spare hand he shook mine. Sticking his tongue out Antonio blew a raspberry, just to show that he could. It made Alfie laugh. 'And that, you definitely get from your father.' Wiping his feet on the door mat Alfie pushed my jaw closed. 'It's good to see you Spencer, I hope that I am not intruding.'

Looking back along the hallway I saw Lola and Mary exit the kitchen. The moment that Lola saw Alfie she flew down the hallway hugging him with Antonio still in his arms. Joyfully she kissed his cheek turning to Mary. *'You must believe me now when I tell you that miracles do exist!'*

Having regained my composure after the initial shock that Alfie was alive I was undeniably happy to see him again. 'We never thought that we would see you again!'

Mary took her turn to step forward and kiss Alfie's cheek. He returned the gesture.

'Coming home to find two beautiful women throwing themselves at me was worth all the sleepless nights and cramped conditions that I had to endure to get here.' Alfie noticed the bump showing on Lola. 'And just in time by the looks of it...' he winked at me, 'you've been busy Brand!'

'Come on in Alfie, the hallway is not the place to be asking questions and we have some more surprises in store, Christmas surprises.'

Alfie grabbed my arm. 'I'm sorry, but I've not brought anybody any presents.'

Sitting alongside Lola she looped her arm through his. Having you home safe and sound is the best present and the children had so much from Santa.'

Although arriving late and totally unexpected Alfie was a big hit with all four children and he was interested to hear about Thomas and his art gallery. He was surprised to see how much Amelia had grown. Mary watched as Guy and Skye vied to be close to the stranger who needed a shave.

'You must have returned with a sprinkling of magic,' remarked Thomas, 'or they think that you're the big man.'

Alfie mouthed, *'big man'.*

'He lives at the North Pole and comes out once a year with reindeer for company,' I replied.

Patting his stomach where he had distinctly lost weight since I had seen him last, he laughed as Skye put her hand up and touched his beard. 'You're like a pussycat,' she said.

He scooped Skye up onto his knee. 'There were times when I felt like a panther in the night princess.'

'Was it that hairy?' I asked.

Alfie nodded. 'Lets' say that I won't be returning to the dark continent anytime soon. Not if I value my life.'

Mischievously Lola asked. 'And the two parallel scars, have they healed?'

'Yes, although every time that I look in the mirror after getting out of the shower they remind me of how close a shave it was getting married.'

'And the Ahumbra tribe, I take it that you're still top of their hunting list?'

Alfie grinned. 'And the menu.'

'We didn't sell the flat and a cleaner has gone in regularly to keep it clean and check for water leaks.' Alfie thanked us for looking after his home. He winked at Skye who giggled back.

'And the art, how's that going?' Alfie asked Thomas.

'Good thanks, although it's always slow around Christmas, but it'll pick up again around February when people have different needs.'

Alfie nodded, but I had known my school friend long enough to know when ideas were running around inside his head.

'With these lovely additions to your family you're gonna need somewhere bigger soon.'

Mary responded. 'One day we'll be able to afford a house and have a garden for the children to play in.'

In admiration of his exploits we listened as Alfie went on to describe his escapades in Africa and how he had escaped the trackers from the Ahumbra tribe. His journey mostly on foot had eventually landed him at the sea port in Morocco, it was there that he veered from his course and ventured across to Greece where he had been recuperating renting a beach hut before coming home.

'Why go to Greece and not come home straight away.'

'I'd caught something nasty in Africa that made me unwell. I had lost weight as a result and the doctor that I saw in Morocco suggested plenty of sunshine, as if I'd not had enough. I looked a real mess so I opted for a Greek island.' He looked around the room.

'This is a really lovely house, you both chose well.'

Sat alongside Lola looped her arm through his once again. 'We wouldn't have it, if it wasn't for you Alfie, we owe you so much.'

With a flick of his free hand he dismissed the fact that he had been our guardian angel. 'If we have anybody to thank it's my late dear aunt Ellen Claire, she was one with all the money and lots of it. The flat down by the river was hers originally although she only ever used it when she came up to London to take in a show. She left me the flat and her bank account when she died. I only use it when I'm in London which is rare these days.'

'But, it's a home,' explained Mary.

'Yes and no really Mary, you see I'm like a wandering minstrel with a mission.'

'To find what?' she asked.

'Adventure in every quarter of the globe. I like to look back and see my footprints in the sand.'

I saw a glint in his eye knowing his footprints meant much more.

'Did you meet somebody on your travels, besides your native wife?'

Alfie grinned, he looked at Lola. 'Marrying you has made him sharper.'

'Yes, she shared the rented beach property with me. Like me she is bewitched with a restless spirit for travel and adventure.'

'Then you'll make the perfect couple,' replied Lola.

With Skye sat on his knee she had laid her head on his chest and we watched as her eyes drooped. Alfie made sure that she was safe and wouldn't fall.

'Maybe one day I will experience all of this for myself, but for the moment I still possess a restless soul looking for that one special star in the sky.'

'You've certainly found a little star tonight,' I replied as Alfie gently stroked Skye's hair away that was covering her eyes.

'You should all come over to Greece for a holiday in the spring before we move on. There's a large property down on the beach with at least five bedrooms. We know the owner and he hardly ever uses it. Bring Danielle and Martyn too.'

'By then they'll have a baby as well.'

It was Alfie's turn to look surprised. 'Danielle a mum, you're kidding. You see what happens when I go away.' We laughed and Skye stirred although she didn't wake.

'So what happens with London, I've a feeling that we won't see much of you in the future unless the lady in Greece is from here too?'

'No, she's from Sweden. Part of my heart will always belong to London, but I'm not sure about the rest. Erika I know has a chunk already.' He looked down at Skye sleeping with her head resting on his chest. 'If this little angel can hear my heart beating then I'll never fully leave town.'

'And Thomas Barringer, will he ever find peace?'

Alfie responded giving a gentle shake of his head. 'Probably not Spence, you see he lived his life one day at a time and I believe that down the tunnel of time some of his wild spirit latched onto me.'

Alfie suddenly opened the flap of his shirt pocket, it caused Skye to murmur, but she didn't wake. From his pocket he took a wrapping of parchment. He asked Thomas to come and collect it. As Thomas took the parchment Alfie grabbed his wrist. 'Before you unravel it and look inside, will you promise me not to refuse what I have to give?'

The air was thick with mystery as Thomas sat back down beside Mary. They both looked at Alfie and agreed. 'Yes,' Mary replied.

'Good.' Alfie nodded happy that they would. 'Now what you hold in your hand was something that I found on my travels although for reasons known only to me I can't say where, but I promise you that it wasn't stolen. It's of no use to me, but I think that you will benefit greatly me from the parchment.' With his free hand he gestured with his index finger. 'Remember you said that you promised.'

Mary reiterated that they would abide by the promise. Gently pulling back the folds of the parchment Mary gasped.

'Alfie this looks like a piece of cotton muslin, the type that wrapped the body of Jesus after his crucifixion.'

Alfie grinned. 'That's exactly what I thought when I found it. Go on Thomas open it up fully. You'll find that what is inside isn't from his tomb, but perhaps under it.'

Mary frowned as Thomas very carefully unwrapped each strand until the linen parchment was open for all to see. In the middle of the cloth sat a diamond, an uncut stone. The colours emanating were the most beautiful that I had ever seen.

Again Alfie raised his index finger. 'You promised remember.'

Amelia, Guy and even Antonio went across to Thomas to look at the diamond.'

'Get used to those Amelia,' said Alfie, 'they're supposed to be a girl's best friend.' Mary who was sat with her mouth open was lost for words. 'Take it to Hatton Garden and make sure that you fetch a fair price on the stone. It should be enough to secure a garden for the children.'

Lola went to the kitchen to collect the tissue box for Mary as Thomas and Guy hugged her. When Thomas looked up again at Alfie his eyes were also moist.

'I look upon you all as my friends and my family. It's the one thing that draws me back London.' Mary and Thomas both thanked Alfie.

I got up and patted my friend on the shoulder, like a highwayman Alfie was full of surprise and he knew how to deliver. 'So what comes next?' I asked.

'A decent breakfast at the café cooked by Vera.'

We sat drinking coffee and wine, talking and bringing Alfie up to date with everything that had been happening during his absence including the romance between Robert and Stephanie until Antonio had climbed up and fallen asleep on Lola's lap, with Amelia and Guy both yawning. Thanking Alfie once again for his generosity Mary and Thomas took their young family. Later with the children in bed they would begin making plans of their own. With Lola upstairs with Amelia and Antonio I poured Alfie and myself a whiskey.

'You were always one for surprises Alfie and you certainly know how to take the wind out of a couple's sails.' We chinked glasses. 'You have made my future secure.' I thanked him. 'And then like a breeze passing through you make Mary and Thomas's dreams come true overnight.'

'That's what adventure is all about Spence. Strictly between you and me I literally found the diamond on the roadside outside of Morocco. Some bugger must have dropped it and my guess is that it will serve Mary and Thomas, and the children better than some unscrupulous dealer.'

'You have a heart as big as a whale my friend.' I topped up his glass.

'I've done some bad things too Spence, things I'm not proud about, but maybe this is my way of making amends, at least that is how Robert would see it.' He raised his glass. 'To Danielle and Martyn.'

'Who would have thought that when we were at school we would be sitting here today, you an intrepid explorer and writer and me the owner of a café, and with a family. Schools should have replaced the school nurse with a clairvoyant.' We laughed.

Just prior to Christmas I went to see a solicitor where I made arrangements to have the flat put in Danielle's name. I know that she's that she's been looking after the flat in my absence. I've really no need for it and they could certainly do with it now that a baby is on the way.

'If you can put me up for the night, I would like to come with you tomorrow and see Danielle and Martyn so that I can give them the key officially.'

When Lola reappeared I poured her a drink. Alfie told her about his visit to the solicitor. This time it was Lola's chin that he had to push up.

'But where will you stay when you return to London? She asked.

'In a hotel. I'm never in town long enough to settle the dust beneath my feet before I'm away again and I only ever come back to see you all.'

'Just make sure that you steer clear of Africa,' Lola advised, 'it was bad enough losing you the first time around without there being a second lot of heartache.'

Alfie grinned. 'The trouble is Lola, that's where most of the mystery is buried.'

'Yes, but consider the odds if you ran into the father of the bride again, he might not see it quite how you do and especially if he has a grandchild.'

For all his bravado, his generosity and heart the size of the moon Alfie was a sensible man and I honestly believed that any future adventures would be where he felt the safest, especially if he was taking Erika along. Alfie suddenly stood, undid the belt of his trousers dropping them down one side to reveal two long scars on his buttock.

'I have these as permanent reminders and not to go boldly where others have not been before. I'll let then take the risks, then come along after and take the spoils. Erika speaks five different languages so she's a handy interpreter to have alongside.'

It was very late by the time that we got to bed mainly talking about his relationship with Erika and their plans to see parts of the world that neither had seen. Lying in bed with Lola asleep and the moon sitting in a theatre surrounded by stars I couldn't wait to see the expression on Danielle's face when she saw Alfie alive and then when he handed over the keys to the flat to her.

Explorer and adventurer, general risk taker and unequivocally a generous friend, whatever Alfie Wilson was or he had achieved throughout his exciting life I felt that there was much more to come. And like Thomas Oliver Barringer the highwayman Alfie would one day realise that chasing dreams was exhilarating and good for the soul, there comes a time when a man has to settle down and consider having a family of his own. I did hope that when that day arrived he too would have a daughter like little Skye. In time Alfie would remember her sleeping on his chest and want the same although for now he was content knowing that soon she and Guy would have a garden of their own to play in.

Reflections

We all helped Danielle and Martyn move into their riverside apartment and around lunchtime Vera and my mum provided the food, fussing over the children as they ran around playing happily together.

Having been collected from the children's home by Mary and Thomas, Guy and his sister Skye had spent as much time as possible with Amelia and Antonio becoming inseparable. Mary had also settled into a more relaxed routine and her sister Anna had flourished grabbing the opportunity to manage the florists. After closing up she would visit to see her niece and nephew in their new house.

Day dreaming as I stood behind the counter in the café I was aware of an elderly couple as they walked on by giving me a brief wave before resuming with their conversation. Arm in arm I wondered what stories they could tell. I smiled to myself as I watched them disappear from sight as I doubted either had ever used the red bicycle stood outside. They might have wanted to take it for a ride around the block, but physical restrictions prevented that adventure. I rubbed my shoulder where the cold weather had affected an old injury.

'What are you thinking about Spence,' asked Danielle standing alongside, 'you were miles away.'

'I was watching an elderly couple walk up the road and at the same time wondering why you are still here. You can hardly fit between the tables.'

Danielle looked at me, a determined look to suggest that I should mind my own business. 'The baby and I have worked out a successful regime, he or she moves left or right and I follow suit. I am okay Spence and if I get breathless I have plenty of chairs to sit down on.'

I placed two mugs under the Fracino Contempo. 'I'm only thinking of your welfare and that of the baby.'

She sat herself down on the chair that I had put behind the counter.

'I know, thanks. I reckon that when this little bugger makes an appearance it'll come out dancing the way that it moves about.'

'Does the baby keep you and Martyn awake?'

Danielle looked towards the kitchen.

'I hope it does, it's his fault that I'm in this condition...' We laughed as I added a shortcake biscuit to the saucer.

'Life changes all the time don't it Spence!'

I leant back against the counter top, there were only a few customers in and they were happy having been fed and watered.

'It never stops revolving I know that much, but you've so much to look forward too now and Alfie has made everything right for us all.'

'I know, but every so often I reflect when I'm alone.'

'About Paris and wondering what Emily Follingdale is doing?'

'Sometimes, but mainly about life in general. Although I've no regrets.' I remembered Lola going through the same phase when she was heavily pregnant and wondering if she would miss out on life, events and ambitions.

'Wondering *what if* never works although we've all done it. Trust me, you have to grab whatever the day and the future presents and be grateful for everything.'

'I am Spence. I have the most amazing flat overlooking the river. Martyn who does anything for me, the café, all of you as friends and now a baby coming. I'm just fed up that I can't get into my jeans!' She held the underside of her belly as the baby moved.

'Are you okay, do you need me to get Vera?'

Danielle breathed in deep several times. 'No, I'm okay only whenever I mention my jeans the little one moves. I'm sure that they can hear me and give me a kick as a reminder of what they're going through.'

'When was your last scan?'

'Last week and everything's fine.'

'And you still don't know the gender of the baby?'

'No and we both don't want to know. Boy or girl we want this little one so much.' I watched as Danielle put her arm on the counter top for extra support. She was breathing a lot heavier.

'I think I should get Martyn to take you home.' I was about to move past when she suddenly grabbed my arm. *'Wow... that was more than just a kick.'*

I called out for Vera. Instantly she and Martyn appeared. Vera took one look at Danielle then told Martyn to call for an ambulance.

'Is the baby coming,' he asked.

'YES...' cried Danielle, *'now call the ambulance and tell them to hurry!'*

Luck would have that there were two middle-aged ladies left in the café and one told Vera and myself that she was a retired nurse. They helped in making Danielle comfortable and to relax her breathing like she had been shown at the pre-natal classes. The nurse also kept a count of the contractions. Five minutes later the ambulance arrived. I could see the relief in Danielle face as it parked outside.

Grabbing the bag that she had prepared and was in the back cloakroom Martyn stood to one side as Danielle was helped into the ambulance. I asked Danielle if she wanted to go with her, but Vera held onto my arm, holding me back.

'She and Martyn will do just fine Spencer, let them enjoy this moment together and later when the café is closed we can all go up to the maternity hospital.'

'She'll be alright, won't she?'

Vera looped her arm through mine and squeezed it tight. 'Danielle's a woman now and very soon she'll have a baby to look after, the same as Lola will. You have to learn to relax more Spencer. Life changes with a new baby, you should know that.'

Yes, I did remember when Antonio had been born. It was getting quite close to Danielle repeating the event and having her baby in the café. The ambulance disappeared from sight leaving just the four of us in the café, although moments later we were joined by Anna and Thomas.

'Danielle?' asked Anna.

'Yes,' replied Vera, 'so you'd better think about getting a bouquet together.'

'I need to phone Lola and Mary,' I said heading for the kitchen.

'They already know, I sent them both a text message as the nurse was making Danielle comfortable. Phone your mother instead.'

'Why mum?'

'Because with Martyn gone I will need some help in the kitchen with the lunchtime trade.' I did as Vera asked and mum arrived within minutes. With me pacing back and forth Thomas suggested that I go home to see that Lola was okay. Taking the red bicycle from outside the café I cycled as fast as I could.

By the time I had arrived out of breathe and with my leg muscles aching Mary was already there too.

'Has anybody told Danielle's mum?' Lola asked.

'Vera was calling her as I left the café.' I had just put my mobile on the kitchen worktop when Martyn called.

'It's a girl,' he cried, the excitement evident in his voice, 'Danielle had it in the back of the ambulance.'

'Congratulations, is Danielle and the baby okay?'

241

'They're great Spencer... really great. I so wanted a little girl.'

'And Danielle?' I asked.

'Secretly she did too!'

'Then your wish came true.' I told Martyn that we would all be along later to see Danielle and the baby.

'You didn't ask if they had named the baby,' said Lola as I put the phone back down on the worktop.

'No, I didn't, I forgot. I am just so relieved that they're both alright.' I had to sit down to absorb the news. Doing so made Lola and Mary smile.

'You're not good around babies being born Spencer, You should really leave it up to the women. We know what we're doing.'

Mary made a pot of tea as I listened to them talking accepting that Lola was probably right. I had seen many changes take place and none more so than Danielle go from a teenage girl and blossom into a beautiful young woman. I had to accept also that now for the time being she would be missing from the café and that motherhood would become her priority. We would need some extra help.

When they went to collect the children from school Amelia was first in through the door followed by Guy, Skye and Antonio who had been held back being strapped in the push chair.

'Does this mean that with Aunt Danielle's baby we have another auntie?'

I laughed as I opened the cake tin for them each to select a slice.

'I think that as the baby will be the youngest of you all Danielle will want you to call the baby by her first name.'

Amelia looked at the other children, 'that's good only with so many aunties and uncles, we'll get a little confused.' Standing behind the middle island Lola and Mary were grinning.

Mary laid out four plates for the cake slices. 'Uncle Martyn will tell us the baby's name when we speak to him later.'

242

With an exasperated sigh Amelia took off her coat. 'I know and daddy forgot to ask.' Like mother, like daughter I thought. Mary tried to hide her smile as she unbuttoned Skye's coat.

Martyn saved the day by texting me the baby's name. *'Emily, it was Danielle's choice and I like it.'*

'It's a beautiful name,' said Mary as I showed the children the text message. I grabbed my jacket from the back of the chair.

'I had best get back and see what's happening at the café. Vera has a set of keys, but she'll want to close early today and besides somebody else might have use for the bicycle overnight!'

The return journey was slower than my previous encounter with the potholes in the road and the odd dog barking as I cycled past. I was so pleased for Danielle and Martyn and Emily was indeed a beautiful name for a little girl. Weighing in at just over three kilogrammes, Emily was a nice healthy baby and I couldn't wait to see mother, baby and the father.

So much had taken place since taking custody of the keys for the little red café, so much perhaps that I had run out of pages in the two books that you have kindly read. There will undoubtedly be more stories to come as the seasons come and go, and time will march on as the children grow.

Arriving back at the café I parked the bicycle in its usual place making sure that the tyres were properly inflated and that the seat was steady. Thomas opened the door for me and offered a coffee. 'It's great news.'

His smile was as exuberant as his paintings. 'I have really enjoyed working in the café. You know there's something very magical about this place. No wonder customers are attracted here every day.' We were enjoying a coffee together with my mum, Vera and Anna when Robert Styles entered.

'I hear that we have occasion to celebrate a new birth.'

Reaching up to the shelf beside the coffee machine I took down a clean cup.

Vera's Ginger and Orange Cake with a splash of Rum (optional)

Ingredients for the cake:

- 100 grammes (4 oz.) golden syrup
- 100 grammes (4 oz.) black treacle
- 100 grammes (4 oz.) softened butter
- 100 grammes (4 oz.) caster sugar
- 250 millilitres (9 fl. oz.) water
- 275 grammes (10 oz.) plain flour
- 1 large egg, beaten
- 1 orange, grated for the rind
- 1½ level teaspoons of bicarbonate of soda
- I level teaspoon of ground cinnamon
- 1 level teaspoon of ground ginger
- 1 splash or cap full of Rum (optional)

Ingredients for the Icing:

- 100 grammes (4 oz.) icing sugar
- The juice of 1 large orange

Bringing the cake together:

- Pre-heat the oven to 180° C / Fan 160° C / Gas Mk. 4
- Prepare a 23 cm (9 inch.) deep round cake tin, greasing the inside and lining the sides with baking parchment
- Pour the golden syrup, black treacle and water into a saucepan slowly mixing in and bring to the boil but do not overheat otherwise it will set

- Place the remainder of the ingredients in a mixing bowl and beat thoroughly until you have a consistent blend
- Add the syrup and treacle mixing again thoroughly until you have a smooth blend
- Add the splash of rum (optional)
- Pour into the cake tin
- Bake in the oven for about an hour or until the blade of a knife is clean
- Leave to cool for a quarter of an hour before you remove the baking parchment
- Finish cooling

Preparing the icing:

- Sift the icing sugar into a mixing bowl and add the juice of the orange mixing until you have a smooth mix which should be relatively thick in texture
- Spoon the icing over the top of the cake
- Leave to set for an hour
- It is advisable to stand the cake on a wire rack and have a large tray or plate underneath so that when you add the icing any extra will be caught

For best results:

Vera suggests that for this particular cake, when the cake has been baked and cooled, leave the parchment in place and add foil then let the cake stand for a good two days. This period will help the cake to mature and at the same time become nicely moist and sticky.

Top tip:

A slice of this cake should be served with a pot of tea or coffee and shared with family and friends. The cake is easy to make a delight to behold and it will have your phone ringing to see if there is any left!

We at the little red café hope that you have enjoyed our time together, remember that are always welcome and please let us know what you think as we are always open to suggestions, comments and recipes.

Other Books by Jeffrey Brett

A Moment in Time
ISBN – 979 - 8642194461
Barking Up the Wrong Tree
ISBN – 978 - 1073495290
Beyond the First Page
ISBN – 978 - 1980681991
Leave No Loose Ends
ISBN – 978 – 1549552984
Looking for Rosie
ISBN – 978 - 1980369400
The Little Red Café
ISBN – 978 - 1980912583
Rabbits Beside the Track
ISBN – 979 - 8635555187
The Road is Never Long Enough
ISBN – 978 - 1794541948
The Moon, Balloon and Stars
ISBN – 979 – 8634519852
Shadow of Blame
ISBN – 979 - 8672633008

©

About the Author
Jeffrey Brett

I was born in London during the middle of the last century. I follow no particular genre writing my short stories, psychological thrillers and humour.

After working for so many year in the public service sector I have finally found the time to enjoy my writing and publish my books. I wish you many hours of happy reading and if you have any comments regarding any of my books please email me and let me know.

Magic79.jb@outlook.com

www.Jbartinmotion.co.uk

Printed in Great Britain
by Amazon

56343097R00142